“Are you *senseless?*” she demanded. “What on earth do [illegible] this? Nearly everyt[illegible] wrong did, and we [illegible] have been killed!”

“Yeah, but we *weren’t*, and frankly, I’m delighted as hell about that. Aren’t you?” he asked, still with the big grin, which she found as annoying as it was attractive.

“Are you sure you didn’t fall on your *head*? You scared me half to death, tumbling down like that. *They* scared me, shooting at us, with real bullets. I’ve seen up close exactly the kind of damage those things can do.”

“I’ve seen more than my share, too, but—”

“But nothing, Jude,” she said, her entire body quaking. “Did you get a look at the back window? *This?*” She gestured angrily toward the shattered rearview mirror. “That could’ve just as easily been one of our skulls. And I— And I’m not— I can’t do this—”

Unbuckling his harness, he reached over and clasped her arm. “Callie,” he said, gently pulling her closer. “Don’t you understand? You already have, and you were brilliant. *We* have, working together.”

* * *

If you’re on Twitter, tell us what you think of Harlequin Romantic Suspense! #harlequinromsuspense

Dear Reader,

As the wife of a first responder, I have spent years watching these brave, resourceful men and women rush off to assist others during what are very often the most stressful moments of their lives. I've even had the opportunity to do a ride along late one night, which gave me the chance to see my husband's work as a firefighter from a whole new vantage. I also got to see the work of the paramedics and EMTs whose apparatus ran out of his station. Each of these positions, in addition to medical flight crew members such as those depicted in *First Responders on Deadly Ground*, require outstanding problem-solving and people skills, along with incredible stamina and compassion—and the ability to deal with stressful situations that can change everything in the blink of an eye.

Like many first responders, flight nurse Callie Fielding finds herself bearing the unseen scars of one such "eyeblink"—a tragedy that cost the life of her own beloved husband. Even years later, she is still deeply affected, emotionally isolated from the very support system that helps many navigate the worst life has to offer.

At first, when handsome new flight paramedic Jude Castleman attempts to reach out to her, she rebuffs him. But later she begins to see Jude as something else—a means to the justice she's been denied against the powerful family she blames for setting the crash that destroyed her life. As the two work together to defeat a common enemy, she discovers Jude may hold the keys to so much more, including a love with the power to bring them both the healing they deserve...

Happy reading,

Colleen Thompson

FIRST RESPONDERS ON DEADLY GROUND

Colleen Thompson

HARLEQUIN®
ROMANTIC SUSPENSE™

Recycling programs for this product may not exist in your area.

ISBN-13: 978-1-335-75939-9

First Responders on Deadly Ground

Copyright © 2021 by Colleen Thompson

This edition published by arrangement with Harlequin Books S.A.

For questions and comments about the quality of this book, please contact us at CustomerService@Harlequin.com.

Harlequin Enterprises ULC
22 Adelaide St. West, 40th Floor
Toronto, Ontario M5H 4E3, Canada
www.Harlequin.com

Printed in U.S.A.

The Texas-based author of more than thirty novels and novellas, **Colleen Thompson** is a former teacher with a passion for reading, hiking, kayaking and the last-chance rescue dogs she and her husband have welcomed into their home. With a National Readers' Choice Award and multiple nominations for the RITA® Award, she has also appeared on the Amazon, BookScan and Barnes & Noble bestseller lists. Visit her online at www.colleen-thompson.com.

Books by Colleen Thompson

Harlequin Romantic Suspense

First Responders on Deadly Ground

Colton 911: Chicago

Colton 911: Hidden Target

Passion to Protect
The Colton Heir
Lone Star Redemption
Lone Star Survivor
Deadly Texas Summer

The Coltons of Mustang Valley

Hunting the Colton Fugitive

Cowboy Christmas Rescue
"Rescuing the Bride"

Visit the Author Profile page at Harlequin.com for more titles.

To all the first responders who dedicate their lives
to being there on the worst days and
nights of our own...

Chapter 1

It was pitch-dark outside the helicopter, thick clouds swirling past them, when Jude Castleman's voice came over the headset, that deep, rich voice that brought to mind old bourbon and polished burl wood every time she heard it. "Hey, are you all right?" he said over the helo's hum. "You look a little…"

"Worry about yourself, Rookie. I'm just running through my checklists." As queasy as she was distracted, veteran flight nurse Callie Fielding cut him a look meant to warn the recently hired paramedic that she wouldn't welcome further attempts to engage her in any conversation beyond what was necessary for the care of the young patient they were on their way to pick up. She'd thought she'd made it clear enough during their previous two shifts together that she had no interest whatsoever in any personal chatter.

Apparently, Jude was a slow learner. Or maybe he figured he was worth whatever it would cost her to risk getting to know him. Which only proved he didn't know her yet at all.

"Your hands are shaking," he challenged, the LED lights of the instrumentation reflecting off a square, masculine face and a pair of intelligent blue-gray eyes, their corners fanned with the fine creases of a man maybe a few years older than her own thirty-four. Locked in on her face, his gaze cut straight through the frostiness that would keep a wiser man at bay. "You sound a little hoarse, too. You're not coming down with something, are you? Because if you might be contagious, we'll need to make sure you don't infect the—"

"I don't know how your crew ran things back in Arizona." Swallowing back bile, she pasted on her sternest stare. "But let's get one thing straight now. Here in Texas—and especially at LifeWings—patient safety's our top priority. I'd never show up for a flight sick."

"Got it, Red," he said, proving that he would never be the kind who recognized when shutting his mouth would be in his best interest. "Adding invincibility to your list of superpowers, right under warmth and charm."

Rolling her eyes, she resumed pretending to study the checklist she could recite forward or backward if awakened from a sound sleep. Better to focus on the work—and her annoyance with the sort of man who believed it clever or original to tag a woman with a nickname based on nothing but hair color—than to continue staring into the curling mass of clouds that reflected back their lights. And wondering whether it was the impenetrable dampness or some trick of sound, with the muffled noise of their own rotor—or perhaps even their rural Kingston

County, Texas, destination—that had tricked her into imagining that the voice she had heard from the pilot's seat, speaking to their contact center over the radio, was her late husband's.

She reminded herself that it had been four years since she'd last heard or seen Marc. Whatever momentary glitch of memory had caught her off guard, the breathing techniques she'd been taught had gotten her through the jolting moment. Yet when she glanced up again, for just a moment, Jude Castleman's annoyingly keen gaze shifted. *Reality* shifted, putting her back onboard that doomed chopper, where that night's flight medic screamed, "We're going down! Hold on!"

As a gust buffeted her present, Callie reached for the nearest grab bar and fought to keep from crying out. Fought to anchor herself to the here and now, as chills rippled over her sweat-soaked skin beneath her jumpsuit and her pounding heart threatened to burst free of her chest.

"Hey," came a soft voice, slightly distorted by his headset. Jude again, only this time, he reached out and laid a hand atop her wrist, the simple human contact wrapping warm tendrils around her icy heart. "It's okay. You're fine. Just a little turbulence, but Charlie's bringing us down now."

Choking back a whimper, she latched on to their pilot's name. *That's right. Tonight it's Charlie Stenhouse, ex–coast guard, flying.* Glancing forward, she assured herself that it was only his helmet and night-vision goggles, and possibly her own fatigue after a series of exhausting shifts in the emergency department back in Corpus Christi, where she'd filled in several days this week, that had tricked her into believing, even for a moment, that it was Marc behind the controls. Alive again, as they had all been when they'd been called out that stormy January night.

Still, the cacophony replayed in her brain: metal twisting, glass exploding, the dying echo of the men's shouts all around her. She felt the ghost of old pain bursting across her legs and forearm, followed by inhuman shrieks she hadn't recognized as her own. The terrible crescendo came, as always, in the far more horrifying realization that, aside from her, no one else remained capable of screaming.

Over now. It's over. Her throat constricted painfully, tears piling up behind her eyes.

Fighting back the pain, she reminded herself she hadn't melted down in years—not since the hospital, which ran LifeWings, had forced her to suffer through six months of therapy and physical rehabilitation, followed by a psychological examination to assess her fitness for flight. The process had been a nightmare, costing her a chunk of her soul.

"Still with me?" Jude asked her, his keen eyes scrutinizing her for any sign of weakness.

And why wouldn't he? During their interactions thus far, she'd answered the new hire's good-humored friendliness with brusque efficiency, never asking a single question about his work history or what had brought him here from Phoenix. And she'd never for a moment wondered about his personal life—though she'd have to be dead not to notice the strong cheekbones, the cleft chin and the long, ringless fingers that now burned like fire where they touched her flesh.

Abruptly self-consciousness, she snatched back her icy hand. "I've been a flight nurse—and doing just fine without your help—for seven years now," she said, hearing—and hating—the defensive edge in her voice.

And hating even worse the knowing look he returned, the hint of a smile that didn't touch the sadness in his eyes. "Yeah, but how many of those years have you been flying with PTSD as your copilot?"

Her heart pounded as visions of forced leave and the drawn-out process of a psychologist's reevaluation flashed before her eyes. "It's not—" Anger shook through her voice, along with the vibration of their descending helicopter. "I don't know what you've heard about me, who's been spreading ugly gossip, but I swear I'm back. Giving everything I've got to my patients—everything. And I intend to stay on—"

"I haven't *heard* anything." Never breaking eye contact, Jude kept his words calm and steady. "And I'm not here to cause anybody any trouble. But I do know a flashback when I see one, just like I know you're not the ice queen you pretend to be."

Fear pulsed through her, hot and urgent. Because that cold night four years ago, she'd not only lost her colleagues and patient but the husband who had introduced her to the world of flight medicine. Having her wings clipped now would sever her last connection to the man she missed so sharply, it still sometimes hurt to draw breath.

"But for right now, all *you* need to know," Jude added, his handsome face radiating sincerity, "is that I've got your back. Tonight and any time we fly together... Callie."

The lump in her throat more painful than ever, she hesitated, both wanting and at the same time scared to death to trust him. But a glance out the lightly frosted window, where the headlights of emergency vehicles and lit flares marked a section of two-lane, rural highway that had been blocked off, told her this was no time for indecision.

She fussed with the straps of her safety harness and murmured, "I'll hold you to that… Jude."

At her use of his name, his smile was warm and genuine, the open smile of a man longing for connection. But he was barking up the wrong tree if he hoped to find it in her.

Switching her focus, she thought of the sixteen-year-old female they'd been called to transport, who was believed to have sustained a serious neck injury in a motor vehicle accident. With her quality of life or possibly her survival at risk, the girl deserved a flight nurse who was fully on her game.

As soon as they were on the ground and Charlie cleared them for a safe exit, Callie and Jude unplugged the communication links from their helmets and exited the helo. The shock of the low-twenties windchill had Callie hunching her shoulders and shivering, wondering if they'd accidentally overshot South Texas and landed in Antarctica. After piling their jump kit and gear on top of the stretcher and lowering its wheels, they spotted a tall, powerfully built deputy waiting beyond the edge of the blade radius, who waved for them to follow his lead. Bending forward at the waist, he held his Western hat to his head to keep the wind from snatching it away and led them past a fire truck to the spot where an EMS rig was parked with its rear doors open.

"Patient's on the ambulance," he called over his shoulder. "Her mother's with her—she's the one who found her daughter in the wreck and called us to the scene."

Callie followed his nod, glancing toward a bend in the road ahead and the inky-dark depression that lay about thirty yards below it, a wash likely formed by erosion, or perhaps there was a creek down there among the grassy, coastal hills. At the bottom, she made out the still-lit taillights of a passenger car, its rear end pointed like an arrow skyward.

The rescue crew must have had one heck of a job hauling a possible spinal injury up out of that gully, over mud and rocks and heaven only knew what. Glad that extrication wasn't part of her duties, she asked the deputy, "How's our patient? Breathing? Vitals?"

"Oh, she's breathing, all right," he answered, "what with all the noise she's making."

As they approached the rear of the ambulance, Callie heard it for herself—and caught her first glimpse of the sixteen-year-old, her long, blond hair disheveled and her face red and tear-streaked as she struggled against the restraints holding her slender body to the backboard. "It's my shoulder that's killing me, not my neck! If you'll just quit torturing me and let me off here, I'll—"

"Baby, calm down," an older version of the teenager urged as she struggled to tuck her platinum hair out of her face and back up under a fur hat so fluffy it seemed to take up half the ambulance. Other than a nose tipped red from the cold and a single smudge of dirt across a soft-looking tan coat Callie thought might be real cashmere, the woman managed to look flawless, with her long lashes, understated makeup, and fingers that sparkled with diamonds and the plum-colored polish of her elegant manicure. "You *could* hurt your neck if you keep struggling. You could be *paralyzed*."

"It's not my neck! It never has been. I told you before

you made them truss me up like some bondage queen in a porno!"

"Daphne, please!" her mother cried, face flushing. "You've never watched a— Whatever will these people think?"

Realizing that their *critical neck injury* was nothing of the sort, Callie ignored the patient's and her mother's squabbling to cast an accusing look at the EMT, a wiry male with the bulging brown eyes of an overcaffeinated gerbil. "You're the one who called us out tonight?"

He cringed at her tone—or perhaps it was her irritated look that had him so quickly shaking his head and gesturing out the back, toward the vanishing uniformed officer. "Don't blame me. It was the deputy. He made the call before I even got here after talking with the mother. By the time I'd assessed the patient, you were already in the air, so…"

"There's no stuffing that genie back into the bottle, is there?" Jude remarked from where he stood behind Callie. Clearly, he meant to remind her that, once the decision had been made that there was a medical necessity and the weather fell within acceptable parameters, the air ambulance wouldn't be recalled…

No matter how the weather conditions, the time of year and the destination conspired to retrigger the post-traumatic stress disorder she had prayed she'd left behind. Or the fury that boiled to the surface every time it hit her how perfectly avoidable the tragedy that had triggered it had been.

Callie nodded to indicate her understanding—at least until the patient's mother spoke up from inside the ambulance. "I told that Deputy Kendall," she announced, "I wouldn't have my Daphne hauled over an hour of bumpy back roads only to wind up at some little Podunk county hospital and risk her senior volleyball season on some second-rate general surgeon's handiwork."

"Mother, *please*," the girl warned.

As the frigid wind tugged at the fabric of her jump-suit, Callie felt heat climbing up her neck at the idea that this woman had dragged them out here after midnight, risking lives and diverting their chopper from *actual* emergencies, over the chance her daughter's volleyball season next year might be impacted. Reminding herself she was a professional—and that sometimes during times of crisis, patients and their families could be confused, upset or just plain awful—she tamped down her temper, turning her attention to her patient.

"Mind if I check you over, Daphne? I'm Nurse Callie, and this is my partner, Jude, here, right behind me. I know you're having a rough night, but I'd like to make sure we aren't dealing with anything too pressing before we're on our way."

"Um, sure. Why not?" the girl said, sounding tired and cranky but young and vulnerable, as well. "Everybody else's been pulling and pawing at me all night. Just be careful of my right shoulder, please. It hurts so bad and feels like—it's like popped out of place or something."

"It's not only her volleyball," her mother explained while Callie checked her patient's vitals, "but Daphne's backhand—and of course her golf swing. She's a gifted young athlete. You can't imagine the years of lessons, the scholarship prospects at the very best schools—and we do support the LifeWings drives each year with a *generous* donation from our foundation."

"Just when I thought this night could not get *more* embarrassing!" Daphne groaned.

"As the whole community appreciates, I'm sure," Callie forced herself to respond to the mother, removing her stethoscope from her ears and giving Jude Daphne's blood pressure, which was somewhat elevated—but probably not as high as Callie felt her own climbing.

"I doubt it very much," Daphne's mother grumbled. "As far as I'm concerned, the family's been taken for granted far too long by the sort of people who contribute nothing."

"The—the *family*?" Callie looked up sharply from her examination of her patient as cold waves of suspicion rippled through her. Because she might not know her patient's name, but she was all too aware of the family that ruled this part of South Texas. The same family whose patriarch had leveraged his own money and influence to get LifeWings' helicopter sent out four years prior—in defiance of the safety parameters that should have kept them from flying in such weather.

And kept three people alive—and my life worth living. Deep inside, the thought set off a tremor, threatening to shake her professional composure all to pieces.

Jude caught her eye. "Excuse me, Nurse Fielding— Callie—but maybe we'd better get loaded and get out of here before the temp drops any lower."

He was right, she knew. Nodding her agreement, she told their patient, "Let's get you to the hospital, where they can check you out and take care of that shoulder." Nodding to Daphne's mother, Callie managed only, "You'll have to excuse us."

Once they had the girl on their stretcher, Callie and Jude wheeled her toward the waiting chopper.

Running to keep up, the mother shouted, practically in Callie's ear above the rotors' noise, "Is there room for me to hold my baby's hand, or will I fly up front with the pilot?"

Though it was by now spitting cold rain, Callie stopped the stretcher's progress. "I'm sorry if it wasn't made clear, ma'am, but you'll have to arrange your own transport to Corpus Christi. Regulations forbid—"

"I'm sorry," the woman said, straightening her spine and thrusting her smudged face forward. "But do you know who I am, miss? Does the name Tammy Kingston-Hoyle mean anything to you?"

"Kingston?" Jude blurted, clearly taken aback. "You're—you're one of those ranching Kingstons?"

"I certainly am," she said, her sniff of disapproval combined with an arched brow, "and my child clearly needs me, so if you'd just—"

"I couldn't care less what your name is," Callie interrupted, burying her true reaction to a name that she would always hate. "It's your weight that has me worried."

The woman drew back with an offended gasp that had her daughter, on the stretcher, cackling with glee. "She means *for the helicopter,* Mother. She isn't calling you *fat!"*

"No, ma'am, I would never do that," Callie truthfully assured their patient's mother. "But that doesn't change things one iota. You are not. Coming. On. This. Flight."

Clutching her coat beneath her chin, Tammy Kingston-Hoyle accused, "You're being ridiculous. And I don't care for your tone, either. What's your name?"

"I'm Callie Fielding, ma'am, certified flight nurse—"

"And the one in charge tonight. Not you," Jude said,

partially redeeming his initial reaction to the woman's name. "So if you'll excuse us, ma'am, we need you to stay well clear of the LZ—that's the landing zone as marked off by the flares, you see—so we can get your daughter safely to the hospital, where she'll be thoroughly examined by the trauma team for any unseen injuries."

"Who knows?" Callie added as the dam finally burst on her temper. "They may even find there's a legitimate, air ambulance–level issue somewhere in there, though for your daughter's sake I hope it isn't serious enough to justify your throwing the mighty Kingston name around in the service of young Daphne's backhand."

The moment their shift ended at seven in the morning, Jude rushed to his locker, where he changed into jeans and pulled his Phoenix Suns hoodie over a long-sleeved T-shirt. Spiking his dark golden-blond hair with a careless gesture, he scowled at the stubble his reflection showed him, wishing he could spare the time for a shave and shower. But if he wanted a shot at catching Callie Fielding before she lit out for the day, he couldn't afford to delay. Not if he wanted to talk to her about last night's clapback at the Kingston woman.

Heading for the door, he chuckled, recalling his surprise to hear the nurse whom coworkers had warned him could be a real firecracker when riled pop off so bluntly at their patient's mother.

Cold and aloof as she'd been around him until that point, he'd begun to wonder if human iceberg would be a more appropriate description of the stickler of a flight nurse. But Tammy Kingston-Hoyle had successfully ignited the long fuse of Callie Fielding's temper, prompting her to let fly with a sentiment that she'd have probably been wiser to keep to herself.

That was only one reason why Jude rushed down the hall in the hope of catching his famously standoffish colleague. Not ideal, he knew, hanging outside the women's locker room like some sort of low-grade stalker. But he needed to be here before she made a beeline for the deep-blue GT Mustang she kept parked in the farthest corner of the garage.

The first day he'd spotted her driving off in the convertible, he'd exchanged a glance with Pete Stillwagon, an ER nurse who'd been walking out with him that morning, before commenting, "For a woman who doesn't like attention, she sure does flash a lot of chrome."

"That car was her husband's baby," Pete had said, scrubbing at his short, dark beard while staring after the vehicle with deep longing in his basset hound eyes. "So it doesn't matter what the offer. She'll never sell it to you."

But unlike Pete, a recovering car nut currently relegated to a minivan, thanks to his growing family, Jude had only had eyes for the long, lean redhead tucked behind the wheel. Not that he intended on doing anything about it, but he'd heard enough about the sole survivor of the LifeWings air disaster of four years prior— despite what he'd told Callie—that he'd like to think the two of them had one thing in common…

A serious vendetta against the wealthy and powerful Kingstons of South Texas, one that last night's outburst had gone a long way toward confirming. And one that just might make her the ally he was looking for—*if* she'd hear him out.

"Since you're new around here, it's only fair to let you know you'll want to have a care with that one," Pete had warned that morning when he'd noticed Jude staring after Callie's departing car for too long. "She's not half as tough as she acts—and considering all she's been through, nobody's going to take it kindly if you give that woman another second's grief."

As he cooled his heels outside the women's lockers, idly pretending to check his cell for messages, Jude thought about the promise he'd made to keep his distance from the tall redhead—unless she decided otherwise. Pete had laughed and shaken his head, making a scoffing noise that indicated his estimate of Jude's chances ran somewhere south of zero.

By the time ten minutes had ticked past, Jude began to wonder if Callie had somehow spotted him and found some way to duck out another exit unseen. With a sigh of frustration to have missed her, he hoisted the strap of his duffel bag over his shoulder and was just turning toward the exit when he caught movement out of the corner of his eye.

Sure enough, it was her, aiming her long strides not so much *at* as *past* him, her gaze glued to the glass double doors of the hospital exit. With her sleek auburn ponytail bouncing along her back, dark-wash jeans hugging a pair of long and slender legs, and an evergreen fleece jacket zipped halfway up the modest swell of her chest, she more closely resembled an actual human woman, undeniably attractive despite the fatigue around her amber-brown eyes, than the helmet- and jumpsuit-armored figure he'd flown with last night.

"You're late getting out of here," he remarked, trying to hide the relief in his voice.

Her gaze flicked in his direction, betraying reluctance before she paused. "I wanted to check on Daphne Hoyle, make sure she was really okay."

"The *Kingston* girl, you mean?" he asked, thinking that however Callie had reacted to Daphne's power-tripping mother, the flight nurse had treated the girl both professionally and kindly. He'd even overheard Callie apologize for her sharp words to the girl's mother before the teenager, to her credit, had responded, *"Obnoxious as my mom was acting, she ought to be grateful you didn't bring her up here and push her out the door. I know the thought crossed* my *mind."*

"Our *patient*," Callie corrected, giving him a stern look, "is feeling a lot more comfortable, now that they've reduced her dislocated shoulder and given her a sling and something for the pain."

"But otherwise, she'll be okay?"

"If her mother doesn't kill her for stealing her aunt's keys and driving away from the family lodge retreat to go meet up with some town boy." Shaking her head, Callie pinched her lower lip between her teeth

"Oh man," Jude said. "Hormones, high school and regrettable decisions. That brings back a few memories. Young Romeo wasn't there in the wreck with her, was he?"

Callie shook her head in answer. "She never made it to their rendezvous before a coyote jumped out in front of the Mercedes."

"She's lucky to be alive. And even luckier her mama found her way out there on that dark road. She and that giant hairball of a hat of hers make it here yet?"

He figured Tammy Kingston-Hoyle must've had about a two-and-a-half-hour drive to reach the hospital here in Corpus Christi. During which he hoped the woman had forgotten all about how furious she'd been over Callie's remark—and her refusal to bow to what Kingston-Hoyle clearly considered her family privilege.

Callie's sigh suggested otherwise. "Oh yeah. She caught me just in time to assure me she's filing a complaint with the hospital administration about my *'rude, insulting* and *completely unprofessional* behavior.'"

He snorted. "I'll certainly vouch for you."

"I doubt that'll do much good, since she also mentioned she was including your—how was it she put it? Oh yes, your 'insubordination' in the complaint, too."

"Insubordination? So she imagines she's our boss or something?"

"She did point out that as a member of the Kingston Family Foundation's board, she feels absolutely certain that her concerns about the *staff's* dealings with the public will be taken seriously. They *are* major donors, and trust me, I've already learned the hard way how very much that matters to the powers that be."

He hesitated a beat before admitting, "I know you did. I'm sorry."

She put a hand on her hip. "I thought you said you hadn't participated in any gossip about me."

"Is it really taking part in gossip to read up on an air ambulance company's safety record before you submit an application?" It had gone a lot further than that, but the last thing he could afford to do was cop to that now—not if he didn't want to forever shut the door on any shot he had with her.

She pursed her lips until the color bled from them before sighing. "I—I suppose that does make sense."

"Damn straight it does, for any flight crew member who doesn't want to end up splattered somewhere over Southeast Texas," he said. "When I recalled that the chopper that went down had been leaving an emergency on Kingston ranch property that night, in weather that should've made the former safety coordinator think better of the whole idea, I don't blame you a bit for your reaction to last night's—"

"You're not worried about your job, new as you are?" Callie asked, lowering her voice as a pair of silver-haired women, burdened with huge purses and the owlish expressions of visitors, passed by. "I know you're still on your probationary period—"

He frowned at the reminder that new hires could be let go for almost any reason, or no reason at all during their first six months of employment. But when it came down to it, there was a principle that went beyond employment. "We're damned well not the help here. We're trained professionals. I don't care how damned rich or well connected that woman is."

Callie studied his face, a mixture of curiosity and distrust in her expression. "Don't you? Because you acted like you did care last night. You sounded like you'd seen a ghost the moment she mentioned the name Kingston. What's your beef with them?"

"What makes you think I—"

"Don't play coy, Jude. Or pretend you just so happened to be hanging out here when I walked by. What's a guy who's only moved to Texas from Phoenix three months ago even *know* about the Kingstons?"

"Because I'm— I might be—" He went quiet as a food service attendant pushed a loaded cart past them, trailing the scents of prepared patient breakfasts. His empty stomach, never one for subtlety, gave a hungry growl.

"How about I buy you some coffee in the cafeteria," he asked Callie, "and we talk more about this?"

Just as he'd expected, she shook her head. "Sorry. I don't do caffeine—"

"Are you serious? I've never known anybody who works our hours who doesn't practically live on the stuff."

"I really need to get going," she said, edging toward the door. "I've got to go pick up my—"

"You eat food, don't you? How 'bout breakfast?" He'd been warned by others as well that he'd have better luck cozying up to a rabid bobcat than engaging the lone survivor of the LifeWings air disaster in casual conversation. But there was nothing casual about his interest in this woman—or in the justice he'd come to Texas to seek.

"C'mon, Callie. Fifteen minutes of your time. That's all I'm asking here," he lied.

Adjusting the daypack on her arm, she paused and turned. In her low-heeled boots, she barely had to look up to meet his eyes, though he was nearly six three. "You know, Rookie," she said, "when you came on, it caused quite a stir around here among some of the female staff members, and not even just the single ones. I'm sure you could find one of them who'd be thrilled to find you waiting outside the ladies' lockers with that disarming smile and the friendly invitation—at least, I'm hoping it's the friendly kind, because from what I've seen so far, you're a damned good paramedic."

He shrugged. "I do my best."

"So I'd be seriously disappointed if you were the type who didn't understand that when a woman tells you she's not interested—as I am in no form or fashion—"

"I'm not hitting on you here, Red. I swear I'm not some creeper."

"Wise move, Rookie, since I'm no stranger to a scalpel—or HR complaint forms, either." Raising one sleek brow, she added, "As a certain emergency physician in this building could attest."

He chuckled. "I'd expect no less of you, but I still need a shot of hot caffeine before I climb into my freezing truck. And a few words with you about our mutual issue with the Kingstons— *if* you're interested."

Her face paled, a constellation of faint cinnamon-colored freckles dawning across the bridge of her nose and fanning out across her cheekbones. "And if I'm not?" she asked.

"Once you've heard what I have to say, if you decide you're out, you're out. I'll never bother you again about it. And I'll continue backing whatever story you care to tell about what happened last night—"

"It won't be any kind of *story*. The truth is good enough for me," she insisted.

"Fine, then. You have my word."

"Your word?"

He gave a shrug, "It's what I've got. Maybe the only thing of value I have left to offer."

Callie gave him a measuring look, her golden-brown eyes thoughtful. And disarmingly beautiful, with their frame of thick, soft-looking lashes.

"So do we have a deal?" He extended his hand, hoping she would take it. Hoping, too, in the back of his mind, for the chance to see if that surge of interest he'd felt last night, the war drum of his pulse the moment his fingers had touched her cool flesh, had been more than his imagination.

Ignoring his outstretched hand, she frowned and ducked a nod. "Okay, Rookie. Here's the deal. Yes to breakfast, but not at the hospital. I don't want anybody seeing us and figuring we're getting our stories straight about Mrs. Kingston-Hoyle's complaint."

"Sure thing. Where do you want to—"

"Sally Joe's, over across the bay bridge on Mustang Island. Know the place?" When he shook his head, she gave him the street address before adding, "Wait here for five minutes. Then leave and meet me at the corner table, over by the palm trees."

"That's a lot of cloak-and-dagger for a simple break-fast, Red," he said.

She zipped the front of her jacket and gave him an offhand shrug. "You can never be too careful. Or at least I can't, if I don't want my coworkers suddenly spreading the foul rumor that I've reverted to my human form."

Chapter 2

Callie had just taken her order—an herbal tea and a couple of spinach-pepper egg white bites—back to one of about a dozen tables and was sitting and looking out at the still-chilly morning mist when Jude showed up and headed for the counter after confirming her presence with a glance. Apparently serious about his coffee habit, he ordered their largest size and didn't waste time doctoring the drink before making his way to the table.

"No breakfast?" she asked, swallowing the mouthful she'd been chewing.

"Food can wait for a bit," he said, "but the need for java's approaching critical—especially with the heat out in my clunker."

"Gotcha," she said, watching as he blew across the surface and sipped appreciatively at the dark brew, which had always tasted too bitter and made her too jumpy for her liking.

The warm, rich scent of it, though, wafting her way, and the sight of a man so obviously enjoying his first hit of the morning, set off the echo of an old ache. Though sometimes the grief packed into such moments still had the power to level her, making her wish that she, too, had died on impact that night, this morning she felt only bittersweet nostalgia and a faint pang for the kind of bond she could never bear to risk again.

Certainly not with Jude Castleman, a near stranger who clearly wanted something from her. But what? And how quickly could she convince him she had nothing left to give?

He rubbed the back of his neck and grimaced, looking oddly nervous for a guy whose breezy confidence had struck her as almost cocky the first couple of times they'd worked together. "I'm not—I'm not quite sure how to start."

"Quickly, would be my suggestion. As I mentioned, I have somewhere I need to be."

Remembering his kindness in the chopper, she refrained from glancing down at her watch and instead sipped her tea, savoring its minty flavor.

With a sigh, he set down his coffee. "I guess I can start with my grandfather's death. He passed away this summer, back in Phoenix."

"Sorry to hear it," she murmured out of reflex.

"Don't be. He was a bitter, abusive man when he was well, and I can't say the dementia made dealing with him one bit more pleasant."

"You were the caregiver?" she asked, unable to keep the surprise from her voice.

Jude shrugged. "He did raise me. Reluctantly, I know, but after my mom took her life—"

"Oh, Jude—I *am* sorry." Raised by a tumbleweed of a single mother, who'd dragged the two of them from town to town as she'd chased a dream of breaking into the big-time as a singer, Callie had known uncertainty, even deprivation in her younger years, but her mom had always been there, her first and often only friend, trying her heart out for the both of them.

"After her death when I was eleven," he said with a nod to acknowledge Callie's words, "he was pretty much stuck with me, just the way I ended up stuck with him after the memory care facility kicked him out for being overly combative."

"That kind of thing's a big problem," she said, sympathizing.

"Sure is, especially when they drop off your half-naked, practically psychotic grandfather at your apartment as you're just about to head off to work for the day."

She winced at the appalling—and illegal—action. "What did you do?"

"What *could* I do? I arranged for family medical leave—most of it unpaid, but that was what I had—and moved with him back into his house because I couldn't find any caregiver who could handle him, and all the other facilities were either full or— But you don't want to hear about that nightmare, trust me."

"How long did you—"

"Almost eight months, until one afternoon, when I begged a neighbor to keep an eye on him while he napped so I could go pick up some prescriptions and a grocery order..."

By the way Jude's blue-gray eyes glazed over, she knew the errand hadn't gone as planned.

"What happened?" she asked, already dreading the answer.

"The fire trucks were lined up by the time that I got back after my neighbor called me. He'd woken up, freaked out, and started shouting abuse and throwing things until she'd ended up fleeing for her safety. She left her cell inside, though, and in the time it took her to get to another phone and come up with my number, he'd managed to figure out where I'd hidden the stove knobs and light the damned place up."

"Oh no... Was it the fire that killed him?"

Jude shook his head. "Heart attack, probably from a combination of smoke inhalation and the stress of the firefighters breaking down the door to try to save him. All while I felt like such a piece of garbage."

"It wasn't your fault. You couldn't possibly be with him every second. And you had asked someone responsible to—"

"Not that, so much. I'm talking how damned *relieved* I felt, knowing I wouldn't have to go on any longer, listening to him rage about how I'd never been anything but a worthless bastard. A bastard who'd all but driven my mother to—to end things the way she did."

Raising her hand to her mouth, Callie felt the horror of such cruelty threatening to choke her.

"It's understandable you'd feel relief," she said once she had found her voice. "It doesn't make you a bad person, only human. *Superhuman*, as far as I'm concerned, for taking care of a man who treated you so badly in the first place. Not everybody does, believe me."

She'd seen it in the emergency department, elderly

and incapacitated men and women abandoned without ID, or brought in off the streets in deplorable condition.

"I know that," Jude said, the roughness in his voice reminding her that as a paramedic, he'd no doubt seen the same, "but whatever else he was to me, the man was family. The only family I knew, and I'd be damned if I was going to leave him."

She reached out, brushing his knuckles with her fingertips before she could stop herself. "Then somebody instilled some good values in you."

"*She* did," he said quietly, his gaze drifting to the window and Corpus Christi Bay beyond the parking lot. In the wake of last night's cold front—a rarity in an area better known for its mild winters and hot and humid summers—it formed a misty gray expanse, a bit calmer than the Gulf of Mexico would be on the other side of the narrow north-south-running strip that made up the barrier island.

But as much as she felt for Jude, she had to know where he was going with this. "So what does any of this have to do with the Kingstons?" *And the chance that after everything I've lost already, one of those soulless jackasses means to get me fired from LifeWings.*

Her stomach spasmed at the thought, robbing her of what little appetite she had.

After another swallow of his coffee, Jude set his cup down, his big hand shaking slightly as he looked into her eyes. "I know this is going to sound strange, but I believe it's possible I'm one of them. And not just some bastard from a one-night stand with one of the distant cousins, either, but a legal heir to the bulk of the empire that Big Jake Kingston, the man I believe to've been my father, left behind last year."

* * *

Jude managed to steady his hands, but inside he was shaking, waiting for her to laugh her head off at his outlandish claim. To tell him it was nothing except wishful thinking to imagine that a scabby, scrawny throwaway who'd been verbally—and sometimes physically—beaten down until he'd been unable to take it and had taken off at seventeen, was the lost prince of some billionaire ranching legend's family. Would she, like his grandfather, take one look and proclaim that he was nothing?

Instead, she frowned down at her watch before saying, "If you'll excuse me for a minute, I've gotta let my mom know I'm running late to pick up Baby. Because however long this story runs, I want to be here for every bit."

He gaped, surprised to hear that the accident that had left her widowed and injured had also left her a single mother. Or had the child—she had said *baby*, after all—come afterward, maybe resulting from some rebound relationship in the wake of her grief? No wonder Pete had warned him off messing with the woman.

He thought about the risks he was considering, if he moved forward to the next phase of his plan. Thought of how they might all too easily spill over to affect this woman—this *mother*—if she decided she wanted a piece of this action. Could he really live with the risk of getting her flat-out fired—or possibly worse, if things went sideways—with the welfare of a child at stake, too?

By the time she'd finished sending her text message, his gut had given him his answer. Shaking his head, he pushed up from the table, saying, "Never mind, Callie. You go on home to your kid."

Looking up, she laughed. "You want to see my baby? Hold on a second. Let me show you."

Gritting his teeth, he lowered himself back into the chair. And chuckled when she showed him a photo on her cell of herself, grinning in an upholstered chair, her arms overflowing with a dappled bluish-gray and white hairball sprawled upside down on her lap.

"Meet PB, which is actually short for his very favorite food on earth—Peanut Butter, but my husband and I had a running joke that it could also stand for Practice Baby," she said, her eyes tinged with sadness in spite of her smile. "We adopted him just three months before the…" She shook her head, as if to shake off the memory of the incident that had ended the couple's hopes so tragically.

"Gorgeous animal," Jude said, admiring the dog's bicolor eyes, one coppery brown and the other icy blue. And relieved as hell that her so-called *practice baby* wasn't human. "What is he?"

"Australian shepherd," she said, "and my lifesaver. That big hairy mess's love and his energy have gotten me through some very rough times."

Jude grunted his approval, wishing—not for the first time—that his schedule and living arrangements would allow for the kind of companion who wouldn't run off looking for a better offer the moment life got rocky.

"So back to what you told me," she prompted. "I'm going to need some explanation."

"Yeah," he said, taking another swig of coffee. "The fire damage at my grandfather's house ended up being pretty much limited to the kitchen. While I was cleaning out the place after his death, I ended up coming across some papers. Divorce papers for my mother, though I'd never had any idea she'd been married. Jacob Kingston, of Pinto Creek, Texas, was listed as her husband."

"Big Jake Kingston?" Callie's body tensed as she spat out a name that most people from this part of Texas knew well, since he'd owned a good chunk of it. As his heir still did, in the form of a legacy that stretched back almost 150 years, to the historic cattle ranch that spawned it. "You're absolutely sure it was the same man?"

Jude nodded. "At first I had no idea who he was, but I did some more digging, even talked a friend of mine who works as an insurance investigator into helping me dig up some verification I couldn't access on my own. It didn't take Leo long to confirm that my mother was definitely married to *that* Jacob Kingston—and had lived with him up until about seven months before my birth."

"Yet she never mentioned your father?"

He shook his head. "When I'd ask her who my dad was, she'd only tell me, 'A big mistake—but at least I got you out of the bargain.' But afterward, she'd shut herself into her bedroom and I could hear her crying, so I learned pretty young it wasn't a question I wanted to be asking."

"I definitely get that," she said. "My mom's never been into discussing her past relationships, either."

"And my grandfather had me convinced I was a bastard—'what a woman gets for falling into sin,'" Jude said bitterly, though nothing about the statement jibed with his memory of the sweet, churchgoing mother who had turned away any potential suitor so she could focus on what she'd called her "duty as a mother."

"My investigator friend dug up some custody orders that ruled against my mother—and a court transcript implying this was on account of her supposed history of adultery."

"*Custody* orders? So Jake Kingston knew about you?"

"They were for my mother's firstborn child, not me." Jude went on to confide that his mother had had another son in the early years of her unhappy marriage—a son she'd been forced to walk away from by her powerful ex's claims about her infidelity.

"The shame of it, being driven from her child, her home, being forced to live with her father's judgment— she never spoke of it, but when I think back, I'm absolutely certain that it broke something inside her."

"No wonder she didn't tell anyone she'd been carrying a second son by Kingston," Callie speculated, her eyes widening. "She couldn't bear the thought of having you taken from her, too."

"But I wasn't enough—no kid ever could've been— to fill the hole left by the son she was forced to leave behind."

"Forced by the late, great Big Jake Kingston." Callie's lip curled with contempt. "The same man responsible for my flight crew being ordered out on a night we never should've flown."

Callie's phone vibrated on the table, making a buzzing sound against the wood. "Sorry," she said, before flipping it over and frowning down at what Jude could see was a text message.

"Something wrong?" he asked.

She sighed. "I totally forgot that my mom has a can't-miss appointment this morning. Long story about why, but if I can't make it over there to pick up PB in the next twenty minutes, she'll have to lock him in his kennel for hours—which'll feel like a century to my boy without his morning run on the beach to burn off energy—and then call and wake me after she gets home this afternoon."

Disappointed as he was to have their conversation interrupted, he admitted, "That sounds like a pretty bad deal. But I was really hoping we could finish—"

"Listen," Callie said, already crumpling up her garbage, "as much as I'd like to keep this conversation going, I'm not having my dog tortured—or my shot at sleep before my evening shift wrecked—"

Raising his cup of coffee, he said, "Hey, I get it, really, so how about— You said you're taking your dog for a morning run, right? What if—would you mind if I came with you?"

His heart was pounding, he realized, feeling as awkward as a junior high kid.

"You're seriously suggesting going for a beach run in this weather? Wearing jeans and those boots?"

He shrugged. "I never promised I could keep up, only that I'd appreciate the chance to tag along."

Lips pursed, she narrowed her eyes, as if to gauge his sincerity for a moment, before huffing out a noisy breath. "I don't have time to hash this out with you now, so I'll tell you what. If you'll follow me, in a couple of miles, I'll tap the brakes at the beach access turnoff to your right. Take that and then wait for me, and I'll be back in five, ten minutes tops with Baby. Deal?"

"Thanks," he said. "You won't regret this."

But the dubious look she gave him mirrored his own doubts.

As he left the building, he huddled deeper into his hoodie against the cold wind and started toward his old truck before, behind him, Callie called, "Hold up."

Looking back, he felt a moment's embarrassment,

seeing her look of amazement as she stared past him at the more than twenty-year-old pickup, with its collection of primer-brown and electric-blue patches and its numerous scrapes and dents. With the Arizona plate still on the crooked rear bumper, there was no denying the automotive eyesore, once used in his late grandfather's painting business, was his, but pride made him straighten his spine and ask, the word coming out a little more defensively than he meant it. "Yeah?"

"Nothing," she said with a shake of her head. "I was just remembering about how you said your heat's out. So why don't you hop into my car and we'll go together? There's no need for you to freeze your tail off waiting for me on the beach. I'll drop you back here later. Okay?"

"Thanks," he said, deciding she wasn't such an iceberg after all. Which *he* would definitely be if he had to sit too long waiting in that tin can, which had all-weather air-conditioning, thanks to a rust hole through the passenger side floorboard. Plus, time alone in the privacy of her vehicle would be a very good thing: another chance for him to finally get to the point.

As she started toward the gleaming Mustang, something made him add, "And, um, I don't usually drive such a—or I didn't used to— My last ride was a lot—a lot less likely to warrant calls to the police to check out a suspicious vehicle when I park it on the streets."

"It got you here, didn't it? All the way from Phoenix." She clicked the fob to unlock the doors. "I couldn't care less what you or anybody else rolls around in. All this flash and horsepower were my husband's priority, not mine."

As he buckled himself into the comfortable leather seat inside, he felt like a fool for having brought it up.

Why should he care what she thought of his damned truck? Even if she hated it, what did it matter?

On a personal level, he assured himself it didn't. But if Callie got the idea he was some lowlife loser simply out to scam money from the Kingstons, his hopes for gaining her trust—and help—were over before they'd even begun.

After turning off her music—some alt-rock band that she'd had blaring when the car first started—she pulled out onto the two-lane road, heading farther from the city. As they proceeded, the thin needle of land that made up this end of the barrier island widened somewhat, and the low dunes to his right mostly blocked his view of the gulf.

As they passed the sign pointing out the beach access road she'd mentioned, he spotted two small deer prancing across the otherwise deserted track, their delicate forms partly obscured by blowing sand.

"What I need to know before we get any further into all this," Callie said as they continued in the direction of what he saw were the first beach houses, all of them built up on pilings set back toward the right, "is why you've come to *me* with this story and why now?"

"Because you've suffered at the Kingstons' hands, too. I've known that from the start, but after what I witnessed last night with that patient with the insufferable mother, I *knew* you saw the Kingstons for what they truly are—and it finally gave me hope that you might listen—and consider helping when I—"

"Do you have any idea what kind of man this person you say was your father *really* was?" she spat out bitterly. "LifeWings' management *warned* him it was dangerous for everyone involved, sending out a helo on a night the weather was so bad, but the only thing he cared about was getting his friend patched up so he wouldn't end up charged with homicide."

"What?" Jude shook his head, icy shock waves detonating in his stomach. "I never read anything about that in any of the papers. Are you saying that the patient killed in the chopper crash, this Walter Winthrop, *wasn't* injured in a hunting accident the way they reported?"

"In the middle of the night? *Please.* Deer season had closed weeks earlier, so there was no reason for the two of them to be way out in the backcountry, hunting trophy bucks the way he claimed. Which means that Winthrop's facial gunshot wound might not have been an accident at all."

"Surely there must've been an investigation? Were you ever interviewed by the police?"

"It's only sheriff's department down there, and no. They never talked to me in the hospital while I was recovering. Just the transportation people investigating the crash later, which was what killed Dr. Winthrop."

"Did you ask about it? Call the authorities?"

"I'd just lost my husband and a colleague and was pretty seriously hurt myself, so as you might imagine, for months I was—I was far too—" She swallowed audibly. "Let's just say it was all I could do to get myself through the day. And the nights were—if it hadn't been for PB…"

"I'm sorry," he said gently.

She waved off the sympathy with an impatient flick of her hand before slowing to take a left, turning into a small neighborhood of homes built on somewhat higher ground. Some were older, vacation places, modest and weather-beaten wooden structures, while some of the newer, more expensive-looking homes were larger, far more modern and built up on berms or pilings.

"When I was finally able to think halfway straight again," Callie told him, "I eventually did contact the sheriff's department down there in Kingston County, but everyone I spoke with seemed to have developed laryngitis. Or maybe collective amnesia. But they must've run straight to their overlord, because a few days later, I received a call from this attorney on the Kingston payroll by the name of Ed Franklin. I'll never forget how icy cold his voice was when he promised to personally destroy me if I didn't quit making waves."

"Those sons of bitches *threatened* you?" A rush of anger burned his face. "After everything you'd been through? Everything you'd lost because of—"

"Yeah...and I was too damned broken to— I had nothing left to fight with—and nothing left to fight *for*, either," she said, pulling up in front of a modest, elevated yellow beach house. "You understand?"

He ached to reach out to her, but knowing she wouldn't welcome it, he could only say, "I do get that, and I'm sorry. I wish I could have been there for you. I'm sure you could've used a friend."

"I didn't want *friends*," she blurted. "I wanted my *life* back, or at the very least, my husband."

"I get that," he said, wondering if the raw edge of her grief and anger would ever fully heal.

Blushing, she blew out a breath. "I'm sorry. Sorry I'm so— I'd better run inside and get my dog now before my mom has a conniption— *There* they are."

The relief in her voice was palpable as she caught sight of a tall, blonde woman in boots and an oversize, colorful sweater descending the wooden staircase with a large woven handbag draped over one shoulder and a fluffy bluish-gray-and-white dog at her heels.

"Sorry I'm running late, Mom. Thanks for waiting!" Callie was telling her as she sprang from the vehicle and ran over.

Seeing his mistress, the excited Australian shepherd, a good-sized animal about the size of a collie, woofed and nearly bowled over Callie's mother, a curvy fifty-something blonde, trying to get past her. Pulling the leash from her hand, he raced to Callie, his rounded rear end wagging as he danced clownishly in front of her in greeting.

Jude couldn't help grinning, seeing how she slapped her shoulders and gave him an ear-scrubbing when he jumped up to plant his big paws on her. After ordering him off and kissing her mother on the cheek, Callie waved goodbye and hurried PB toward the car.

Jude noticed her mother's less than subtle lean as she gave him a curious once-over. He smiled and waved, trying to look friendly— or at least nonthreatening. Eyes sparkling, she smiled back and nodded before turning away, reassuring him that he'd passed some unspoken test.

Callie hurried back and loaded PB into the rear seat of the car.

"Is he friendly?" Jude started to ask her before PB answered the question himself, thrusting his shaggy head between the seats and snuffling all over the side of Jude's head and face before he could fend him off.

"Cool it, Baby," Callie said as she buckled into her own seat before telling Jude, "I'm sorry. In the morning, he has a ton of pent-up energy. Once he burns it off, he'll quit being such a goober."

At least the dog listened, so Jude chuckled and wiped off the drool. "What's a little slobber between friends—and I consider all dogs potential friends."

"You have one?"

Still petting the dog's head, he shook his head and answered, "I hope to someday, if I can ever get into the right living situation."

"Well, until that happy day, I can assure you PB will be happy to shower you with as much drool and dog hair as you can stand. And probably a little extra for good measure."

The knot of tension inside him loosened slightly at her statement, at her implication that this might not be the last time she deigned to speak with him. Or had she only forgotten her usual standoffishness for the moment because he'd taken to her dog?

By the time she buckled in and put the car back in gear, her mother was backing her SUV out of the driveway, her head practically on a swivel as she scoped out Jude on the way past.

Jude felt a smile tug at one corner of his mouth. "She seems a little…*curious*."

With a chuffing sound, Callie said, "If my mom were any more curious, she'd blow off her appointment to come pound on the window and demand a proper introduction. Along with a side of light grilling, if I know her."

"You told her that I'm just a—" He caught himself just in time to keep from saying *friend*, which seemed too much of a presumption.

"A *coworker* that I'm giving a ride home," she finished for him. "But you have to understand, she's spent the past year trying to set me up with any male who has a pulse." With a sigh, she followed the SUV back out of the small division. "You'd think she'd have enough to worry about with the state of her own marriage."

"Not so great?"

"Let's put it this way. This morning, she's off to meet with their marriage counselor alone while the big jerk sleeps in on his day off," she said, "not that that will stop her from texting me later to give me the third degree about you. Or giving me that same tired lecture about how it's high time I quit moping and get back in the game. And it's not just her trying to peddle some coworker's brother who loves kids or some guy with a nice boat they met at the marina."

He winced. "Well, I can promise you I'll never do that, mostly because I hate it, too. Although for me, it's usually somebody's sister they're out to hook me up with, or that hot sonogram tech who just moved down here from Houston."

Callie laughed. "You mean the one who's so smitten with her equally cute girlfriend? Your fix-up buddies need to check in with the emergency nurses if they want to keep up with the latest developments in hospital gossip."

He shrugged. "Makes no difference to me, because I've got way too much going on to be interested in anybody right now."

But that was garbage, he knew, all too aware that there was one woman who *had* definitely intrigued him more every time he was around her. Not that he intended on complicating the situation by doing anything about what he'd convinced himself was a seriously unwise attraction.

Nodding her understanding, the woman in question

started driving back in the direction of the beach access. "I'm sure you've had a lot weighing on you, with this discovery about your mother's marriage and then your move to Texas to deal with it."

He felt the pressure of it now, riding like a boulder in his lap as they traveled back in the direction of the causeway. For the next few minutes, they rode in silence, the only sounds the dog's eager whimpers from the rear seat and the faint sizzling hiss of a misting rain against the windshield as it rolled in off the gulf.

"I have a question about your move, though," she said.

"Go ahead," he said, peering into the uniform grayness—the sky, water and road seemed to meld together.

She slowed her speed and flipped on the car's intermittent wipers. "If you wanted to find out more about the Kingstons, why come here instead of going straight to Pinto Creek, where they live?"

He shrugged. "Not much in the way of jobs for me, for one thing. And I couldn't exactly show up in that tiny little town, a stranger, and start asking a lot of awkward questions. Think about what you already found out about how the Kingstons even have the law down there running to tattle to them."

She nodded. "From what I gather, just about everybody in that county's somehow dependent—or has a close relation who is. That probably explains why that deputy last night was so quick to call us out for Daphne Hoyle's popped shoulder. Speaking of which, how's the girl's mother related to your brother?"

Jude's gut clenched hearing her refer to his mother's firstborn as such. It made the theoretical relationship, one that still made his head spin to imagine, somehow seem real for the first time. "I'm afraid Jake Jr.'s dead, too. He was killed in a motorcycle wreck a few years before his father's passing."

"That stinks, Jude—that you'll never get the chance to meet him." Grimacing, she slowed before making the turn onto the beach access road and proceeding slowly, mindful of the ruts in the narrow, sand-blown surface.

"Yeah, it does," he said, wondering what that meeting might have been like—whether his brother would have welcomed him or cursed the fact of his existence.

"So, with your brother gone, what happened to the ranch after Big Jake's death?"

"Everything went to Big Jake's son from his second marriage, Beau Kingston."

"So he'd be your half brother, right?"

"I guess so, assuming Big Jake really is my father." It felt disorienting, admitting such a thing out loud, though he'd spent more time thinking of it lately than he cared to admit. "Beau's actually only about a year younger than I am."

"I'm with you so far," she said. "So, Tammy Kingston-Hoyle? Daphne's mama?"

"A cousin—" *My* cousin, though the snobby blonde with the fur hat would probably rather scrub off her own skin with a wire brush than admit to such a possibility. "—from a branch of the family that sold off its interest in the ranch a couple generations back for big bucks. But she does serve on the board of the charitable foundation set up to benefit the community with a certain number of grants each year—"

"Like those donations to LifeWings she was trying to lord over us last night."

"Exactly." Jude scowled at the thought that the Hoyle woman would be petty and vindictive enough to go after

Callie's job and maybe his, too, over some ridiculous power play and a few hours' inconvenience.

Finding the parking area as empty as she expected, she nosed into a space where a sliver of gulf was visible between two low dunes. Though she put the car in Park, she left the engine idling to tell him, "Big Jake Kingston was even more high-handed. Or at least he was that night four years ago, when he pressured LifeWings' safety director to get him to send out our chopper in spite of the conditions."

"People have been known to go to great lengths," Jude said, "to get away with murder."

Callie's expression darkened, her gaze hot with fury and her eyes shining with moisture. Though the dog whined in the back seat, she didn't seem to hear him.

"*Three* murders, as far as I'm concerned," she burst out. "There was Larry Higgins, too, the flight medic who was with us that night. And I'll never forget my husband, Marc. Not as long as I live."

Turning over her right wrist, she yanked up the sleeve of her dark green fleece, exposing a small tattoo on her lower forearm. Delicately wrought in plain black ink, it depicted the infinity symbol—similar to the number 8, lying on its side. Except the simple image was interrupted by the tiny, tilted figure of a silhouetted helicopter.

Jude swallowed past the lump in his throat, and wondered if his own ex-wife had ever loved him with a fraction of the intensity he saw in Callie's beautiful amber-brown eyes. A devotion that clearly hadn't faded in four years. "*Three* then, yes—just the way he got away with emotionally destroying my mother, driving her to take her life with what I damned well mean to prove were lies. But then, destroying lives clearly means nothing when you've owned a big chunk of South Texas for 150 years."

Callie's gaze burned into his as she bared her teeth in a mirthless smile. "So I guess the *real* question is what do you intend to do about it now, Jude Castleman? And just how soon can we go with this to the media and finally cut the high and mighty Kingstons down to size?"

Chapter 3

Jude lifted a hand as if to stop her, his eyes flashing alarm. Or maybe panic, Callie realized, at how swiftly she'd jumped at the chance to finally *do* something. Something other than numbly tiptoeing through each day, struggling to avoid any move that would cause the fragile grip she had on her pain to crumble.

"Let's slow down a minute," he warned, his face paling in the morning light. "Before we get too far into this."

"What do you mean, before we get too far?" she demanded. "*You're* the one who came to me, aren't you? The one who wanted my help—because you already knew enough about my history to figure this would light my fuse."

With the words, she visualized the spark igniting, bright against the bleak, unchanging background of what she'd thought of as survivorship, not living.

From the back seat, PB whined and yelped, his limited patience at its end. Shaking her head, she sighed, realizing she couldn't delay his run any longer—not if she didn't want the upholstery clawed out of frustration. "I'm not up for running in this mess myself this morning, so I'm just going to walk a little while he runs up and down here. If you want to wait here in the car, I don't blame you, but—"

Casting a stubborn look in her direction, he said, "A little rain won't melt me."

Together, they left the car, and for the next few minutes, Callie's attention was on getting PB to the beach before allowing him off leash for a romp. True to form, he raced up and down the stretch, never venturing beyond the range of recall before turning back and zigzagging in the opposite direction. Kicking up sand beneath his paws, he amended his pattern, making figure eights whose edges splashed into the cold and frothing surf.

"I'm guessing you go through a lot of dog shampoo at your house," Jude said as he watched. "Towels and bathroom cleansers, too."

"You have *no* idea," she admitted, noticing that, now that PB had slowed his manic zoomies, he was presently snuffling at a heap of brown seaweed washed in on the tide. But along with his energy, the misting rain had eased, too, and the chill wind died down to make their stroll more bearable.

"So why'd you freak out, back in the car?" she asked. "What's the issue about going public with this? I thought you wanted to do something."

"Not go straight for the nuclear option," Jude said, "not before I've given him a fair chance to respond."

Confused, she shook her head. "Fair chance? Given who? Explain yourself right now, Rookie."

After snorting at the way she'd put it, he pushed back the hood of his thick sweatshirt before giving a stumbling account of, how a couple of weeks before, he'd sent a letter to Beau Kingston, telling his potential half brother what he had discovered.

"Wait—you mean, you just came out and *told* the guy? In writing?" she asked, stunned to imagine him taking such a risk. "Are you literally *insane*?"

"Not so I've noticed." Jude shrugged, his hands shoved into his pockets. "But I figured if I just let him know what I did, without being confrontational or issuing any demands, he might—"

"Did you send him proof of your claims?" Distracted, she slowed abruptly, scarcely noticing PB's presence until he trotted up beside her and pushed his slightly damp head beneath her hand.

"Of course I did. Copies, anyway," Jude said, his tone defensive. "The originals are in a safe-deposit box at my bank. And my friend Leo, the insurance investigator, is keeping copies for me, too."

"Well, that's *one* thing you've done right, but why?" she demanded, her heart beating harder than it should as she rubbed her dog's ears for comfort. She winced, upset with herself for falling into the trap of caring about a coworker, even just a little. "Why tip your hand that you're a threat to them instead of finding a lawyer to run interference?"

Jude rubbed his fingers together, making the universal sign for money. "I've talked to a few, but the moment they realize who they'd be dealing with, they all want a huge retainer, way more than I could possibly come up with."

"Then what about going through the press or something? This is just the kind of juicy story some reporter'd love to get hold of."

"You think that's what I *want*, my mother's name dragged through the mud in public?" Pain crackled through his words, burning so intensely in his blue eyes, she found them hard to look at. "A bunch of online trolls judging who she was, calling her a slut and a gold digger? It's bad enough it happened to her once already, back in Kingston County, when she first tried to fight what he was saying. I'm sure it's what drove her to— to— I'm the one who found her, you know? After she had—after she had…"

"All right. I understand. I'm sorry," she said honestly, catching a glimpse in his haunted face of the eleven-year-old who'd so clearly been traumatized by the discovery. Over the years, she'd seen too many loved ones arrive in the emergency department or at scenes where LifeWings had been dispatched with that same shell-shocked expression, watching their hopes extinguished after they'd learned help had arrived too late.

"I'm *not* a threat to Beau," Jude insisted. "I told him I wasn't after money. I didn't ask for anything. All I want—all I need is his—"

"It's all right. Take your time," she said, stopping to look out at a strand of golden sunlight piercing the low clouds to light up a greenish patch of water.

"The family needs to come out and admit, publicly and officially, that it was all a lie," Jude said, "that my mom wasn't anything like Big Jake branded her, that she was loyal, heart and soul, until he—until he made his accusations." With a shrug, he added, "That's what I need your help with, convincing Beau to do the right thing."

"Are you *serious*? You're talking about this half brother of yours—a man raised by Big Jake Kingston—as if he might have morals and a conscience. And the admission you're asking him to make would make *you* legitimate," Callie pointed out, seeing that as focused as Jude was on the great wrong he was hung up on righting, he was totally missing the larger point. The one that could so easily come back to bite him if he wasn't careful. "As well as the eldest surviving son, and, I'm absolutely certain, a legal heir to his estate."

Shaking his head, Jude went on to explain that he'd never set out to threaten anyone's inheritance, only to inform—and to give his potential half brother the chance to prove he was a cut above the Kingston who had sired him. "I offered to take a DNA test, to cooperate in whatever third-party interviews or background checks Beau prefers to verify my identity, thinking that maybe he would—"

"And what have you heard back?"

Jude sighed. "Nothing yet. Not a damned word."

"Because he's freaking out at the idea that some nobody out of nowhere—I'm sorry, Jude, but that's how these silver-spoon types see working people like us—is going to cut his billion-dollar empire in half."

"But that's not what I—"

"Wake up, Jude. For all you know, Beau Kingston's huddled right now with a team of cutthroat lawyers, trying to figure whether they're better off bribing some underpaid tech at whatever lab they hire to test your cheek swab or digging up—or simply *inventing*—the kind of dirt that'll eliminate you as a threat forever. After what they did to your mother—"

"If they mean to try that kind of bull with me," Jude vowed, "I'm ready for all comers. And more than ready to confront them personally, to make them pay for what they've—"

"Maybe you think you've got this covered," Callie told him, "but somehow I doubt it, Rookie. And the longer you give them to dream up ways that you and I would never think of to destroy you, the worse it's going to be for you —unless we come out swinging hard, before they get the chance."

The January sky had already gone dark by the time Jude locked up his apartment, located on the second floor of an older, smaller complex along the edge of Oso Bay, and headed for his truck for his 7:00 p.m. shift. Keys in one hand, he was juggling a fresh cup of the coffee he'd brewed to make up for his near-total lack of sleep that day. He'd done his best to rest after a meal of steak and eggs and an intense workout he had hoped would burn off his excess energy, but his mind wouldn't stop replaying how the conversation with Callie had ended.

He still remembered the mixture of disappointment and frustration in her eyes when he'd told her he'd have to think through his next step—along with whether he really wanted to involve her, now that she'd so thoroughly pointed out the full scope of the danger.

"Why bother telling me all this in the first place," she had blurted, "get me all excited about the idea that there's finally something, *anything*, I can do to help, when you're not even fully committed?"

He'd clearly ticked her off—maybe even blown his chance with her—but he hadn't given her an answer. Hadn't been able to put into words the dim hope he'd been holding on to, the foolish fantasy that Beau Kingston might be willing to explore the possibility that the two of them *were* brothers. That after a time, the billionaire ranching heir might even welcome him into a clan that Jude had learned included Beau's two sons and his second wife.

Jude cursed himself for a fool, reminding himself he was a grown man—and far too old to hold on to some childish notion that there was a family somewhere, even the family whose patriarch had caused his mother so much suffering, waiting to welcome their lost scion with open arms.

After his old truck started on the second try, he zipped the light jacket he had thrown on, grateful that last night's bitter cold had eased into the low fifties—what he understood was a far more typical winter cool snap this far south in coastal Texas. As he pulled out onto the road that would take him to the hospital, the thin clouds overhead veiled all but the brightest stars. But in the murk of the marshy waters rimming the bay along the roadside at his right, he caught a glimmer of lights reflected from several passing vehicles.

Glancing into his rearview mirror, Jude noticed that, dark as the road was, the SUV that had pulled out behind him had switched its headlights off. Accelerating quickly, it came up on his bumper fast.

Did the idiot mean to pass or—

His heart raced along with his pickup as he pressed down on the gas to avoid an impact from behind. Yet the shiny black SUV pulled to his left, drawing even with Jude's rear tire—despite the fact that they were approaching caution signs warning of a blind curve dead ahead.

He doesn't mean to pass me.

If the darkened headlights and the vehicle positioning weren't enough to convince Jude, a split-second glance over his shoulder did. In that blurred fraction of a second, two details jumped out at him: the driver's glowing cigarette and the emergence of a long gun barrel from the lowering window just behind him.

"No!"

Jude mashed down on the pedal, praying that the pickup– though scratched and faded and old enough to vote—had a little more juice in it. With a rattling sound, the truck lurched forward, speeding into the curve.

The SUV behind him roared up on his left again, just as a small car- –a tiny econobox model—came around the curve. Certain the occupants would be killed in the collision, Jude yielded the lane, braking as the heavier SUV swung into his path.

On a wider road, he would have made it. Or during a span of drier weather, when the marshy shoulder didn't extend nearly to the pavement. But with a series of wet, wintry days this past week, his right-side tires sank deep into the muck.

As he fought for control, the SUV sideswiped his truck's bed, the crunching impact lifting the left side from the road…

The pickup rolled twice before the side of Jude's head smacked hard against the door frame. Yellow-orange spangles burst across his vision a fraction of a second before his reality went inky black.

Jude didn't know how long he was out—seconds,

maybe minutes—before the world returned. A world of deep shadows, dark reflections and—was that water, sloshing, dripping, *pouring* in beside him, through a broken window to his left?

Uncertain where he was, he grew aware of his discomfort—the thudding of his heart, the painful pulsing of his left temple when he moved his head and the aching of his arms, which seemed to be raised above him for some weird reason.

No, not raised *above* him. *Dangling*. As he himself was drooping, suspended upside down from his lap and shoulder harness.

Memory crashed in on him with a sickening jolt. The SUV rushing up with its lights darkened, the driver with the wraparound shades and the glowing cigarette. The ski mask guy with the gun barrel that had emerged before the vehicle went flying off the road. Flipping into the shallows adjacent to the bay.

When his hands clenched involuntarily, their cold wetness made him jerk them upward, lifting them dripping from the water that had flowed inside—and was still filling—the inverted top of his truck. Cursing, he felt for the seat belt and found the straps encircling his thighs where he'd slipped partway out of the harness.

Even if he could get himself out, would the men who'd tried to kill him still be out there, waiting for their chance to finish the job? *The job Beau Kingston surely sent them to do...*

Unable to imagine anyone else who would want to harm him, Jude groaned, cursing himself for a fool. If he somehow survived this, he swore to himself he would take Callie's advice and come out swinging before the Kingstons found another way to shut him down for good.

Painfully, he craned his neck and saw the dim glow from his dashboard—with the engine dead, every idiot light was burning—illuminating the thick, mud-choked water spilling into the cab below his head. Now about four inches above the flipped roof, the quickly rising tide reeked of dead fish and rotting vegetation. Clearly, if he didn't get himself out of here soon, he was going to drown—or choke to death—in the slimy muck.

From outside the pickup, he heard the muffled sounds of urgent conversation. Male voices, they increased in volume and intensity, as if they were coming closer. *Good Samaritans or first responders*, he prayed—but a dark chasm opened in the pit of his stomach, insisting that the first to be on hand were far more likely the pair who'd put him here, eager to make sure they left no witnesses behind—or their job unfinished.

Pushing his feet against the floor above the pedals, he reached down and plunged his left hand through the cold ooze and braced it against the roof of the truck. Gritting his teeth with the effort, he placed his right hand on the buckle of his seat belt and breathed a silent prayer that the action he was taking wouldn't be his last.

Chapter 4

With her heart pumping as if she'd just finished a 10-K run instead of the short walk from the parking lot, Callie feigned a confidence she wasn't feeling. She knocked at the office door of the Thorn, as the HR director was known among the hospital's veteran employees. Answering the door at once, the rail-thin Myra Thornton smiled, the sprayed wings of her full silver hair, flowing skirt set and pastel scarf as unchanged as her deceptively friendly ways.

"Lovely roses," Callie said, trying to keep her voice from shaking as she nodded toward the full vase—the ever-present blooms a delicate ivory today. One of the first things new employees were told by more senior hospital staff was the importance of not showing weakness within this scented realm.

She was rewarded with a nod as Mrs. Thornton gestured toward one of the two comfortable chairs in front of her scrupulously neat glass-topped desk. "Coffee? Water? Or—oh wait, I remember, you prefer lemon tea, don't you?"

"Right now, I'd just as soon get straight to the point." Callie said, choosing the seat that was closer to the door. "I wouldn't want to inconvenience the nurse I'm relieving by being late."

"As you wish." Nodding curtly, the Thorn retrieved a file from the credenza and sat down next to Callie rather than behind her desk.

Crossing her ankles, which looked impossibly thin atop the high-heeled pumps she wore, the older woman silently flipped through the pages, pretending to refresh her memory of Callie's history. As if anyone else who worked for the hospital shared it.

Callie bit her lip, refusing to add more ammunition to the case she knew had already been made against her. Refusing to allow her nerves or temper to accomplish what Tammy Kingston-Hoyle's complaint couldn't.

Smiling up at her, Mrs. Thornton said, "You're an outstanding nurse, Mrs. Fielding, a credit to the hospital and your profession. Your files, both before and after the—the incident four years ago are commendable, with your advanced certifications, awards for mentoring new hires, and letters of commendation from grateful patients and their families—"

"Along with the occasional complaint," Callie admitted, knowing it would be foolish to deny the grievances that had been filed over her conduct toward those co-workers she felt were slacking—or even incompetent.

The Thorn's smile only widened. "Your only fault is that you don't suffer fools gladly." She chuckled dryly.

"To be honest, you rather remind me of a younger version of myself."

Horrified by the comparison, Callie made a mental note to bring in cupcakes or maybe order pizza delivered to the ER before her next shift. *And make an effort to be kinder.*

"However," Mrs. Thornton went on, "this does not mean we can afford to ignore a complaint about your conduct from the mother of a patient."

"'Afford to' being the operative term," Callie said, "when the mother of that patient happens to be a big-time LifeWings donor."

Frowning at the accusation, Mrs. Thornton pulled a complaint form from the file and handed it to Callie. "Do you deny this?"

After holding up a finger to signal for a moment as she read, Callie thought of her vow to Jude after he'd offered to back whatever story she chose to tell. A vow to stand by the truth of her own words and actions.

"It's pretty accurate," she admitted. "*But* it doesn't explain my reasons. If you had only been there and heard that woman—there was no legitimate reason for us to have been called out on a night like that one."

"I'm not interested in your excuses. The decision to send for LifeWings had already been made by the first responder on the scene."

"Sure, some ill-trained deputy who's probably in the Kingstons' pocket." *Just as you are*, Callie wanted to add but didn't dare.

"That's not the point. The call for LifeWings had come in. It was signed off on shortly thereafter by the supervisor in charge, and *you* were sent to the scene to assess and prepare a patient for transport—*not* to pass judgment."

Something about the woman's tone, or maybe it was the way she peered up over the dark rims of her reading glasses, had Callie flashing back to other meetings. Meetings where the Thorn had made her little considering noises as she'd flipped through medical reports related to Callie's physical therapy, reviewed the psychologist's evaluation following her PTSD counseling and asked intrusive questions about how she was "handling" widowhood before deciding whether to allow her to return to duty.

The memory left her vibrating with resentment and unable to hold her temper. "You know what? If you don't think that I, of all people, have *earned* the right to a little judgment, especially when it comes to some woman risking both her daughter's and our crew's safety on another foul night over her kid's *backhand*, you can deal out whatever punishment you think fit. Because I'm not one bit sorry."

Mrs. Thornton frowned back. "Then I take it the apology I'm about to suggest is—"

"Out of the question. I'm not groveling to some entitled donor." *Especially not a Kingston.*

The frown lines deepened. "Then we have very little to discuss, other than your suspension from the LifeWings flight schedule until your formal disciplinary meeting, thirty days from now, where we will discuss whether your continued work in the same environment that resulted in your husband's tragic death remains in anyone's best interest."

"But you've said yourself, I've done my job and done it well," Callie railed, her hand encircling her tattooed wrist. "And if you'll take a closer look at the advanced training I've done, you'll see it's all about flight medicine. *I'm* all about it." *Because it's the one thing I can do that keeps me feeling close to Marc.* "And I'm not about to let some spoiled rich woman who can't deal with being denied a request that would have put her and her own kid in danger mess this up for me."

Mrs. Thornton dredged up a sympathetic look from somewhere. "Perhaps it would be best, in light of the circumstances, for you to take some of that vacation time you've accrued. As I've already advised you more than once, if you don't start using those days, you'll end up losing them."

"Don't do this to me," Callie pleaded, imagining weeks stretching out before her without the strict routine she relied on to keep from remembering too much and feeling it too deeply. "Especially not this time of year."

Though it killed her to let down her guard in front of the Thorn, the thought of spending the upcoming anniversary of Marc's death with only her dog, along with her mother's *helpful* encouragement to replace her husband with virtually anything with a Y chromosome and a pulse, had Callie erupting in chill bumps.

With a stiff nod, the Thorn proceeded. "Then confine your future work to the emergency department. Or perhaps you could continue to assist with LifeWings' employee training. At least, with you, there are some options—"

"Wait. What do you mean, 'at least, with me'?" Belatedly, alarm shot through her as Callie realized she'd been referring to Jude, who as a newer hire, could be terminated for almost any reason. "Don't tell me, that woman had something to say about my flight medic, too, because Castleman's behavior last night was *beyond* reproach. He was completely professional from start to finish."

"You know I can't speak about any other employee," Mrs. Thornton responded crisply. "I can only advise you to see to your own career by making certain your work in the ER remains exemplary. Otherwise, I can't vouch for what your future holds."

But Callie knew she wouldn't *have* a future with this hospital if they wouldn't let her fly.

As the ambulance crew wheeled him into the emergency department of the same hospital that employed him, Jude's teeth chattered uncontrollably, in spite of the blankets that had been strapped over his wet clothes. For all the years he'd spent working as a paramedic, he was completely disoriented by the whoosh of the doors opening, the clamor of voices. Even the electronic chiming of a hospital tone and the thump of approaching footsteps made him squeeze his eyes shut. Still, flashes of light and movement seeped through his closed lids, including a torrent of words that exhaustion prevented him from making any sense of.

Instead he was immersed in fighting to keep his shivering muscles from seizing against the restraints. In fighting—unsuccessfully, it turned out—to keep his stomach from bringing up the mucky water he must've swallowed when he'd—

Drowned?

No, that couldn't be right, he thought after he'd brought up a bellyful on the floor. Thinking back, though, he remembered nothing from the accident after the searing panic he had felt when his foot had tangled in the shoulder harness as he'd worked his body free of the submerged truck. Flooded again with emotions, he bucked against the restraints, his lungs spasming as he tried to cough up what felt like half of Oso Bay.

He felt a hand on his shoulder, plucked his own name—spoken in a familiar, feminine voice—out of the clamor. *Callie*, saying, "I'm right here, Jude. Let's get you onto the bed here and see what we have."

The noise expanded once again, washing out whatever else she might be saying. Still, the oasis of recognition allowed him to quit fighting the pain and confusion and trust the capable, competent and surprisingly passionate woman he'd confided in that morning to sort this all out for him.

Soon, several sets of hands lifted him onto what he realized must be an exam room bed, and a new oxygen mask was fitted to his face. He felt things being done to him—vitals taken, sodden clothes cut from his body—and for a moment, he felt shame at having his coworkers, or more specifically Callie, see him so helpless.

But even that small burst of emotion took more energy than he had, so he drifted for a while, too weak to open his eyes, much less to respond to questions. He must have slept—for how long he had no idea. He only knew that when he woke, his shivering had eased, thanks to the warming blankets tucked around him.

Someone had turned down the lights, too, making his eyes less painful as he adjusted to his surroundings. Judging from the layout of what was surely an exam room, he remained in the emergency department. When he turned his head too quickly, the dim space seemed to spin around him, causing him to groan aloud and triggering a spasm of coughing.

The curtain slid open slightly, and he raised an arm to cover his eyes, hissing at the sudden brightness. "Can—can you—?"

"Sorry about that," said a stocky male, judging from the voice and silhouette. "Let me grab your nurse for you, let her know that you're awake."

Callie came rushing in a few minutes later, as he was sitting upright, the blankets puddling around his middle as he tried to clear his lungs.

"Here, let me get you a little water," she offered.

He winced. "Don't you think I've had enough damned water?" But it was true, his mouth was somehow parched and his throat scraped raw, so he didn't argue when she insisted.

After she had helped him drink a few sips and re-checked his vitals, she asked, "Do you know where you are and why you're here?"

"Of course I do. I'm at the hospital," he said irritably, even though he knew she was only assessing his mental status as they both were trained to do. "And I'm here because I—"

Choking on phlegm, he once more coughed until she again passed him the cup.

"It's all right. There's no hurry. You've aspirated water—and probably a bit of muck, too, from the look of the chest X-rays. You can tell me all about your accident later."

He grabbed her wrist—clamping down when she reflexively pulled back. Refusing to let go, he stared hard into her brown eyes, which had flared wide with alarm.

"No—no accident," he choked out, his voice straining and his head pounding with the effort, but he *had* to make her understand. "Two men in a big black SUV ran me off the road on purpose—and that was—that was *after*—" He fought off another spasm of coughing. "The masked guy stuck a big gun out of the window and—and pointed it straight at me."

"*What* masked guy? Who?" she asked, her eyes huge against her pale face.

"I— No idea, but—but who else would want to? Like you said before—"

"Kingston's men—it has to be," she hissed, her gaze flicking toward the curtain as if to check to make certain they were still alone.

"You—you're the one who warned me h-how damned ruthless they'd be," he said as he released her.

"But I never imagined they'd send someone here to—to try to kill you." Shuddering, she rubbed at the gooseflesh visible along her arms. "If it weren't for those college students who pulled over and went in after you— Thank goodness one of them knew mouth-to-mouth."

Jude's already unsettled stomach squirmed.

"This changes everything," Callie told him. "We have to call the police, tell them everything you know before this goes any further—"

"No!" he blurted before being taken with another coughing fit.

As he struggled to calm his breathing, she passed him the water again. As he sipped, she shook her head. "I'm sorry, but I'm not sure I can let this go—or take the chance that the Kingstons will send someone else to finish what they've started—"

"It's not your call—not your story to tell," he insisted, "so you can't—"

"All right, Jude. Calm down before you make yourself even sicker."

"You won't talk, will you, while I'm laid up?" he asked, uncertain whether to trust her quick agreement. Uncertain he'd made the right call in trusting his business—his intimate family secrets—with this woman, this virtual stranger, in the first place. Locking eyes with her, he pleaded, "Promise me."

Before she could respond, a petite, dark-haired woman pushed aside the curtain. After introducing herself as Dr. Elena Diaz, she explained to Jude that in light of the immersion injury to his lungs and a possible mild concussion, he was being admitted. "At least overnight and most likely for a day or two for treatment."

"But I'm still a probationary employee with the hospital system," he protested. "I c-can't possibly miss—"

Dr. Diaz shook her head, her expression sympathetic. "I don't know who the LifeWings program has conducting their flight physicals, but I can't imagine they're going to let you back up in a chopper for at least a month or two."

As he gaped in shock, Callie's hand, which had been helping to support him as he'd drunk the water, gently squeezed Jude's arm.

Chapter 5

Armbruster hated working with a partner, and he detested failure even more, since in his experience, the presence of the first, especially the buzz-cut young muscle neck he'd been stuck working with on this job—who couldn't even shoot straight, despite the fact that he called himself Trigger—all too often led to Armbruster having to explain the second to the client.

"I wanted him *eliminated*, not just soaked and rattled." The man's Texas accent was as unmistakable as his irritation as he complained over the burner phone Armbruster would use for this task only.

Though he could have cast blame on his partner's poor aim, Armbruster would never undermine their profession with a client, and he was especially loath to risk infuriating a man with hands who could pop his head off like the cork on a champagne bottle. Particularly when that man was currently next to him and chomping an onion-laden takeout sandwich. He sat behind the wheel of the car he'd hotwired to replace the SUV they'd ended up rolling into the bay elsewhere following Jude Castleman's untimely "accident."

"We were contracted for a single unsolved, low-profile kill," Armbruster reminded the client as he tapped the ash off his cigarette—a habit he had tried for many years to give up, not unlike the profession he'd retired from and then returned to no fewer than three times already.

"I know that, but you know, too, I want him gone fast—"

"So when those Good Samaritans showed up out of nowhere and dived right in after the target," Armbruster continued, forcing himself to ignore the interruption, "our window of opportunity closed…unless you would have preferred to absorb the cost and attention a triple would've brought without further consultation?"

"Of course I don't want a trail of dead innocents getting the media and, God forbid, maybe even the Texas Rangers dragged into this." The client's sigh rattled over the phone connection, his anger and impatience not quite masking his fear of the legendary Lone Star lawmen. "But I have pressing needs, and with the target currently hospitalized, I was thinking you might—"

"You know as well as I do there'll be cameras everywhere there, and far too many witnesses." Though he was well aware of the whisperings that had made him a legend within certain circles—a reputation both he and his handler had carefully cultivated—Armbruster often wondered if his clients imagined that he had the ability to turn himself into smoke and ooze through ventilation systems. Or perhaps they watched too many of those ridiculous movies where black-clad ninjas did handsprings past machine-gun fire, eliminated unprotesting victims and disappeared into thin air.

"I'm not suggesting anything of the sort," the client protested, "but while you're waiting for a better opportunity, there is something I need you to take care of."

As the client described what it was he wanted, Armbruster felt the sear of indignation. "You were told that I'm a *specialist*," he said, cutting a warning look toward his partner, who seemed oblivious to how loudly he was chewing on his reeking sandwich. "This is hardly in my purview."

"You haven't accomplished your *purview* yet, though, have you? In spite of the more than generous retainer your—um—arranger or whatever he is negotiated to guarantee results."

"Because I *get* those results," Armbruster said, with the confidence of a man who had over his many years in the business persevered through countless temporary setbacks, but always found a way to do exactly as he promised, "as I'm certain you were made aware."

"Perhaps, but we both know that now that our quarry's been alerted, that may prove more difficult and time-consuming. And *my* time is a valuable commodity—as is my patience at this moment. So will you or will you not handle this detail and report back with results?"

After a moment's consideration, Armbruster named his price, to be paid in the form of a bonus after the completion of the original assignment.

Following the expected protest and counteroffer, they arrived at a new deal.

"But remember," warned the client darkly, "you won't see another penny until Jude Castleman is dead."

A little after ten in the morning two days later, Jude was cooling his heels in his hospital room, wearing the faded jeans, long-sleeved T-shirt and old running shoes that Pete Stillwagon had grabbed for him from Jude's locker. After numerous tests and treatments to deal with the gunk in his lungs, a surprising number of visits from concerned coworkers and a meeting with the police detective assigned to investigate his so-called *accident*, he was more than ready to get out of here, now that he finally had his discharge papers.

Instead, he kept peering out the window into the parking lot and glancing at the clock, wondering what had happened to Pete, who had promised to arrive more than a half an hour earlier to give him a lift to his apartment. They'd spoken just last night, after Pete's shift in the emergency department had ended, and his coworker had assured him, "It's not a problem. You can count on me."

But given Pete's failure to at least touch base— and Jude's own recent experience—he couldn't help the knot of anxiety in his belly warning that something could have happened to his friend.

Jude tried to tell himself there was no reason to be so paranoid. After all, Pete wasn't the one who'd managed to get himself on the wrong side of the Kingstons. Still, the worry built until Jude found himself digging out the new prepaid smartphone that Pete's wife, a fellow hospital employee from the radiology department, had been kind enough to purchase for him to replace the cell phone that had been lost in the wreck.

Just as he was pulling up Pete's number, Jude heard the room's door open, along with the jingling of car keys.

"There you are," he said as he canceled the call. "I was about to check on you."

But instead of the bearded, dark-haired nurse he had expected, Callie Fielding stood before him, looking freshly crisp in a light cotton tunic with charcoal leggings and retro royal-blue sneakers with white laces. Her hair was down again, and the loose waves tumbled, as if the breeze had tousled them on her way in from the car.

His fingers tingled as it unexpectedly hit him how much he'd like the chance to use his fingers to untangle all that chestnut silk, to explore its texture and the warmth of her lightly freckled skin.

"Nice kicks, Red," he said, buying himself time to remind himself—not for the first time—that this was one woman he had no business thinking about that way. And to get past his surprise, since he hadn't seen or heard from her since he'd been brought in to the emergency department. "But I thought you were Pete. He was supposed to be my ride home."

"I'm afraid Stillwagon's got a sick kid," she told him, dropping her keys into the pocket of the small handbag she had slung over one shoulder. "Nothing serious, but I guess the school calls if they're running even the slightest fever."

"So he asked you to come?" Jude guessed.

She bobbed a quick nod. "It's my day off, so Pete figured I might be available. Although..." As she surveyed the grouping of cards, balloons and a plastic container of home-baked cookies dropped off by various female coworkers, her amber-brown eyes glittered with amusement. "…it seems like he might've chosen one of our more *appreciative* colleagues."

Jude snorted. "I'm not sure I'd want some of those ladies knowing where I live. Evidently, my *accident* has convinced them I need some serious taking care of."

Glancing at a couple of the more prominently displayed cards, she smiled. "Trust me, Rookie. The only needs that pack of man-eaters are interested in having taken care of are their own. Although if you're into that sort of thing, I hear that Sharon also makes an outstanding Texas sheet cake. At least that's what her husband says. *Big* guy, short fuse—we've see him in the ER after a couple of pretty nasty Saturday night honky-tonk dustups. If I remember right, he came out of both incidents in a lot better shape than the guys he mixed it up with."

"I'll be sure and keep that in mind," Jude said, wincing at the thought of how unabashedly that particular flight nurse had been coming onto him since his arrival. Without ever once mentioning a spouse or the young daughters he'd heard others pointedly ask her about within his hearing. "I appreciate your concern for my virtue—and the lift, too, Callie. I could've called for a car."

"Then we wouldn't have had the chance to talk business," Callie said, her gaze burning into his, "which is something we very much need to do, if you're up for it."

"What business?" he asked.

She shook her head an instant before the door opened and an attendant arrived, pushing a wheelchair inside. Though Jude told the younger man he was more than capable of walking, Callie shook her head. "You know it's hospital policy, so just get in the thing and let's get going. And don't you dare leave behind those cookies, because that particular individual's chocolate chip pecan caramel have been known to cause minor riots in the break room when she brings 'em..."

"And here I thought you were some kind of health nut, with your herbal tea and Goody Two-shoes low-carb breakfast."

Callie rolled her eyes. "If that's really what you think, try standing between me and a plate of fresh-baked pastries, Rookie."

The attendant chuckled but had sense enough to stay out of their conversation as Jude reached for his jacket.

"You probably won't need that," Callie advised him. "That cold front's cleared off, and the sun's burning off this haze fast."

She turned out to be right, he was happy to discover, the soft gulf breeze and warming temperatures making him grateful that coastal South Texas's occasional blasts of winter were normally as short-lived as those he'd left behind in Phoenix.

Inside Callie's Mustang, she asked Jude where his place was. "Or would you'd rather grab a bite first? It'll have to be quick, because I have a thing I promised I'd do a little later, but—"

"If it's all right with you, I'd just as soon head straight home," he said as he adjusted his shoulder harness to accommodate his still-sore muscles. "When they're not waking you up to poke and prod you around the hospital, they're stuffing you full of mediocre food."

"Fine by me," she said as the engine rumbled to life. "As long as I can score a cookie or two in exchange for the lift home."

"Happy to share my spoils," he said before giving her the name and location of his complex, which lay more or less between the hospital and her own neighborhood on Mustang Island.

"I know those apartments. A friend of mine used to live there." As she pulled on an oversize pair of sunglasses from her console, she tilted a look in his direction. "So I guess we'll be driving right past…right by where they pulled your truck out of the water."

"And me, too, I guess." He grimaced. "Not that I remember that part."

She started driving, turning in the direction of the smaller of the two bays that lay between the city and the gulf. The bay that had swallowed one man and given up another, considerably less naive one.

"Have you heard anything from the police yet?" Her voice was sober as the hospital fell behind them. "I suppose they've been investigating what—what happened to you."

"They sent a detective to ask me what I remember. It seems the college kids who witnessed my truck flying off the road—"

"The same ones who resuscitated you?"

"Yeah," Jude said. "I'm trying to see if I can meet them by the way, to thank them—though a handshake seems— What do you say to a pair of strangers who'd risk their own lives to do a thing like that?"

"'Thank you' is a great start," she said, sounding completely earnest. "They must be amazing young people."

Jude blew out a breath, still scarcely able to wrap his head around how close he'd come to dying. To ending his existence with nothing, neither wife nor girlfriend, a real home or even a furry best friend he could call his own to show for thirty-seven years on the planet.

"You okay?" she asked.

"Sorry, yeah. Just a little... A near miss like that makes you think. But I'm sure I don't have to tell you." He thought about the tiny chopper inked over the infinity symbol on her wrist and how much more she'd lost than he had.

"I—ah—after my physical injuries were healed, they made me go to see a counselor before they'd let me fly again." Though she had to stop for a traffic light, she kept looking straight forward, the rigidity in her back and shoulders giving away her discomfort. "She's actually not half-bad, if you decide you'd like to talk to somebody about it."

But not to Callie herself. He heard that in her voice, heard her practically pleading for him not to drag her back to the edge of that precipice again.

As the light turned green, he cleared his throat before returning to a safer subject. "Anyway, those college kids—the witnesses—reported to police that a black SUV forced me off the road, but they were too busy worrying about me to catch the make and model or plate number."

"Sounds reasonable."

"I'd say so. Mostly because I'm here to say it. But the detective was disappointed to know I couldn't tell them any more than they had already, and since there were no other witnesses or surveillance footage..."

"So you really didn't mention anything to them about your beef with the Kingstons?" she asked.

He shook his head. "I haven't told anyone besides you. Seriously, who else would believe that a guy like me could be a real threat to people like them, and that even if I somehow was, with all the lawyers in the world at their disposal, they'd try to—to take me out directly like this?"

"You're right about that," she said. "Let me guess. This detective that you've talked to—he's probably imagining this was road rage or maybe the culprits were drugged up or drunk—"

"Detective Judd's a woman, but you're right. She also mentioned the possibility of gang activity, too." Jude sighed and shrugged. "What is it the doctors are always saying? When diagnosing a patient, you look for horses, not zebras—and I'm thinking that to a cop, a murderous billionaire ranching heir would have to sound more like a unicorn."

"Which is why," Callie ventured as they passed a bait shop and marina, allowing him a glimpse of sunlit water, nearly as blue as the clearing sky above, "I went ahead and took the HR director's advice to take some vacation time, as long as I'm grounded from LifeWings for the next four weeks."

"What do you mean, *grounded*?"

"Tammy Kingston-Hoyle's complaint, remember?" The sharpness of her voice, combined with her flush of color, betrayed her emotions. "Pending a hearing to determine whether I'm a *liability*, working the same job that killed my colleagues and my..."

When she couldn't finish, he jumped in to say, "But you've been doing that job—and damned well, from everything I've seen and heard—ever since you returned to duty after your recovery. What's it been? Over three years now since you came back?"

"If anybody else were griping about me, I don't think it would be a problem. But when you attach the name *Kingston*—" she choked out the hated name with effort

"—and enough dollar signs to a complaint, it tends to take on weight."

"That isn't right," he said, "and if there's anything I can do to help—"

She shook her head, her expression so stricken that some instinct told him there was more she wasn't saying.

The road turned toward a marshy natural area, one of the few spots where houses, vacations condos and other development didn't extend to the tidal waterline.

"Wait," he said. "You warned me before. This is about to blow back on me, too, right? What've you heard?"

Callie hesitated a few moments before huffing out a sigh. "Human Resources wouldn't come out and say, but I'm afraid—afraid that because of your probationary status, whatever consequences you face could end up being even more serious."

"You mean like termination?" Jude could ill afford to lose this job now, especially with these new medical bills coming in. "No one's said a word to me."

"And I'm sure they won't, until you're cleared for duty."

"That buys me a few weeks, at least…"

Grasping the wheel harder, she gave a growl of pure frustration. "The whole thing is ridiculous, considering that you've done absolutely nothing wrong."

"That wouldn't be the point," he said, grasping the broader ramifications in an instant.

"Then what *would* be? Because I sure as heck can't see one."

"Don't you? To appease this Kingston-Hoyle woman so she doesn't jeopardize LifeWings' funding, maybe the hospital feels they have to make a grand gesture and make an example of *somebody*. You're a veteran flight and emergency nurse with all kinds of advanced training. Way harder to replace than some newly hired flight-certified paramedic from out of state."

"Don't sell yourself short, Jude. You're experienced in the field, *and* you deliver outstanding patient care."

He waved off her praise. "It's not the same as experience in this job, within this system, and you know it, especially at your level. Plus, there's the social component."

"*Social* component? What are you talking about?" she scoffed. "It's not like I'm exactly known for being the life of staff parties. I can't remember the last time I spoke to anyone—except for you, and Pete this morning—outside of work, and trust me, neither time was my idea."

"Yeah, but you weren't always like that, were you? Or that's what I've been told."

"You've been asking around about me," she accused, an icy edge to her voice.

He shrugged. "People talk when they care. And people around here care about you a great deal."

"They *pity* me. There's a difference."

"You've got that wrong, Red. Your friends and colleagues respect the hell out of you and, yeah, they do feel for what you've been through, just the way I'm sure that you would for any fellow human who'd gone through something like that. So maybe try cutting yourself a little slack sometime and remembering that you're just as worthy of compassion as anybody else."

For a span of time he marked off in the drumming of his heartbeat, she said nothing, her mouth drawing into a thin, tight line and her eyes inscrutable behind her sunglasses.

"*Compassion...*" As they reached a bend in the road,

she pulled over so sharply that he was certain she was about to demand that he get out of her car and walk the rest of the way home.

Instead, she took a deep breath, seeming to collect herself before asking, "Is this it?"

"Is this what?" As he stared out the passenger window, his heart skipped a beat before punching hard against his sternum at the sight of multiple sets of tire marks—probably both his truck's and those of the tow vehicle that had winched it free of the muck—leading down into the water.

At the bay's edge, he saw a spot where many of the tall, tough grasses had been mashed down and several leggy shorebirds poked their long beaks hopefully into the disturbed silt. Without another word, Jude unbuckled his seat belt and exited the car, every nerve ending in his body electric as he stood looking down and watching the sun glint off the wavelets.

It was piercingly beautiful, the blue of the water, the cry of the gulls kiting on the breeze. Still, when the wind shifted, a stagnant breath of marshy salt air hit the back of his throat, and he felt himself choking. Drowning.

He heard Callie's door close moments before he felt her touch his arm.

"I know how hard it must be, facing this place again so soon," she said. "I'm sorry to have made you do it, but I'm afraid we don't have much time left."

Straightening, he stared at her. "Time left before what?"

"Before Beau Kingston's thugs try again to end you." She cut him a concerned look. "Unless you believe that detective's nonsense about some random lowlife targeting you on your way to work along this quiet little stretch of waterfront road."

"Not for a minute. But the question is, what am I going to do about it—because other than coughing all over Beau Kingston, I haven't exactly come up with a solid plan for forcing him to admit who I am to him."

"You've done one thing very right, though." The breeze stirred her long hair, which glowed an even brighter shade in the brilliant winter sunshine.

"What's that?"

"Picked me to confide in." Excitement lit up her eyes. "Because have I ever got a plan for us —but it'll only succeed if we're brave and bold and work as partners."

"As partners," he echoed, the two words resonating in a place inside him that had been too long bruised and hollow.

She brushed a lock of stray hair from her cheek. "Partners in finally putting the Kingstons in their place and in finding justice for my husband and your mother. So are you in, Jude Castleman?"

This had been what he had wanted, what he had dreamed of from the moment he'd first thought of trying to enlist her as an ally. But there was a wildness in her expression that made him hesitate a moment, wondering how far she might be willing to go for her revenge. "Does it involve violence? I'm not talking about defending ourselves, but I'm not about to waylay and ambush somebody in cold blood even in order to—"

"No unprovoked bloodshed or excessive mayhem," she promised. "Though a little deception and the tiniest smidgeon of light larceny—nothing of real value—might come into play."

Intrigued, he felt a smile tugging at one corner of his

mouth. "I'm liking the sound of this already. So when do we get started?"

She smiled back at him, so beautiful that he knew he'd follow her to the gates of hell, just for another chance to feel the raw excitement he felt building inside him.

"Do you want the details now?" Callie asked as they pulled into the entrance of the two-story apartment complex. With its boxy, older wood-frame structures weathered by sun, salt air and the coastal storms that occasionally rolled in off the water, the place was looking a little rougher than she remembered it, but the quiet location couldn't be beat—or the view of the bayshore, where, even at this time of year, she spotted a couple of dedicated anglers fishing in their waders. "Or would you rather wait until I come to pick you up for our trip, after you've had a few days to rest up and recover?"

As eager as she was to get going, she knew Jude wasn't ready to make the leap straight from the hospital to the plan she had in mind. Or at least his still-healing lungs weren't.

"Our trip?" Jude shook his head, a look of mild confusion troubling a face she wished weren't so distractingly handsome. "So I take it we're driving down to Kingston County?"

"If you want your half brother's DNA sample, I know of no better place to get it."

"A—a DNA sample? Are you *serious*?" His normally deep voice, still somewhat hoarse after days of coughing, filled the confines of the car. "*That's* what you're talking about stealing? A DNA sample from a billionaire rancher who already more than likely has hired guns out to kill me?"

"We'll be in and out before he knows what—"

"In and out of where? The ranch itself, you mean? Are you crazy? That place is surrounded by miles of fencing and keep-out signs, all of it totally off-limits to anyone but authorized personnel."

"Not all of it," she corrected. "I'm not sure if you came across this information in your research, but they've recently opened up a little visitors' center with some historical information and a self-guided nature walk, about a mile from the mansion where the family lives."

"I did read about that," he admitted. "Some pet project of Beau's wife, Emma. I understand she's a teacher of some sort."

"A professor and researcher of wildlife biology," Callie said. "She personally goes out there a few times a week with a volunteer or two to lead talks with schoolkids and ecotourists about the coastal prairie habitat and efforts the ranch is making to conserve native birds and other species. The thing is, she and her volunteers have been casually chatting back and forth about their schedules on their social media page."

"You mean where anyone can see it?" he asked.

Callie grinned. "Exactly, which is how I know the perfect time and place for the two of us to make our move."

"Not to hurt or scare this lady, though. She may be a Kingston, but she's *not* our enemy," Jude insisted.

She made a face. "Give me a little credit, will you?"

He gave her a look. "All right, but I'm going to need to hear the details. I'm right up there on the second floor." As they left the car, he looped a bag over one arm and carried his container of cookies in his hands. "I'm warning you, though, if you're expecting a fancy bachelor pad, you're about to be sorely disappointed."

She fluttered a hand across her forehead, feigning a Southern belle–style swoon. "Oh dear. How will I *ever* survive my very first glimpse of a manly mess?"

He chuckled. "I never said I was a slob, only that Brenda—that's my ex-wife—was the one who ended up with all the furniture." His expression soured. "And every other damned thing, including my best friend from the job."

"Ouch." The pain she saw flash through his eyes told her he was a long way from being over the betrayal.

"Yeah, well, she made it clear from the start she wasn't going to be a part of the whole 'taking care of Grandpa' routine. And I can't say as I blame her for that, since he was almost as nasty to her as he was to me."

"That's no excuse for bailing on you when you needed her the most," Callie said as they started up the staircase. "Partners are supposed to have each other's backs when times are toughest."

"You know what?" Jude said, slanting a dark look in her direction. "How about we change the subject? This one's doing nothing for my mood."

Callie nodded. "You've got it. Sorry if I…"

"We're good," he murmured, not meeting her gaze. He shifted the items he was carrying to pull out his keys as they approached a blue door.

"Here, let me get that for you," she offered, taking the box from him.

Jude's hand froze before his key ever reached the dead bolt. "What the—?"

Her pulse accelerated, her breath hitching when she spotted the pry marks in the wood. The door was slightly ajar, she realized. Could that mean someone might even now be waiting inside?

Jude's gaze found hers, and his fiercely determined look assured her he'd had the same thought.

"Head downstairs and keep your phone out," he whispered, "while I check things out inside."

"You're just out of the hospital!" she hissed. "Don't go in there. We'll call the police—unless this place has a security officer?"

Jude snorted. "This place? Are you kidding?" he asked, still keeping his voice low. "Besides, whoever broke in is probably long gone."

"Which is why I'm staying right out here on the landing if you have to go inside." *Where I can be of some use if things go sideways in there.*

Jude pounded on the door frame and bellowed, in a voice so menacing, it made Callie flinch, "If anybody's in there, this is your one shot at getting out in one piece! Hands up!"

From inside, they heard a thump. Had it been a footfall…or something falling to the floor?

"Last chance!" Jude thundered. "Unless you want the police hauling you out."

When nothing happened—with the exception of one neighbor timidly peeking out of his door a few units down before slamming it again and audibly turning the dead bolt— Jude went in. Callie, who'd set down the box, stood with her phone shaking slightly in her hand, the digits 9 and 1 already pressed.

When he emerged a couple of minutes later, looking troubled but none the worse for wear, she breathed again as he waved for her to join him inside. The destruction she saw on entering took her breath away.

"Oh, Jude," she said, peering around at the upheaval and realizing that the thump they had heard earlier must have been some item toppling from its precarious position among the wreckage. "I'm so sorry. After everything you've been through—"

"They must've been looking for the originals of the documents I sent Kingston." Jude peered around at the emptied drawers and cabinets of the kitchen and living room, where all the contents from plates and cutlery to bills and paperbacks appeared to be scattered on the floor or broken. The largest knife from the kitchen block had been used to disembowel the cushions of a once modest but serviceable sofa. "And of course, to send a message. And not a very subtle one…"

Following his gaze, she saw where he was staring: at what looked like a graduation photo of Jude himself from his paramedic training program, a serrated steak knife impaling the shot through one blue eye to pin it to the living room wall. Disturbed to see the much younger, almost heartbreakingly hopeful version of the man beside her skewered, Callie shuddered before reaching for the knife's hilt to remove it.

"Better not," he warned. "Don't touch that."

"You can't imagine they'd leave fingerprints?" she asked him. "Not if they're professionals. And seriously, what are the odds that this is random?"

"What I'd really like to know," Jude said, "is where the hell my neighbors were when these clowns were turning this apartment inside out. I know Mrs. Menendez works nights, but this had to've made one heck of a racket."

"However they got in and out, they've certainly made their point—" When she saw him wince, she added, "Ah, no pun intended. But there's absolutely no way you can stay here now."

"They've accomplished one other thing, as well," he told her, stepping in through the bedroom doorway and then emerging with a handful of scraps, which she recognized as the torn fragments of what looked like older photographs.

As he let them fall to the floor, she saw the confettied bits of people—most likely irreplaceable memories—and a lump formed in her throat. Seeing a fragment of a woman's face, she wondered, could it have been his faithless wife? But judging from the hard set of his jaw and the furrows dug into his forehead, the picture had been of someone that meant far more—possibly the mother whose honor he was so bent on restoring.

"Oh, Jude…" Reaching for him, she stopped just short of contact, fearing that as angry as he was, he wouldn't take kindly to compassion.

"You remember how, back in the car just now," he said, a dark intensity in his gaze as he stared into her face, "you promised me this plan of yours wouldn't include any 'excessive mayhem'?"

"Yes." A shiver of foreboding, as sharply cold as dry ice, rippled up her backbone.

"You leave that part to me," he told her, "because if the Kingstons are willing to fight this dirty, the gloves are damned well coming off."

Chapter 6

After the arrival of the police, who had apparently been called by the neighbor who'd heard Jude on the landing, Callie answered some questions, leaving out—as Jude did—anything about the Kingstons. The two uniformed officers at first to seemed to be going through the motions as they half-heartedly examined the damage and jotted down a few notes, their noncommittal responses offering little hope that the case would merit serious attention, let alone result in an arrest.

That changed abruptly the moment they asked about the bag containing Jude's few belongings, with the hospital's name printed on it. Once he admitted he'd just been released after a crash that had been intentionally caused, Officer Alvarez tensed before exchanging a look with his deeply freckled younger partner.

"Who was the detective working on your case?" Office Alvarez asked Jude. "You get his name, by any chance?"

"Hers, you mean. It's Detective Judd, from the Robbery/Homicide Division," Jude said.

The word *homicide* sucked the breath from Callie's lungs. She'd known, of course, that whoever had run Jude off the road after aiming a gun at him had meant business, but the realization that the police were taking the attack so seriously made her wonder if she and Jude were doing the right thing, withholding information.

Or if she'd been right, insisting the two of them drive on their own to Kingston County to steal a murderous rancher's DNA? *Could I get the two of us arrested?* Or would they both simply vanish, their bodies disappearing somewhere beneath the massive swaths of South Texas rangeland where the powerful family had grazed its herds for almost 150 years?

"I'm pretty sure the detective's gonna want to see this," Alvarez said, "and ask a lot more questions about this so-called *accident* of yours."

Inside her handbag, Callie's phone signaled an incoming message. Pulling it out, she felt the air rush from her lungs as she read the text. "Oh no…"

"What's wrong?" Jude asked, coming to her side.

She shook her head rapidly, the room closing in on her as her tears pricked at her eyes and her thoughts flew to her mother. But she was all too conscious of both officers' gazes to go into the details. Or maybe keeping such a secret was the wrong move, protecting the one person who didn't deserve her—or any decent person's—consideration at this moment.

"I'm sorry to interrupt," she said, "but my mother's having a bit of a crisis with her husband. He's locked her out of the house again, and if I don't hurry and get her away from there before she tries to get back inside and he…reacts—"

"Has there been abuse, Ms. Fielding?" Alvarez asked, suddenly all business.

"Not physical that she's admitted," Callie said. "But things have been escalating, I'm sure of it. Controlling behavior, and I've seen some marks, bruises she's explained away, none too convincingly. If I can get her to pack up some things and leave, to stay at my place, where she'll be safe—"

"You can't go alone," Jude said, sounding ready to head over to take care of business himself.

"He's right," Alvarez agreed. "When an abuser knows his partner's really leaving, that's often when he's most dangerous. Are there firearms in the home?"

"Not that I'm aware of," Callie told them. But she didn't know for sure. How could she?

Alvarez nodded. "If you'll give me the names and the address, we'll have another officer meet you on the scene."

"I—my mother will be so embarrassed, seeing the police come. And I can't imagine she'll be willing to press charges." She could almost hear her mother's litany of excuses. *He's under so much pressure at work. He hasn't been sleeping well. If you only knew the real Lonnie the way I do…*

"She doesn't need to know you've sent us," his younger partner, whose red hair was a more orangey shade than Callie's, put in quickly. "You can tell her a neighbor must've called after hearing the disturbance."

Callie nodded before admitting, "It wouldn't be the first time."

"And anyway, *embarrassed* is far from the worst outcome in these cases, believe me," Alvarez said, with the grim eyes of someone who'd seen plenty, "so let me have that information so I can make the call."

After only a moment's hesitation, Callie said, "It's Lonnie and Rhonda Stringer." She then pulled up the address on her phone and passed it over.

While Alvarez made the call, Jude came up and opened his arms, offering the embrace she hadn't known until that moment how very much she needed. As she leaned against his broad chest, she exhaled a shaky breath and murmured, "I'm so sorry. You have enough problems of your own to deal with right now."

"Family always takes priority," he told her, sounding as if he meant it as he rubbed her back in a slow circle. "I'm only sorry that they won't let me leave here and go over with you."

"Let's swap numbers and touch base later," she suggested, "then make arrangements after both of us get our other business taken care of. Okay?"

Once she had her phone back from the officer, she created a new contact for Jude, then passed her cell over to let him plug in the digits. After finishing, he pushed the call button so his phone would have a record of her number, as well.

It was the most innocent of interactions, she told herself, a simple exchange of digits with a colleague. Once their business with the Kingstons was concluded, she assured herself that she could easily purge his number from her contacts, delete any lingering personal attachments and return to the cocoon of isolation where she'd lived these past four years.

Yet as she left the apartment, she wondered how much

longer it would take to banish the memory of the relief and safety she had felt for those few moments, with his strong arms wrapped around her.

When the knock came that evening at nine thirty, Jude's hair was still damp from the shower and he was buttoning his long-sleeved shirt, one of the few garments still left on its hanger in the closet, over the pair of jeans he'd also found undamaged. He'd managed to scrape together several other items to throw into a duffel, but he would definitely need to do some shopping in the near future.

The need to replenish the trashed contents of his apartment, however, was the last thing on his mind tonight, especially when he opened the door and saw the tightness around Callie's mouth and the way her gaze shifted uneasily as she stepped into his living room.

"Are you really still up for this?" he asked, suspecting that she'd left out a great deal when she'd texted him a couple of hours before that *everything's okay with my mom.* "If you need to, we can hold off, or—"

"Really, it'll be fine. My mother will be staying at my place, taking care of Baby. And PB will be taking care of her, which is something my boy's very good at."

At the mention of her dog, some of the tension eased in her expression. Or maybe she was faking it. Jude didn't know her well enough to be sure.

"You're not worried about your stepfather coming around and bothering her there?"

"First of all, please don't call him my stepfather. That two-bit bully's nothing to me and never has been." She sighed and shook her head. "And he knows he isn't welcome on my property. The only real worry is that my mom—that she might get it in her head to try to smooth things over with him when I'm not around to shore her up."

"She'd do that?"

Callie nodded. "She has before. She'll talk a good game when I'm with her, but—she always sees the best in people, to believe in their capacity to change, no matter how many times life has tried to teach her that men don't make good fixer-upper projects."

He grimaced. "It's no crime having too big a heart," he said, having known other women—and at least one male friend— who seemed to make the same mistake repeatedly. "I'm only sorry that she's having problems."

"Thanks, and right now, I'm not too worried," she said, "since the police've warned Lonnie that if he doesn't keep his distance, he's going straight to jail. And if there's one thing that freaks him out, it's another arrest on his record."

"So he has a history?"

"A couple of intoxicated assault charges from his younger years, but he stays clear of the bars these days. He's at least kept that promise to my mother. And he's just recently scored a nice promotion over at the refinery, which I can't imagine him wanting to risk by getting himself thrown behind bars."

"Glad to hear it, but if he ever needs any extra convincing and the cops aren't handy, you have my number," Jude offered.

A sad smile warmed her beautiful eyes. "That means a lot. But what about you? Are you really still up for this trip tonight? After all, you've clearly had a rough day when you really should've spent it resting."

When he gestured broadly to indicate the several

large trash bags he'd managed to fill with debris after the detective and the evidence team she'd called in had finally left the place, she shook her head in wonder. Much more remained to be cleared out, cleaned and repaired before the apartment would once more be back to anything like normal.

"I'm plenty wiped out," he admitted, recalling the doctors' advice to take it easy for the next few weeks to recover fully from the aftereffects of the crash, "but way too wired to sleep."

"I see the door's been fixed, but I can't imagine you'd feel safe sleeping here, no matter what," she said. "Now that they know where you live—"

"Cops advised against that, too," he said, "though I'm pretty sure at this point Detective Judd's decided I know way more than I'm saying."

"You aren't worried about getting into trouble with the police, are you?"

He shook his head. "What's to worry about? We're just taking a little road trip, right? To get away from all our problems."

"And maybe to get to know each other," she put in abruptly.

"You—you mean…?" he stammered, his heart staggering for a moment before the bright peal of her laughter had him flushing.

"I *mean* that's what I told my mother, who was so pathetically excited she forgot to be upset with me for leaving her to dog-sit PB while we're down in Kingston County." Her slender hand settled on his shoulder. "But it was just a cover story, Jude, so there's no need to look so panicked."

"That *wasn't* panic," he grumbled, turning to grab

his bag before reaching inside his bedroom to flick off the light switch. *That was the look of a man's hopes rising—even though I damned well should have known better—just before you crushed them flat.*

Once more, the weather had changed, Jude found, the evening dreary and somewhat cool, with a misting rain that must have blown in off the water. But Callie seemed undaunted as she climbed behind the wheel.

"Need to stop for anything? Dinner or anything like that?" she asked him.

"I've eaten," he said, grateful to the neighbor who'd heard about his break-in and shown up with a plateful of homemade chicken enchiladas still warm from the oven, "but I could stand to hit an ATM to pull out what cash I can." To minimize his electronic trail, he intended to avoid using cards as much as possible anywhere near Kingston territory, so he'd have to make do with the bank's daily withdrawal limit.

"You've got it," she said.

After taking care of the errand at a drive-through, they headed farther inland before turning south onto the road that would take them out of Corpus Christi. As the city traffic gave way to the darkness of the coastal plains, Callie went on to describe in detail the plan she had come up with while he'd been recovering in the hospital. By the time she'd finished telling him about the items she'd purchased and had packed in the Mustang's trunk, she finally darted a look in his direction.

"Are you listening to me, Jude? Or have you fallen asleep?" she asked, sounding equally uncertain and annoyed. "Because I've been talking nonstop for, like, twenty minutes, and you haven't made a single comment or even asked a question."

Straightening in his seat, he said, "Of course I'm listening. It's just that I'm sitting over here blown away that after all the time I've spent racking my brain over this, in just a couple of days, you could come up with something so simple, but so perfect. I mean—I knew you were a sharp flight nurse, one of the best I've ever worked with, but *this* is absolutely brilliant, right down to the last detail."

"C'mon, Jude. It's far from perfect."

"You're definitely right. It's still seriously risky. Which worries me, not on my own account so much, but yours. We've already seen how far these people are willing to go, how little lives like ours matter to them—"

"You think I don't know that?" she erupted before warning. "It's *my* plan, so don't imagine for a second I mean to let you push me out in some chauvinistic desire to protect me."

"Easy there," he said, taken aback by her heat. "Nobody's trying to push you out. But I do want you to be certain, to know for sure exactly what you're getting into. Because if this thing goes south on us—"

"It *won't*," she insisted, "because Beau Kingston's scheduled to be out of town for that big stock show in Fort Worth. He's presenting the award for the grand champion. I saw the announcement online."

"Still, this ruse that you've come up with to get inside his house has a lot of moving parts," Jude said, "and one completely unpredictable player."

She shook her head and argued, "Not that unpredictable, not with human nature being what it is…unless you're too scared, Jude Castleman. Or don't think you can pull off a simple bluff."

He snorted. "You obviously haven't sat down to play poker with me."

"Good, then," she told him, "because first thing tomorrow morning, it's going to be time to stack our deck."

Now seated on the passenger side of the stolen Cadillac, Trigger jotted down the license plate numbers of the blue Mustang GT as he'd been asked to.

Looking up, he shook his buzzed, blond head at Armbruster. "I can't think why you'd want this—or give a damn who the target's shacking up with. He's none of our concern now. Isn't that what the client said? That Castleman gets to keep on breathin', at least until he figures out where the guy hid those papers we couldn't find in his apartment."

"For *now* the client wants him breathing, yes," Armbruster admitted, frustrated but not completely shocked by the client's "suspension" of the contract, a notification they had received while watching from an ill-lit corner of the parking lot as Castleman had climbed into the convertible driven by the tall, attractive woman who'd come to collect him.

As he watched the Mustang's taillights disappear into the darkness, Armbruster drew from his lit cigarette and wondered if either of the vehicle's occupants had felt the cool breeze of death's passage fluttering past them, like a bat's wings through the deepest shadow. And did Jude Castleman, just as he did, have some sense that fate would eventually finish what it had started between the two of them along this moonlit bay?

Early the following morning, Callie cried out, the blood draining from her face when she walked in with a bag containing breakfast and her late husband walked out of the motel room bathroom.

"What's wrong?" Jude said as he turned toward her, for of course it had been her temporary—*very* temporary—partner and not Marc who had stepped out shirtless, whorls of steam billowing behind him, as he toweled off his damp hair. "You okay there?"

On that awful night he'd been brought into the ER, shivering and shaking, she'd been the one to help him out of his soaked and muddy clothes, the one to help inventory his abrasions before covering him with a warming blanket. So there were no surprises here, yet in this context...

The sight of Jude now, standing shoeless and shirtless, with his jeans unfastened, stole the breath from her lungs. Or maybe it was this strictly nonclinical view of that light dusting of golden chest hair and an impressive set of pecs and abs—along with the realization that she'd slept only feet away from *all this* last night, while he'd been out cold on the room's sofa—that had her so completely rattled.

Ordering herself to quit gaping, she rasped out, "I'm f-fine," her head feeling so loose that she was half-afraid it might tumble off her shoulders. Because grief was a familiar companion, one she'd almost become used to stealing in to catch her unaware when she least expected it, but this—what she was feeling now, the first time in years she'd found herself in such close confines with a man who was more than just a patient— Her face heated as guilt burned through her.

You don't want him. You can't. You're only missing Marc. And missing sex. It's only natural in a woman

*your age, no matter how you try to pretend that you
don't care about it.*

"Well, you don't *look* fine, not with all that shaking."
Jude lowered the towel and reached for the dark gray
T-shirt he'd left lying on the room's sofa, where he'd insisted upon sleeping after they'd checked in to a small
chain motel about thirty miles west of Pinto Creek late
last night.

Taking a step nearer, he offered a reassuring smile.
"Tell me the truth, Callie. That stupid rinse you insisted
I use didn't turn my hair purple or something, did it?"

Her laughter sounded brittle, as dry as the cool wind
rippling through the tall prairie grasses in the field not
far beyond this rural highway intersection. "Not purple, no. Just a few shades darker. Like my husband's."
She frowned, wishing she'd insisted on separate rooms,
even though they'd both agreed it would have drawn
more notice. "So for just a moment—I know it's ridiculous—but you caught me off guard. Sorry if my yelling
freaked you out."

"We're good," he said, the sincerity in his eyes hazing
the memory of Marc's features...or at least the sharpness of the pain she'd felt, imagining his beloved face
staring at her, the pain of betrayal in the brown eyes
she had loved so dearly. Pulling on the tee to cover an
impressively sculpted set of abs, Jude raked the unruly
mess back from his forehead before making a suggestion. "I could shave my head, you know. If that would
help, I mean."

This time, her laughter was genuine as she slapped
at his upper arm. "Don't do that! This stuff will come
out in a few washes and you'll be back to looking like
yourself again—" *Heaven help me.*

"Just in time for some Kingston goon to hunt me down, if we're not careful," he said, all traces of humor vanishing from his expression.

It gave way to a seriousness that sent chills rippling through her. And made her abruptly aware that her hand was still in contact with his rock-solid triceps.

Withdrawing abruptly, she promised, "We'll be careful," before pulling off the slouchy knit cap she'd worn to pick up breakfast this morning, which she'd used to hide her own distinctive red hair from view. She'd pulled on her big sunglasses as well before heading over to a small mom-and-pop bakery to pick up some pastries, coffee for Jude and a bottled water for herself. "But we should probably get moving if we're going to have everything lined up, our reconnaissance complete and be all ready to go first thing tomorrow morning."

"You sound nervous," he said, his blue-gray eyes assessing her intently.

Studying me for weakness, she realized, remembering that night in the helicopter when she'd come so close to slipping into a full PTSD meltdown. And he'd seen it. Seen *her*, in spite of every prickly defense she'd thrown up against him.

"If you're still sure you want to be part of this—" He reached, not for the coffee, as she'd suspected that he would, but for her hand instead. "Because if you've changed your mind for any reason, now's the time to say so."

His fingers folded around hers, which had gone ice cold and shaky. Though her first impulse was to pull away, she fought it. Fought the scared rabbit part of herself, telling herself that she would and could do this— *to avenge Marc.*

Yet it wasn't her husband she was thinking of when Jude squeezed her hand. *Why does he have to be so ridiculously handsome?*

"I promise you, if you have, I won't be angry," he said. "I'll just find another way to do this."

"No," she insisted, the stubbornness bursting out of her. "I didn't drive all the way down here and listen to you snore for half the night for you to—"

"No way was I snoring." Jude's fingertips, which gently caressed the skin over her knuckles, took the heat out of his protest, as did the teasing smile in his eyes.

"You certainly were," she fired back, trying and failing to ignore the way her nerve endings were coming alive in response to his touch. "But it didn't matter. I couldn't have slept inside a soundproofed vault. I was too busy running my plan through my head over and over, trying to figure out if there was any detail that I might've missed. Any detail that might come back on either of us."

"So you're not sleeping, is what you're telling me? Maybe I should do this on my own."

"You and I both know there's no way any of this will work unless we're both in on it. Emma Kingston would never trust a lone male," she insisted before nailing him with the look she used on her most difficult patients. *"Right?"*

"Then I'll find some other way. One that won't risk getting you hurt," he said. "Because as much as making the past right matters, it's still the past, Callie. We can't change that my mother and your husband have been taken from us, but—"

At his mention of Marc, her breath hitched and she averted her eyes.

Stepping closer, Jude reached to gently turn her face toward his. "You don't have to hide that part of yourself from me, not ever. If we can't be honest with each other, then we shouldn't be doing this."

"What *are* we doing, Jude?" she whispered, her voice shaking, because when he was standing this near, every atom of this large man filled her senses, from the scent of his shower-warmed skin to the way his pupils dilated as they focused in on hers.

"I sure as hell have no idea," he said, stroking her jaw lightly, "except somehow it feels like there's no turning back."

Without conscious thought, she raised herself up onto her tiptoes, meeting him eagerly and, yes, breathlessly, as he leaned in for a kiss that sent sensation spiraling through her. The fresh taste of his toothpaste, the surging of her own pulse, the thrill of hearing how his breathing quickened as he pulled her nearer.

With a murmuring of assent, she ran her hands over his back, heat and pleasure thrumming through her body as he parted her lips for further exploration. The kiss went on and on, until her breasts tingled and need pooled between her legs, a liquid heat that left her aching, wanting more of this…of *him*.

But when Jude's hand skimmed her side, gliding along the flare of her hip, instead of passion, a swirl of nausea answered, and that patch of ink on her right wrist start burning.

This isn't right. Isn't Marc. I can't, I can't. Forgive me!

Panicking, she pushed Jude back, blinking as she filled her lungs and rubbed the burning tattoo, which felt almost hot enough to burst into flames. "Please, no.

I thought that I was—that maybe I felt—but that isn't what I've come to do with you."

Backing off with a look of obvious reluctance, he nodded. "I'm sorry if I—if I misread… You're a beautiful woman, and there's a hell of a lot more than that to you—but I don't want to make you at all uncomfortable."

"You didn't do anything wrong. It's me. I'm just not… available in that way." She wondered, *will I ever be?* If only she could flip some imaginary Vacancy sign above her heart on and off at will, as her mother seemed to imagine she could. "You have to understand, this is hard for me."

"So tell me, then, where do we go from here?" he asked carefully. "What is it you do want, Callie?"

"I want to follow through on my plan. *Our* plan," she said, sounding stronger and more confident than she had been before as certainty crystallized in her mind, "not because I think it's going to bring my Marc back, or your mother, or because I think we can punish a man already dead for the sins that he committed. You're right when you say all that's in the past."

"Then why?"

"Because it's important that I take a stand and stop the current crop of Kingstons from thinking they can keep hurting people like us without repercussions," she said. "They need to know that whether they're threatening to destroy careers on a whim, the way Tammy Kingston-Hoyle is with her ridiculous complaint, or trying to have you flat-out murdered because Beau Kingston's too greedy to tolerate the notion that he might have a brother, we're not about to sit back and let it happen."

"So does this mean," he asked, "we can still be partners?"

"Partners, absolutely," she said, extending her right hand, "as long as you can definitely accept that that alliance will never extend to the bedroom."

He studied her carefully, his gaze so heated and so serious, she could almost feel it like a soft breath against her skin.

At long last, though, he took her hand and shook it, saying, "You drive a hard bargain, Callie Fielding, but you've got yourself a deal."

Chapter 7

The next night was Jude's turn to struggle with sleep. He spent hours tossing and turning on the sofa, though Callie had offered to switch places with him, allowing him a chance to stretch out his tall frame on the more comfortable bed. It wouldn't have helped, though, imagining how she'd slept in it only the night before. And how she was lying so near to him, her long, well-spaced exhalations assuring him she'd finally drifted off.

Though he struggled to empty his mind, he couldn't stop imagining himself beside her, draping an arm over her hip, feeling the silken slide of her hair against his cheek and smelling her sweet scent as he matched his breathing to the pace of hers. He shifted on the cushions, his body tormenting him with building need…for it was all too easy to picture himself reaching to caress her breast, and then her capturing the hand that touched her and pulling it up beneath her nightshirt, a whispered *"Please, yes,"* on her lips.

Unable to curtail more heated thoughts, he headed for the bathroom, where he decided that there were some situations for which a cold shower truly was the answer. Because he'd made a promise to a woman he respected, and he wasn't going to make things any better by continuing to lust after her like some oversexed teenager.

Still, the following morning's early start found him jittery and on edge. Skating by on far too little sleep, he downed the coffee and a couple of spicy breakfast tacos they picked up from a small, colorfully painted stand called Flavio's, located at an otherwise barren crossroads outside Pinto Creek. He'd allowed himself to be talked into trying the egg and *barbacoa* variety, which the cook, a round-faced young Hispanic man wearing an apron, had excitedly sworn were Señor Beau Kingston's favorites.

"You're telling me that Mr. Kingston himself eats here?" Jude asked, trying not to look skeptical as he'd glanced at the humble takeout spot, with its few picnic benches and trash containers outside, damp this morning from the heavy mist that had settled overnight. A far cry from the sort of place Jude could envision a billionaire rancher with a phalanx of cutthroat lawyers and hired killers at his disposal dining.

"You can see for yourself first thing every Friday, when he comes to speak with me and shake my hand as he picks up a big takeout order to bring in to feed the employees at ranch headquarters," the young man boasted, puffing out his chest. "And why shouldn't he? After the diner in town where I cooked closed down and my *madre*, who cleaned the big house for a few years, got her cancer, it was Señor Kingston himself who offered me this plot of land. He signed the deed for only five dollars. Can you believe such a thing? *Five.* And then he helped me with the business plan and the materials to build my own place."

"So you built this stand all by yourself?" Callie said, looking behind the countertop, with its trio of bar stools, and toward the simple but clean and neatly organized grill and register areas.

"These hands may have done the hard work." Flavio showed off his calluses and what Jude suspected was a small burn scar from a hot grill. "But without Señor Kingston, this would still be a rocky patch of barren soil good for feeding no one, not even his cattle. He is the best of men and the most generous, and I will never serve any *pendejo* who says any different."

There had been a defensive edge to the cook's voice, as if he'd gone toe-to-toe with more than one detractor in the past. It was enough to make Jude curious, but there was no way to dig deeper without raising Kingston's protégé's suspicions—or further burning himself into the young man's memory.

Once they returned to the car, Callie asked him, "Do you think it's true?" after he had told her. "Do you think it's possible your half brother could really be the good man this Flavio claims?"

"His favorite taco's pretty tasty. I'll give Beau Kingston that much," Jude said, polishing off the last bite as Callie wiped her hands on a paper towel after finishing her own egg-and-potato taco. "And maybe it's possible he has his kind impulses, that he donates to favorite charities and walks little old ladies across busy intersections now and again to make himself feel like a good guy. Think about all the donations the Kingston Foundation's made to worthy causes, such as LifeWings."

"So they can treat us like they own us, no matter the conditions," she said bitterly. "And even if Beau Kingston does have his moments, I'm still not ready to forgive him for trying to have you killed."

"That makes two of us…if it really was him." As the mist thickened to a light rain, Jude felt doubt chewing at the edges of his previous resolve. Were they really doing the right thing, attempting to dupe Beau's likely innocent wife into allowing them access to the family's home—and her husband's DNA?

"We're being ridiculous," Callie insisted, her beautiful face flushing, "getting cold feet, that's all. Even if the incident on the road turned out to be random, you and I both know there's no way your apartment was trashed and searched by random thieves. Not with the message they sent with that steak knife through your picture."

"You're right, of course. *We're* in the right," he said, needing to convince himself as much as anyone. "This is the only way."

They spoke no more of it as Callie drove them onto the gravel back road the two of them had visited the previous afternoon after discovering it using an online satellite map. There, as a dawn mist hovered near ground level, Callie parked her Mustang behind a large brush pile—apparently the debris from some landowner's pasture-clearing project. The two of them then switched vehicles, moving to the geriatric SUV Jude had purchased from a chain-smoking, white-haired woman who'd had it parked amid the tall weeds in front of her mobile home, a faded For Sale sign in the window.

Jude climbed behind the Chevy's wheel, wearing a

blue T-shirt under a large-pocketed khaki vest and a pair of cargo pants in the same tan color. When Callie had given him the wide-brimmed hat to go with it before dawn, he had complained, "Did you seriously set out to dress me up as a nerd here?"

"You're not a nerd. You're supposed to be a birder," she'd said, passing him the compact binoculars on their lanyard, which now dangled around his neck. "Besides, I think you have a serious Nazi-fighting archaeologist vibe going, especially with that little scruff that you have working."

That at least had made him smile, since he figured that a guy could do a lot worse than being compared to good old Indy, and with his temporarily darker hair and a pair of Wayfarer-style sunglasses, he felt decently disguised.

"Ready?" asked Callie, who looked unrecognizable now that she'd donned a hot-pink cap with a long—and surprisingly realistic-looking—blond-streaked ponytail hanging through the hole in the back. To complete the look, she'd added a pair of vintage-looking sunglasses whose frames matched her frosted pink lipstick, but what really blew him away was the white maternity top she wore, its lacy detail making it look more feminine—and less Callie—than anything he could imagine...

With the exception of the convincing-looking baby bump she'd somehow strapped on underneath it,

"Seriously, *Daddy*," she scolded as she twisted the fake wedding band around her finger. One that she'd been swift to point out, when she'd presented him with a matching ring this morning, was a cheap knockoff and nothing like the real wedding set in her jewelry box at home. "You're going to have to knock it off with the constant staring if we're to have any hope of pulling this off."

"Sorry." He tried for a cocky shrug, attempting to disguise the sick chill that had run up his spine hearing her refer to him as the father of her "child," though he understood she'd only been teasing.

"It's just—it throws me a little, that's all," he admitted, "seeing you…like that. Putting myself back in that mind-set."

"*Back* in it?" she asked, giving him a sharp look. "Are you saying there's a kid you left behind in Arizona? Or maybe a whole bunch of little Judes?"

Mentally kicking himself for the verbal slip, he winced at a particularly painful memory. "I didn't mean to— No, no kids."

"Then why is your face going all red and—you're sweating, aren't you?" she asked, staring until he was forced to look away. "Come on, Jude. We have to trust each other here if we're going to make this work."

"There's no damned time for this if we're going to be in place by the time that Emma Kingston drives past."

Callie checked her watch. "We're fine on time, so tell me. Tell me now, because I'm not going to spend this next hour worried that you're about to melt down on me."

He glanced once more at her "pregnant" belly before looking into her face. "Brenda was never all that sold on the whole motherhood idea, but about five years ago, I talked her into trying. It didn't take long for her to get pregnant. For a while, things were great between us. She started to get more and more excited as we did all the appointments together and the shopping, painting the spare room for the baby. I was sure it was exactly what our marriage needed."

"So the marriage before then…" Callie ventured.

He shrugged. "It was never a great match, to be honest. Can't be, when only one partner is fully committed from the start. Looking back now, I see it. I should've had my head examined, imagining a child as some kind of solution…"

She laid her hand atop his right wrist. "But I'm guessing that it wasn't…"

Jude shook his head and blew out a long breath, his eyes closing. "A stillbirth can be devastating for even the strongest union."

"Oh, Jude." She moved her hand to squeeze his. "I'm so very, very sorry. Listen, if this is too hard for you, I can get rid of this stupid fake belly. We'll come up with some other angle."

"Why, Callie? Will that bring my son back?" he demanded, grunting in answer to his own harsh question. "It won't accomplish anything except destroying any real chance we have of making your excellent plan work, so forget that idea. I'll be fine."

"Really?" she asked, studying him with a look that assured him that all he had to do was say the word, and she'd pull the plug on everything, with no recriminations.

"Absolutely," he assured her. "So let's get this show on the road, partner."

"For luck, then. *Partner*," she said, leaning toward him and giving him a soft and achingly sweet kiss. A kiss that pulled him out of the past and left him more confused than ever about his feelings for her.

It took him a few tries, but the faded gray SUV coughed and sputtered to life on the third attempt, shuddering alarmingly and belching a puff of dark smoke from its tailpipe. Afterward, they made the twenty-minute drive over gently rolling coastal prairie rangeland dotted with red-brown Kingston cattle, few of which looked up from their grazing on the thick, tough grasses, which were more gold than green this time of year.

"I wish this rain would clear out," Callie commented at one point. "It's going to be no fun, standing out there in it."

"As long as it doesn't get too much heavier," Jude said, "I'm thinking it could work in our favor."

After a pause, she nodded. "You may be right. This could be exactly what we need to score an invitation inside the house."

As they crested a rise a few minutes later, Callie pointed out the tops of some wind turbines in the distance. "According to the directions I read online, the public access gate's just about a mile ahead. It's supposed to be open after 6:00 a.m., so we should be good."

They proceeded easily, at least until Jude hit the squeaky brakes in front of the gate to stare up at its overarching sign that read Welcome to the Kingston Ranch, Est. 1872. Below these words, were the famous Running K brand and another line reading Visitors' Parking, 1.3 mi.

But it was the thought of entering the ranch itself, this vast swath of range that had for months loomed so large in his imagination, that had him idling, his pounding heart in his throat as it sank in. *This is it*, he realized. *The place my mother lived once. The place that left her shattered by betrayal.* In crossing onto Kingston land, he was taking the first step to reclaiming the dignity that had been stolen from her.

"So they're rich," said Callie, staring up at the impressively wrought metal sign, "and they've had land and power for ages. So what? *We're* here now, and we're darned well doing this. Because you have the right to get the answers you deserve about your heritage, for one thing—"

"And *we* have the right not to live at their damned mercy," Jude added before their tires bumped over the cattle guard that allowed vehicles to drive over an opening spanned by a metal grate.

Soon they passed another sign pointing toward a small parking area.

"Nice little place they've put up out here," Callie remarked, looking toward the covered area, which had semicircular benches to seat groups. Beyond it, Jude spotted what appeared to be the entrance to a walking loop along the prairie habitat, with informational placards and a number of bird feeders placed at various intervals. "Their website says they plan to expand it in the future, get a bunch of outdoor education classes and wildlife rehab projects going."

Jude nodded, but most of his attention was fixed on the well-worn road that continued past the new center, where a large sign read Private Property. No Visitors Beyond This Point. Not far ahead, an electronic gate blocked further access—one that online satellite maps had indicated would lead those authorized directly to his and Callie's actual intended target.

Jude had read a featured article in the digital archives of *The Monthly Journal of Texas*, which had included a photo spread on the historic Kingston mansion, a sprawling white Mediterranean-style showplace that had for more than a century served as the family's seat of power. According to the write-up, the elegant ranch-style home had in its heyday entertained fellow cattle barons, US presidents and even Hollywood celebrities during a period where the ranch's successes had multiplied with successful forays into Thoroughbred and quarter horse racing, land speculation, and a half dozen other lucrative ventures.

Though the once-large family had since dwindled, fading from view somewhat in recent decades, according to the article, the grand home, with its beautiful fountains and mosaics, remained a symbol of that long-held South Texas fortune—as well as a bastion protecting the few remaining direct descendants from the outside world.

A bastion he and Callie now meant to breach.

"So how are we on time now?" Jude asked, anticipation surging through him.

She checked her watch. "I think we're good to get set up now. On a dreary Tuesday morning at this hour and time of year, there shouldn't be anybody else by until she heads back home from the school run. So all that's left is to make us look as distressed and helpless as humanly possible."

"That last part could be a sticking point," he said, sliding her a nervous grin, "because based on your level of preparation, you're currently striking me as one of the least helpless women on the planet."

Peering through binoculars from behind the raised hood of the SUV, which they'd left parked haphazardly outside the entrance parking area, Jude said, "It's definitely her coming, and right on time. You had her schedule almost down to the minute."

Thank goodness. For all her spying on Emma Kingston's social media account, Callie knew that sometimes plans changed—especially when the woman making them was not only juggling professional and home responsibilities, but the instant motherhood she'd taken on when marrying a widower with two young sons, both of whom she'd just dropped off at the local elementary school.

With no more time for hesitation, Callie breathed a silent prayer before gulping from the vacuum bottle she'd had prepared—a vile mixture of warm salt water mixed with mustard, which instantly had her gagging in response.

I've made a terrible mistake, she realized the moment the stuff hit her stomach. She would've been better off counting on her nursing background to allow her to fake a convincing illness rather than to risk actually overdoing it and fully incapacitating herself. But it was too late for regrets now, as she braced a hand against the rain-damp side of the vehicle and heaved until her ribs ached and the world blackened at its edges.

With her eyes and nose streaming and her ears roaring, she had no idea whether Emma Kingston zoomed past them, oblivious, or if she stopped or called for help. All Callie was conscious of was that someone—Jude, it must be—was physically holding her upright.

"Oh, Callie," Jude said, stepping up behind her to lay a hand on her shoulder. "What on earth have you done?"

"N-nothing very smart," she admitted as she struggled to make her legs cooperate.

Behind the two of them, she heard a woman asking, "Excuse me, but do you folks need some help? I have a satellite cell phone in case you need an ambulance."

With Jude's help, Callie straightened, too exhausted

to care how wet she might be getting. "No, no ambulance," she said, before somehow remembering to angle her body to offer the slim, attractive woman in her midthirties who'd stepped from her four-door silver Jeep a better view. "I—I'm just a little dehydrated, I'm afraid I keep— This morning sickness has been *endless.*"

Blushing to the roots of her tawny hair, Emma Kingston winced. "Oh, you poor thing. I've been there all too recently, though you look like it's hit you a lot harder and longer than it ever did me."

All too recently? Callie eyed the woman's yoga pants and the loose-fitting top that draped a slender frame and wondered, could she possibly be pregnant? *Will she sense I'm faking it?*

"I told her we shouldn't have tried to come this morning, but she insisted," Jude said, shaking his head as he shot a convincingly worried look toward Callie. "She's been telling me all about what you've accomplished out here, but I— Honey, I know between this rain and the nausea, it's not very appealing, but can I get you to try to sip a little of this water?"

When he tried to press a bottle into her hand, Callie staggered another step or two and retched again, while mentally swearing off mustard for life—though she suspected her own nerves had a lot to do with the severity of her reaction. How could she have ever imagined this stupid plan of hers would work?

"I've called our roadside assistance plan already," Jude was telling Emma Kingston. "They said they're sending someone out, but it could be an hour or two."

"She can't possibly wait out here, not in this state, and damp as she is, she'll get chilled for certain," Emma told him before glancing back with a look of uncertainty toward the door of her own Jeep, which still stood open. "And with her being pregnant—I should—I should call someone—"

From inside her vehicle, Callie heard a series of fretful, restless noises that went a long way toward explaining Emma Kingston's unease—and vastly intensified Callie's own. *An infant! And a young one, from the sound of things.*

"Hang on just a second," Emma told Jude. "I need to check on her—I'll be right back."

Turning away, she hurried to open the rear door of the Jeep.

"She has a *baby*," Jude whispered urgently as he stared at Callie. "You didn't say anything about a child being present."

"I didn't — I had no idea!" Callie whispered back. "I saw nothing online about her having a kid of her own."

"We can't possibly go ahead with—?" Jude started, before abruptly cutting himself off as Emma came back, nodding her head.

"I've moved some things around in my Jeep," she said before turning kind green eyes toward Callie. "It's a little messy, I'm afraid, but please hop in. You can wait a lot more comfortably at the house—it's just a mile down the road—than you can out here—"

"That's very kind of you, but we couldn't possibly," Callie said.

Jude shook his head. "We can't impose on you. You have a little one to care for."

"Please. I insist." Looking from one to the other, Emma said earnestly, "I'm Dr. Emma Kingston. I—I'm the director of this center, and my husband's— I'm absolutely sure he'd want me to offer you our hospitality, at least to try to get you into something dry, get something warm for you to drink and let you rest somewhere comfortable until help arrives."

Turning her gaze toward Jude, she added earnestly, "I know it's hard to trust a stranger, but for your wife's sake—and your baby's."

"You're right, of course," Jude nodded, apparently changing his mind about backing out. "Thank you so much, Mrs.—I mean Dr. Kingston. We're incredibly grateful. I'm Christopher James, and this is my wife, Sophie, from San Antonio. We were on our way to visit family down in McAllen when Sophie started telling me about this place you'd gotten going, and—"

"Honey, she doesn't need to hear all that," Callie said, holding a hand over her stomach and willing him not to cross the line between making the woman comfortable and freaking her out by babbling their entire cover story all at once.

"Let's get you more comfortable, Sophie," Emma said to Callie. "I hope you won't mind sharing the back seat with my daughter."

"She—she's adorable," Callie managed, meaning it as she climbed into the back seat to see the infant looking back at her with slightly teary blue eyes, her frowny little face slightly mottled as she raised the volume on her fussing.

"And *hungry*, from the sound of things," said Emma, speaking up as she and Jude both buckled in, "but I'll set that to rights soon enough. Just warning you, though, it sounds as if my daughter is about to give us all a demonstration of why my stepsons keep telling us we should've named their little sister the Velociraptor instead of Dove."

* * *

Despite his preparation, it was impossible not to marvel as Emma drove up a long driveway leading to a massive two-story structure topped with a flat, red-tile roof and some sort of fancy cutouts along the tops of the white stucco walls that made the place look more like a palace than a South Texas home. As they approached, a single shaft of sunlight slanted down through the thick cloud cover, illuminating beautifully maintained palm and citrus trees that competed for attention with other tropical plantings—some browned at the edges from the recent rare frost—and a large fountain drew his eye to an elegant covered walkway.

"This is—this is where you *live*?" Callie blurted from the back seat during a lull in the baby's fussing. "It looks big enough to qualify for its own ZIP code."

Rather than taking offense, as Jude feared she might, Emma only laughed. "You sound *exactly* like me the first time I set eyes on this place—which really wasn't all that long ago. But we have plenty of comfy sofas and nice, clean bathrooms where you're welcome to make yourselves at home while you're waiting for your road service to show up."

Pulling close to a smaller, less conspicuous side door than the grand entrance Jude had spotted out front, Emma hopped out of her Jeep, a modestly appointed model with enough sand, dog hair and kid detritus on the floorboards to convince Jude that this woman's priorities didn't include flaunting the wealth she'd married into. As she grabbed the baby's diaper bag and retrieved Dove from the back seat, Jude went to the opposite rear door to offer Callie his hand.

"Feeling any better?" he asked, genuinely concerned

by her washed-out color and the dark circles beneath her eyes as she emerged into the light drizzle. When she'd told him her plan to use some vile concoction to cause herself to be convincingly, if briefly, ill, she'd assured him the effects would be neither serious nor long-lasting. Now, however, she looked miserable to him.

Pursing her lips, she nodded gamely, but he took her arm anyway, all too aware of how she was swaying—and praying she was exaggerating her weakness—as Emma led them inside and down a wide white-paneled hallway with alcoves decorated with groupings of what appeared to be the current generation of Kingstons' family photos. In several, Jude glimpsed a tall man with dark hair and eyes wearing a broad-brimmed hat, his strong jaw set in a look of supreme confidence as he sat astride his big bay horse. In others, this same man, the one Jude had come to prove was his half brother, stood grinning with his arms draped over the shoulders of two raven-haired young boys or casting a look a pure devotion toward his beautiful new wife.

Though Jude had seen a couple of photos of the man before online, these more personal, up-close shots only served to drive home the fact that he and Beau Kingston looked nothing alike, with their different builds, coloring and facial structure. If the two of them were really half brothers, would that be the case?

Reminding himself that they'd had different mothers and that even full siblings could look quite different, he told himself that he and Callie had risked too much to back off now. Especially considering that if Beau Kingston, brother or not, ever realized they had conned their way into his very home, with his wife and baby daughter present, the man would be sure to send more killers calling. Only this time, Callie, too, would likely be a target.

"Right in here, please," Emma said, ushering them into a comfortable-looking room featuring a large sliding window that looked out over a beautifully landscaped central courtyard with a rectangular reflecting pool, a big desk with a computer on it, a sofa and a rocking chair, and a number of framed Audubon bird illustrations gracing its pale green walls.

Jude spotted a couple of large dog beds, along with a good-sized chew toy, which had him cursing under his breath. The presence of canines, along with their tendency to bark at strangers, was something neither he nor Callie had taken into account.

"I thought you'd be more comfortable right here, in my study." Emma paused to soothe the fussing infant before nodding toward a door to her left. "There's a little powder room right over there—you'll find some towels inside the cabinet to dry off with. And behind the desk, there's a minifridge with bottled drinks—or I'd be happy to send someone with tea or coffee to warm you up."

Both he and Callie thanked her but declined the hot drinks, since the last thing they wanted was anyone else showing up while they were snooping around.

Baby Dove waved her tiny fists, her protests growing in volume, which caused Emma to cast a longing look toward the rocking chair, where Jude spotted a large pillow and a cloth that made him realize—with a sudden flash of insight that had him feeling suddenly awkward and intrusive—that they were probably in the spot where she normally fed her infant.

"Is there anything else you need?" Emma asked, her feet already turning toward the room's door.

"Thanks so much. I'll be fine here sipping from my water," Callie said, raising the bottle Jude had pressed on her earlier to show that she was working on hydration. "Now, please, go ahead and take care of that little darling."

Nodding his agreement, Jude urged, "Please don't let us keep you. I'll make sure Sophie's situated and then call the road service number back on my cell for an update."

Clearly distracted by her child's needs, Emma nodded. "If you two will be okay for a bit, then, I'll be upstairs for a little while. I need to get this little girl fed, and we do have our favorite spots…"

"Whatever you need to do. Don't let us bother you," Jude said, blessing their luck—and the hungry baby, whom he now saw as a tiny ally in their cause.

Once she left the room, closing the door behind her, Callie sank down onto a sofa and gave an exhausted-looking sigh. "Hooray for nursing mothers," she managed. "She should be tied up for a good twenty minutes."

"And upstairs, too," Jude said, "but before we talk about getting the sample we need, are you going to be okay? I don't mind telling you, you had me pretty worried out there."

"I'll be all right. I managed to choke down a couple of antinausea pills in the car."

"If you can *keep* them down, that'd be great."

"That's the whole idea." Struggling to sit up straighter, she put on an admirable game face for someone who still looked a little greenish. "I just need a few more minutes."

"Rest here, then, while I check the bathroom to see if we might've gotten lucky. Maybe her husband keeps a few toiletries in there, too, or I'll come up with something useful from the trash."

By *something useful*, he meant any identifiable item likely to contain a sample of his DNA. Inside one of the pockets of his vest, Jude had both nitrile gloves, to keep his own genetic material from contaminating any evidence, and small, sealable plastic packets where he could easily stow something like a toothbrush, a used facial tissue or a discarded adhesive bandage.

"I'll make sure to talk loudly if anyone comes in," Callie assured him, giving the closed door to the room a watchful glance.

He returned shortly, shaking his head. "Nothing useful there. Place is super clean, for one thing. And what little I found in drawers and cabinets looks as if it's hers."

"She *did* say this was her study. But wouldn't you suppose, in a place the size of this one, the man of the house would have some kind of home office or den of his own, too—a retreat from the family where he could make business calls or simply hang out?"

"Stands to reason, and I'm sure there are other bathrooms on the first floor."

"Avoid the kitchen at all costs, though," Callie warned. "There's no way they won't have help of some sort to keep everybody fed."

"But we didn't see anybody on the way inside," he said, though it occurred to him that Emma Kingston had deliberately chosen to take them in through the entrance she had and place them in an easily accessible area where they would neither be overwhelmed by the home's grandeur nor have the opportunity, were they so inclined, to case the joint.

"That doesn't mean there aren't people around," said

Callie, "and cameras, too, for all we know. Which means we both have to stick to the same story if anyone catches you when you're out looking. Say I was in the bathroom, so you went looking for another when nature called, right?"

"All right," he agreed, thinking that, inelegant as it was, it worked, especially considering her supposed illness. "If I'm not back within fifteen minutes, you know what to do." *Find your way out. Run. Hide. Make your way back to where we left the car hidden. And whatever you do, don't risk your own life trying to save mine.*

When they'd hashed out Jude's addition to Callie's plan yesterday—which he'd insisted on adding in case things went off the rails at this most dangerous juncture—it had all seemed logical and doable, a contingency that would never happen. Now, however, the two of them exchanged a look filled with anxiety as the enormity of what was at stake made it impossible for either to get another word out.

With no time to waste, he gave her the briefest of hugs before turning and heading out the door into the same hall through which they'd entered.

Chapter 8

As Callie waited in the study, her nausea gradually subsided, but the improvement in her digestive symptoms did nothing to ease the dampness of her palms or the flutter of her heartbeat. She felt breathless and light-headed until she realized she was hyperventilating. But when she tried to regulate her respirations, she found that she had somehow forgotten the trick of breathing normally.

Where was Jude in the house right now? Had he found anything useful, or had all this been for nothing? Or worse yet, had he run into someone and was being questioned— or even worse? While they'd been imagining household help, what if the Kingstons actually had security people on-site? Her imagination dredged up an image of commando types in all black, bristling with weapons.

As five minutes and then ten passed without any sign or word from him, she paced, peering anxiously at the door from time to time—and gasped, stifling a cry at the sound of deep, aggressive barking. *Trained attack dogs?*

But it turned out to be coming from outside the window, where a pair of what looked more like family pets—a glossy, golden retriever type and an even larger flop-eared hound cross—were growling and wagging happily as they wrestled and played keep-away with a lime-green football toy, heedless of the damp conditions.

Hand pressed to her pounding chest, Callie fought to steady her weak knees just as the door to the room opened. Relieved beyond measure, she turned to demand that Jude tell her what had taken him so long.

Except it wasn't Jude who entered but Emma Kingston, who'd returned holding a cell phone instead of her baby.

Looking around the study, she said, "All that fussing, and it turned out that Dove was a lot sleepier than she was hungry. She's out cold in her crib already. But what about you, and— Wait. Where's your husband…?"

As she glanced in the direction of the open bathroom door and then back at Callie, her mouth tightened.

"I—I'm starting to feel better," Callie said before repeating the story she and Jude had agreed upon regarding his whereabouts. But she heard herself stumbling, tripped up by her own discomfort at misleading a woman who'd shown her nothing but kindness. A woman who had trusted them—two strangers in need—enough to invite them into her home.

Emma's green eyes narrowed. "So he couldn't wait long enough for…?" Voice firming, she said, "Stay right here, please. I'll go escort him back. I wouldn't want him startling one of our housekeepers into hitting a panic button."

"*Panic* button?" Callie blurted, feeling her face heat at this new revelation, as well as the caution—or had it been suspicion she'd seen flare to life in their host's face? "But Christopher would never—you can't imagine he'd touch anything—or pose any kind of threat?"

Emma studied her for a moment before shaking her head. "I'm not sure *what* I should be thinking about the two of you at this point," she said before holding up her phone. "I called our security people to see if they could be of any help with your vehicle. Only I just received a text telling me that SUV's not registered to a Christopher or Sophie James from San Antonio."

"Oh, that." Waving off her concern, Callie desperately worked to come up with some credible explanation. "You see, we've only just bought it last week, and Chris hasn't yet had time to deal with the paperwork. To be honest, he's just terrible about things like that."

"No," said Emma flatly, her gaze sparking with a challenge. "*You're* just terrible—at *lying*, Sophie...or whatever your name really is."

Surging toward the smaller woman, Callie turned up her palms. "You don't understand. Please. This isn't what you think at all."

Eyes flaring at the swift approach, Emma sprang toward her desk, where Callie saw her reaching up underneath it.

"Wait, please!" Callie begged, realizing she was about to hit the alarm she'd spoken of—or worse yet, grab a hidden gun.

"I'm so sorry!" Callie cried. "But I promise, no one's

here to hurt you or your family! I just wanted—I was really sick, that's all."

Behind her, she heard the door opening, and she tensed, half expecting the meaty arms of some security guard to grab her and drag her away.

What came instead was Jude's voice, sounding so calm and reasonable that she could've wept with relief to hear him asking, "Hey, you two. Is everything all right?"

Emma swung a look dark with suspicion in toward him. "You tell me, *Christopher*. But first off, did you find whatever it was you were looking for?"

"I did find another restroom, thank you, just a little way down the hall." With a sheepish look, he added, "I'm sorry to've gone wandering uninvited. But with my wife's stomach acting up the way it was, I didn't want to disturb her, and I'm afraid that I'd had too much coffee earlier to hold out much longer. The good news is, though, I just got a call from our road service. They're only a couple miles away, so we'll hike out to meet—"

"Let me see your phone, please," Emma said, her voice as hard and cold as steel. The voice of a mother determined to do whatever she had to to defend her home and child from an unknown threat. "The call log."

Jude shook his head, looking both confused and troubled. "I don't understand why you would— There's no need to be so—"

"*Isn't* there?" she asked, looking from one of them to the other. "Or what about some ID? Do you have ID in your wallet or that little purse you have there?"

Neither of them answered, but Callie could've kicked herself. How had she ever imagined they could pull off such a stunt?

"Listen," Jude said, raising his palms as he recovered

a bit more quickly. "It's obvious we've somehow made you uncomfortable, and I'm really sorry for that, so how about if we just show ourselves out now? It's not such a far walk back to our—"

He was reaching for the door already, feet turning in that direction when the phone in Emma's hand rang and she quickly answered, sounding terrified as she said, "In my study. *Hurry!*"

It was only then that Callie realized that Emma must have triggered a *silent* alarm earlier and that someone would be bursting through the door to detain them—or worse—at any moment.

Jude already had the door halfway open when Callie shouted, "Run! Now!"

As she bolted in his direction, she slung her purse over her shoulder and paused to warn Emma, "Don't try to follow. We're heading straight out, we promise, but—"

Jude abruptly slammed the door shut, swallowing a curse. Though he hadn't yet spotted their *company*, he'd been alerted to their arrival by the echo of heavy footsteps, fast approaching in the hallway.

"The window!" he yelled, racing to open the sliding closure—which immediately set off an ear-piercing siren that completely drowned out whatever it was Callie was trying to say as she grabbed at his arm, shaking her head.

But whatever she meant to warn him about, it didn't matter. They had no other choice except to take the one route left to them, so he stepped through into the courtyard before reaching back to offer Callie his hand.

With a last, regretful glance toward Emma Kingston, who was bolting for the room's door, Callie accepted his help out the window. No soon had Jude turned to look

:or the best escape route when he spotted two large and
somewhat muddy dogs racing toward them, their barking raising the decibel level even higher.

Certain they were about to be torn to pieces, Jude
hesitated for a moment. Jerking free of his grasp, Callie veered off and ducked down before coming up with
something bright green. Giving it a squeeze that made
both dogs stop short to pause and stare up at what he now
saw was a rather chewed and slobbery football, she held
it aloft and squeezed again before throwing the squeaker
toy to the courtyard's opposite side.

The larger, hound-type dog went bounding after it,
while the golden retriever mix remained in place, its
deep barks echoing along with the blaring outdoor alarm.

"This way!" he shouted toward Callie before running
past the animal, which backed off instead of attacking.
Ignoring the other doors and windows that would take
them back inside the house, he instead made a beeline toward what appeared to be the one exit to the outdoors—a
metal gate between two hedges at the edge of a shallow
rectangular reflecting pool.

He reached the gate steps ahead of her and rattled
the dripping bars hard, but the gate was locked tight
and far too well made to have any hope of dislodging
with brute force.

"We'll have to climb over it," he shouted at Callie,
who looked up at the ornate painted metal gate, which
extended a good eight feet high.

"Hurry!" he urged her. "I'll give you a boost!"

"But what about you?" she shouted over the shriek
of the alarm and the golden dog, which had followed to
bark at them.

"Just *go*!" Bending forward, he made a stirrup of his

interlaced hands, and Callie—too shocked or scared to argue, adjusted the purse over her neck before taking the step.

As he boosted her up, she grabbed onto the heavier framework of the metal Running K sign set above the doorway. Pulling up her feet, she braced them against a top rail, which she used to push off against as she wormed her way higher.

Once she started to pull herself over the spiked rails that topped the lintel, Jude took a running jump and grabbed for the same top rail she'd found. As he struggled to hoist his entire weight up using only his arms, Callie jumped to the ground on the other side.

"Jude!" she shrieked a moment later as she stared into the courtyard past him, her brown eyes wide with horror. "Behind you! Here they come!"

Imagining armed men racing toward them, Jude channeled every ounce of adrenaline into a single grunting effort that had him heaving himself upward as he threw his leg over the lintel. But in his hurry, he overbalanced, tumbling over the far side. Callie's scream was even louder than the alarm siren as he plunged headlong toward the walkway below.

Chapter 9

Callie stared in horror as Jude twisted midair to splash down in what amounted to a glorified belly flop in a shallow puddle on the sidewalk. How he didn't shatter his ribs and sternum—or possibly a limb or two—she would never know, but he was already scrambling to his feet, grabbing for her hand and racing for the front corner of the mansion before the scream died on her lips.

"Guns!" she shouted near his ear, that single glimpse of two uniformed men charging toward the courtyard burned into her memory. The space between her shoulder blades tingled in anticipation of the bullet she expected to pierce her skin at any moment—the first of the hail that would surely end both their lives.

Behind them, the alarm abruptly stopped midshriek, and, some distance behind them, one of the guards boomed, "Freeze, both of you! Hands up! Security!"

At the sound of that angry male bellow, Callie's feet rooted to the spot.

"Don't stop!" Jude yelled as he latched on to her elbow and physically hauled her forward. "They aren't allowed to shoot at fleeing—"

His claim was interrupted by the explosion of several blasts—impossibly loud—and a sound she recognized as a loud, metallic rattle.

"You got the keys, Dan?" the same voice called, more muted, as if he'd turned to question his partner.

At last, Callie and Jude rounded the corner, bringing Emma Kingston's parked Jeep into view. But instead of crossing the drive as she expected and hiding amid the landscaping or heading for a patch of scrubby trees beyond the perimeter of manicured grounds, Jude guided her directly toward the vehicle.

"I saw her tuck her keys under the mat before she got out," he told her.

"Wait. We're stealing her car?" Callie asked, far less shocked by the fact that Emma Kingston would leave her keys in her vehicle, way out here on her isolated and normally secure ranch estate, than by the idea of adding a real, honest-to-goodness *felony* to the list of offenses they'd committed thus far.

The sound of the two guards' excited voices, now once more approaching, removed all hesitation. As Jude jumped into the driver's side, she rounded the vehicle just as another heart-stopping crack erupted—

Yet her own heart kept right on trying to jackhammer its way free of her body as she dived into the passenger seat and screamed at Jude, "Go! Go now! Floor it!"

The Jeep took off like a shot, tearing up the long drive.

Shaking uncontrollably, Callie turned to look behind them and ducked reflexively when she caught sight of the two security guards. Instead of firing again, however, they turned to run toward a black pickup truck. Relief whipsawed through her to see it had been parked close to the mansion's main entrance, forcing them to run in the opposite direction.

As she turned to tell Jude, however, her gaze snagged on the rearview mirror. Seeing the bullet hole straight through it, she swallowed hard and then glanced over her shoulder. A whimper caught in her throat at the sight of the circular perforation, big as her fist, through the center of the Jeep's rear window.

Adrenaline punched her hard then, graying out her vision. Because this couldn't be happening. She was a respected nurse—a professional—and leading Jude into this madness had all been a terrible mistake. Chills and nausea gripped her, and once more, she lost the thread of breathing without conscious effort. Her brain plunged her into the ice-water reality of that stormy night, those final horrifying moments, when the helicopter began wildly careening and then spiraling as Marc lost his battle for control.

Rising above the sounds of roaring wind, the shouts of terror, Jude's voice finally captured her attention. "Callie! Callie, listen to me! Buckle up, I told you. Ride's about to get real rough."

Blinking hard, she saw that they'd traveled some distance, all the way back to the state highway, and the rain had picked up, big drops exploding like fat moths across the windshield. As she numbly snapped the buckle in place, he jerked the wheel, taking them off the otherwise empty stretch of two-lane road.

"What's going on?" she asked as the Jeep bucked and splashed through puddled rangeland, cobbled with thick tufts of grass and stony divots. "Where are you *going*?"

"Down there—see that brighter gold line just above that low ridge?" he asked, his voice rasping as he spoke over the crunch and crackle of the fat tires over loose rocks and gravel. "Those're cottonwood treetops, so that'll be a river bottom, or maybe a dry creek bed. Either way, with that bedrock where we left the highway, they shouldn't see our tracks where we exited. So if we can make it to cover before they spot us, we can hide out in the Jeep for a few hours, let them pass us by and wait until they finally give up searching."

She nodded as it dawned on her that Jude was as tough, smart and resourceful as they came. And one heck of a lot cooler under fire than she was. Otherwise, they both would have been caught—or maybe even killed—already.

The rugged terrain slowed them considerably, leaving them exposed to discovery for a span of time Callie spent praying for deliverance as she bounced against the shoulder harness. Eventually, however, the Jeep nosed and wallowed its way downhill, following the drainage patterns to reach the level of the bases of the trees that lined a narrow, hidden creek that had slowly, over time, carved out a hidden layer to what had looked almost like a flat plain from a distance.

After driving to partially hide the Jeep behind the root ball of a large tree that had fallen over, Jude finally shut off the vehicle's engine. As raindrops plunked out a jittery rhythm over the Jeep's metallic hood and roof, Callie stared in astonishment as he pulled off his hat, scrubbed his darkened hair and let out a loud whoop of laughter that ended in a round of coughing, a reminder that his lungs were far from fully healed.

"Are you *insane*?" she demanded, unexpected tears pricking at her lower eyelids. "What on earth do you find funny about this? Nearly everything that could go wrong did, and we almost—we could have been killed!"

"Yeah, but we *weren't*, and frankly, I'm delighted as hell about that. Aren't you?" he asked, still with the big grin, which, at the moment, she found as annoying as it was attractive.

"Are you sure you didn't fall on your head? Because it's obvious you've rattled something loose," she said. "You scared me half to death, tumbling down like that. *They* scared me, shooting at us, with real bullets. I've seen up close exactly the kind of damage those things can do, watched way too many people's lives changed forever—or end—while their family are left devastated."

"I've seen more than my share, too, but—"

"But nothing, Jude," she said, her vision swimming with unshed tears and her entire body quaking. "Did you get a look at the back window? *This?*" She gestured angrily toward the rearview mirror. "That could've just as easily been one of our skulls. And I—and I'm not—I can't do this—"

Unbuckling his harness, he reached over and clasped her arm. "Callie," he said, gently pulling her closer. "Don't you understand? You already have, and you were brilliant. *We* have, working together."

"How are you not—? Why aren't you *broken*? That fall." A shudder ran the length of her body as she saw him smacking down again onto the sidewalk.

"Plain dumb luck, I guess," he said, though when he shrugged, he grimaced slightly. "That's not to say that when the adrenaline wears off, I won't be looking around for the nearest bottle of painkillers and a long, hot shower to loosen up my lungs."

"I don't doubt it, especially with you still recovering from inhaling half the bay."

"What about you? Are you okay? Back when we drove away, I don't mind saying, it freaked me out a little when you didn't answer. For a minute, I was scared— I thought you might've caught a bullet —"

"I—I'm fine. Or I am now," she insisted.

"Flashback?" he asked, his blue-gray eyes far too perceptive. As if he saw past her denial straight to the fault lines she'd spent four years fighting so hard to keep hidden. "It's okay, you know, if that's what happened. There's no shame in—"

"Aren't I entitled to be scared out of my wits with people shooting at us?" she demanded, angry to imagine him pitying her, thinking of her as damaged goods. "Can't I just be upset that we're out here acting like a couple of criminals and nearly getting ourselves killed for *nothing*?"

"It wasn't for nothing. *Look.*" Shifting away, he pulled a small, sealed plastic bag from one of his pockets. Inside it, she spotted a small barber's comb, of the type many men carried. Golden-brown in color, it had several black strands threaded among the teeth, close to the shaft.

Going very still, she asked, "Where did you find this?"

"We were right. There *was* a second study. Judging from the decor, I have no doubt it was a man's domain. The comb was on the floor in there, right underneath the desk chair as if he'd dropped it out of his pocket. I picked up a bandanna, too, that appeared to have a few spots of blood on it—maybe he'd nicked himself doing some chore or shaving. It was the best I could come up with, considering the time constraints."

"With any luck, they won't miss either one and figure out what it is we're up to while we're getting those DNA results."

"*If* we get them," Jude conceded, uncertainty creeping into his voice. "There's no guarantee the lab's going to find enough usable material."

"We've gotten this far, right?" she said, feeling responsible to do her part now to keep up their spirits. "So let's believe we'll have the proof you're looking for within five days after we get this delivered, just as promised."

He made a face. "You're sure about this private lab you found? That seems awfully quick to turn around genetic testing."

She nodded. "It is, but I chose this outfit because I have a personal connection—a doctor I used to work with who's promised me he'll expedite the process himself."

"And this connection's good?"

She nodded. "Absolutely. This is a big-time lab, very well respected. Their results have been used in paternity and other civil cases for decades, and they have one of the best track records in the country when it comes to accuracy. And they're far faster than any of the law enforcement–affiliated crime labs."

"They ought to be fast, for what they're charging," Jude said. "And thanks again for covering that while I was in the hospital. As soon as I get back home, I swear I'll pay you back."

She waved him off. "Don't worry about it, Jude,

please. I know that right now, you have other issues, and I—I *want* to do this for you."

The truth was, she could easily afford it. Her own salary as a veteran flight and emergency nurse was more than sufficient to her modest needs. Between Marc's life insurance and the compensation she'd received from the hospital's own coverage, which she couldn't help thinking of as blood money, her debts had long since been settled and her financial adviser reported she was free to "live a little," as opposed to continuing to go through the motions in order to tick off each and every day.

"I appreciate that, but I don't want to be some loser deadbeat," Jude insisted, frown lines creasing his forehead. "That isn't who I am, Callie. Or who I plan to be, in this life."

"Who do you plan to be, Jude? If this pans out, and you find out you're a Kingston."

"I'm no damned Kingston," he said, shaking his head. "Never was and never will be. I don't want any part of any of it, except to be sure my mother's finally resting easy, with people knowing the good woman that she really was."

"What then?" she asked. "That is, in an ideal world—"

"Such as one where my alleged half brother *doesn't* have me murdered?" He flashed a wicked grin before he turned serious, head shaking. "I've been giving that some thought of late, whether I might make a course correction."

"A course correction?"

"Professionally, I mean," he said. "Just a couple of weeks ago, I had a call from a couple of emergency docs I knew in Phoenix. They've been working awhile to develop their own line of burn wound packaging products for the field, and I'd given them some input, so they wanted to see if I might like to come on board now that they're ready to start marketing the product."

"Come on board how?"

"I'd do a lot of the legwork introducing them to the right people, going around to trade shows and talking to—"

"You mean like a sales rep?"

"For a product I genuinely believe would save a lot of lives," he said, a defensive edge coming to his voice. "And I'd also be getting in on the ground floor of a business that could really go somewhere."

"I'm not knocking it at all," she said. "Or saying it isn't a great job for the right person, but you seem like such a natural with the active, hands-on work with patients. You're making a difference out there, every shift, and you love being a flight medic, right?"

"Sure, but I'm not a kid anymore. There are other considerations."

She frowned, knowing that he meant the salary, which had driven her last flight medic to go back to school to pick up his RN accreditation. Shaking her head, she asked him, "Is that going to make you happy when you're spending your days sucking up to insurance gatekeepers and your nights wining and dining doctors? Because I just don't see it being you, no matter how much they're offering. And anyway, we *need* good patient-oriented paramedics like you to stick around."

"Thanks for that," he said, "but between the divorce and what happened with my grandfather, I'm going to need to save a lot more money if I ever want a house and yard of my own."

"So you're seriously angling for that dog, then?" She

smiled, remembering his delighted reaction to meeting Baby.

"That's on the wish list. Absolutely," Jude said with an emphatic nod as the rain pattered gently outside. "But the thing is, I want the whole suburban dream. The wife—though this time, I hope to do a whole lot better choosing—a couple of kids, the white picket fence with the honey-do list, and maybe a grill in the backyard to do steaks or burgers on weekends while I drink a cold brew."

She laughed. "Funny, I never took you for the domestic type. You get that from your mother?"

The shine in his eyes dimmed. "She did her best, I guess, when she didn't sit still long enough to think about the past."

"My mother didn't sit still, either—literally," Callie said. "She was like a tumbleweed with a dream—a singer. We skipped around from town to town, always chasing after her big break."

"Dad in the picture?" he asked.

She shook her head. "Not for long enough to make much of an impression. I tried looking him up later, when she was dating this guy who used to steal money from her purse and make me feel all creeped out, the way he watched me. That was the day I found out my biological father was never going to be my dad."

Jude frowned and shook his head. "I'm sorry."

"It's all right," she said. "My mom had my back, and I had hers, the way we still do for each other. But like you, I remember how it was to go over to the other kids' houses and wish I had the kind of family that came with a nice dad, or a sister or a brother, maybe a dog or cat, as well. I'd even get jealous sometimes of the family squabbles and the cluttered sheds or basements, like they'd been living in their place long enough to accumulate some junk instead of running from town to town, forever changing schools and always feeling behind."

"So what happened with your mother? What made her finally put down roots in Corpus Christi?" Jude asked.

"She got a gig with a house band on the weekends for a couple of years. By the time that finally petered out, she'd taken a couple of bookkeeping classes and was doing enough part-time work for clubs on the side that she was able to keep us in one place so I could finish high school."

"Then she quit moving to do right by you. Sounds like the textbook definition of a good mom."

Callie smiled at the memory of her mother's sacrifice, along with the parade of disappointing suitors—and invariably worse husbands—that somehow never killed her mother's enduring hope that the next potential partner would be better. "It's a little more complicated than that, but I do love that woman dearly."

She shivered lightly.

"You cold?" Jude asked. "I could start up the engine."

She shook her head. "I'm fine. Just—just wondering if we're safe sitting here."

"They haven't shown up yet," he said, "which means we should be completely—"

He cut himself off abruptly, his forehead furrowing as he clutched the wheel and stared, unseeing, toward the narrow creek.

"What is it?" she asked, her pulse picking up speed. "What's worrying you now, Jude?"

He shook his head, his face suffused with color. "Something I should've damned well thought of sooner.

We can't just stay in place like sitting ducks. What if this Jeep's got some kind of an antitheft tracking device on it? What if they're drawing a noose around us even now?"

Alarmed by the thought, she looked over the dash and rearview mirror. "It's not the kind that comes with onboard satellite, is it? I don't see any of the buttons like my car has."

"It's not one of those, no, but that doesn't mean there's not a hidden system onboard. The kind that keeps sending a signal even if the car's shut off or the battery's removed."

"Maybe we'd better get back to my car sooner rather than later, then, and ditch this one," she suggested.

He nodded his agreement, adding, "Let's just hope we make it that far in one piece."

By the time they returned to the remote location where they'd left the Mustang, patches of blue peeked through thinning skeins of silver clouds. Along with the rain, Jude's mood had lifted, since he'd spotted few other vehicles along their route—all of those at a distance and no signs of pursuit.

It was enough to give him hope that his worries about the Jeep having some sort of tracking system were unfounded. After all, the vehicle was neither new nor a high-end model, so perhaps the original purchaser— likely Emma Kingston back before she'd wed the wealthy rancher—hadn't added that particular option.

I'll do my best to get it back to you in one piece, he mentally vowed to the woman whose home and peace of mind he and Callie had breached, *as soon as we're finished using it to keep ourselves alive.*

But the moment Jude pulled around the brush pile, Callie cried out as if in agony, "No!" at the sight of the destruction that greeted them—her convertible, knocked askew from where they had left it, its side, front end and trunk all crumpled from what looked like repeated high-speed collisions.

Collisions Jude guessed in an instant had resulted from being rammed deliberately, from multiple angles, by the pickup the Kingston security team had been driving, which had had a heavy steel cattle guard welded on to its front bumper.

Slamming the Jeep's brakes, he looked around desperately, heart booming in his ears. But there was no sign of an ambush—no gleam of black paint from the truck or glint of metal from anywhere around them to indicate guns aimed at them from the nearby clump of scrubby trees. Only a second set of tire tracks, which he now spotted—and the clearly totaled Mustang.

"M-M-Marc's car..." Callie's face had gone stark white, the freckles across her nose and cheekbones standing out like cinnamon-colored constellations. "His pride and joy—this can't be."

"Oh, Callie, I'm so sorry. If I'd had any idea they could've somehow found it and figured out—"

Before he could finish, she'd unlatched her belt, which she'd only just snapped back on after removing the fake pregnancy belly she'd been wearing, and left the Jeep to race to the car—or what was left of it. Joining her, he saw that, in addition to the body damage, the convertible's top had been slashed to ribbons, as well.

"How could I have been so stupid, so irresponsible?" Callie asked, making a vain attempt to rub away her streaming tears. "How could I have ever imagined people like us could ever win, that we had any sort of chance against such ruthless—"

"Callie, we shouldn't—we can't stay here," he said, spotting a large hunting knife, its blade snapped off near the haft, lying on the ground nearby. "If those guys decide to come back—"

"All I—all I can think of," she said, staring at the wreckage, "is how long my husband dreamed of buying this car, how excited he was the day we finally picked it up at the dealership. I used to tease him about how he spent his days off waxing it and made all sorts of ridiculous excuses to keep from driving it in the rain. And now, just look at it."

Jude pulled her into his arms and held her tight against him, smoothing her hair with his hand. "Listen to me and listen to me right now. This is *not* your doing—not irresponsibility or stupidity or anything but a simple act of vindictive evil and frustration."

Pushing free of his embrace, she looked up at him with frightened eyes. "What if they aren't finished?"

"That's what I'm worried about, too. That's why we should get back in the Jeep and get clear of here before they come back and do the same to us."

"No, I mean—look at this door, right here." She went to show him the Mustang's passenger door, which had either been pried or popped open from one of the impacts.

As she bent to put a knee on the front seat, he warned, "Careful there. There's shattered glass, and—"

"Look," she said, showing him the open—and currently empty—glove box. Voice strung tight with alarm, she said, "My registration was inside there. My insurance card, too—"

"Which means they have your name now, too," he

said, cursing himself for a fool for involving her in any of this, after Kingston's henchmen had already tried to have him murdered.

"It's not just my name," she said, her golden-brown eyes wide with growing terror. "Jude, these people have my address—and my *mother's* at my house alone."

"We have to go back home," Callie said, panic throbbing red-hot at her temples. "You have to take me right now."

"I can't do that," Jude said, "especially now, when they know exactly where you may be going."

"But what about my mother? PB?"

"Get back in the Jeep," he ordered, "and get on the phone with your mom while we put some distance between ourselves and Kingston County."

"We're taking Emma Kingston's Jeep?"

"What other choice do we have? As soon as we can, of course, we'll get rid of the thing," he said, "with any luck, before we run into law enforcement."

"Right now, I'd almost rather deal with the police than the men who did—this," she said, her voice cracking as she gestured toward the mangled Mustang.

Jude warned, "We have to assume anybody with a badge in Kingston County is reporting straight back to Beau Kingston and his people—which gives us an even bigger reason to put as much distance as we can as quickly as we can between us and them."

As she started to get in, Jude said, "Hang on just a second. Let's see if our backpacks are still in there."

They found them both, dumped out nearby, but at least the contents appeared to be undamaged. Callie noticed Jude pocketing the inhaler he'd gotten from the hospital pharmacy before his discharge and said, "You're sounding like you ought to use that. Being out in the rain and running for your life probably wasn't the healthiest thing for your lungs right about now."

"Healthier than collecting bullets."

"Point taken," she said.

Once Jude had taken her advice and started driving, Callie pulled the phone from her purse and hit the first number from her list of saved favorites. As her mother's line rang, the knot in her stomach tightened.

When her mother's recording finished, Callie left the message, "Mom, please call me right away. I'm not hurt or anything, but this is extremely urgent."

After hanging up, she struggled to come up with some reasonable explanation for why her mother might not be answering her phone now. "Maybe she's got PB out in the backyard or she's taken him for a quick walk or something."

"She wouldn't take her phone with her?"

"She doesn't always. Or she could be on another call—to a divorce attorney, I hope, and not to that jerk Lonnie." Her stomach flipped as she pictured him conning her mother into turning off the security system and allowing him into the house, although he wasn't welcome—hadn't been since he'd shown up one day while she was sleeping off an overnight shift. He'd started banging on her door, demanding to know where she was hiding her mother—who had actually gone out to buy a gift for a baby shower—and wouldn't leave until Callie had threatened to have him arrested for trespassing.

"Is she good about checking her voice mails?" Jude asked.

"Not always, which is why I'm sending her a text, as

well," she said, pausing to do exactly that. "And I think I have my neighbor's number here, too. I'll see if she can walk over and knock on the door and check to make sure everything looks all right, see if the alarm system looks as if it's armed or not."

Jude nodded. "That all makes good sense. Do triage and then move to the next step and the next."

Triage. That's right, she thought. Assess their concerns in order of urgency and attend to them in that order rather than allowing the glut of needs and worries to overwhelm her.

Such as the fear that Kingston's security team had already started making their own calls.

And the chance that one of these had been to the same killers who had attempted to murder Jude in Corpus Christi last week.

Still, she couldn't stop herself from wondering if those same men might even now be on their way to her house, where her perpetually cheerful, trusting mother would surely open the door for a nice chat.

Chewing at her lower lip, Callie fought back panic as she pulled up her neighbor's number. Before she could make the call, however, her cell vibrated in her hand, and her mother's number along with a photo of her from years past, singing with her guitar onstage, flashed across the screen.

"Mom?" Callie answered, her voice so high and tight, it sounded like a stranger's.

"Callie, honey, what's wrong? I was lying down and had the ringer off. You would not believe how many times Lonnie's called me, begging for another chance, swearing that he's going to change his ways forever. He's even promised me a trip to Branson, like a second honeymoon, if I'd come home to him. But don't worry. I'm not falling for it this time."

Callie would feel more confident about that if her mother, who had a long history of selective amnesia, didn't sound so pleased by the attention. But there was no time to rehash the same argument they'd had a thousand times before.

"Mom, I need you to do something for me, please. I'm going to need you to pack up PB's things and yours. Take him and leave, now."

"Leave where? Your *house*?"

"Yes, my house. And whatever you do, don't go back…not for a week, at least."

"A *week*? Why? But you—you *invited* me to stay here!" Her mother's bewilderment came out a near-wail. "I thought you wanted me to stay away from Lonnie."

"I do. You know I do. But I totally forgot about this appointment I'd made," Callie said, scrambling for some explanation. "I have workers coming to repaint the whole interior. Remember, I told you I've been taking bids."

The latter part, at least, was true, though she hadn't yet committed to colors or dates for the work to be done.

"B-but this is ridiculous," her mother complained before her voice grew firm. "Callista Marie, this isn't at all like you. First you tell me you're running off for a few days with some *man* you've never even mentioned to me—"

"I thought you were happy about that."

"Oh, I am. Or I thought I was. As least, I know he has a decent job and, from little I saw, he is *quite* the handsome fellow. But leaving me for some impromptu vacation, and then forgetting something like this painting job you've been talking about forever—"

Callie gritted her teeth, hating being called by her full name almost as much as she did being called out by her mother. Continuing to lie to her was even harder, but Callie could see no other choice—not when the truth could endanger the person she loved most in all the world.

Improvising as best she could, she explained, "Maybe I'm a bit...*distracted* lately, that's all."

The pause that followed went on long enough that Callie's pulse ramped up with the certainty she was about to be called out again.

Instead, her mother giggled girlishly. "Well, I suppose that good sex *will* do that, sweetheart, especially after such a long drought."

"Oh my *gosh*, Mom. We are *not* having sex," Callie burst out, feeling herself blush to the roots of her hair, especially when she spotted Jude glancing in her direction, his eyes alight and his mouth twitching with amusement.

"Ha!" her mother blurted, so loudly that he surely must've heard it, too.

Make that *definitely*, Callie realized as she side-eyed his chuckling face.

"Do you think I was born yesterday?" her mom demanded.

With a sigh, Callie realized she had only herself to blame for the direction of her mother's thoughts, so she was going to have to go ahead and live with the suspicion, at least for the time being. "C'mon, Mom," she pleaded. "Cut me a little slack, please. You know I don't like to— I can't really talk about things like that."

"You always were the little shy one," her mother said fondly. "But I hope you aren't—you're not actually feeling *guilty*, are you? Not after four years? Because you know, your Marc would want you to be happy."

Callie's eyes slid closed, her throat tightening as a memory of the way she'd felt, kissing Jude, pretending, even for the sake of their deception, to be pregnant with his child, speared through her. But she reminded herself she hadn't called about her hang-ups but for her mother's safety, which could be at risk with every additional minute she allowed this conversation to veer off track.

"Please," she said, "just do as I ask. Pack up your things and Baby's and go and stay at Aunt Jane's. I know she'll be glad to have you both."

And better yet, Lonnie couldn't stand her mother's sister, Jane, who'd seen through him from the first time the two had met.

"But Beeville's over an hour's drive," Callie's mother complained, in part, because as much as the two loved each other, she had always keenly felt the disapproval of her staid and stubbornly inflexible widowed sister, who had remained in the same small town where the two of them had grown up, where Jane had taught high school until her retirement. "Can't you just reschedule this painting thing till you get back?"

"No, I can't. I've called to check already," she said. "The crew's picking up materials and they'll be there within the hour."

"Maybe I should just go home."

"No, Mom! Please. Promise me you won't do that— or so help me, I'll drop everything and come back there and personally drag you out of that—"

"All right, all right. If it's that important to you," said her mother, "but I still think, if Lonnie didn't have a good heart, deep down, I wouldn't have married him in the first place. After all, he did remember how much I love Branson."

"*Please* tell me you'll go and stay at Aunt Jane's," Callie begged until her mother, who hated conflict more than she feared the thought of her older sister's judgment, finally relented.

Callie only prayed that this solution would hold long enough for her to get back home and personally sort things out—and keep her mother safe from the dangerous, if not deadly, problem she might have inadvertently led to her own doorstep.

Chapter 10

Determined to give Kingston's security goons the slip and lie low somewhere out of sight, Jude headed south as Callie sat staring at her phone beside him. When she made it clear she didn't want to talk, he left her to her thoughts, eventually stopping at an intersection where a road sign pointed southward toward the bustling border city of Brownsville, Texas. The rain clouds had by now burned off, leaving little more than a thin haze that dulled the golden-brown scrubland. A dust devil spun sand into the air when a single semi sped by, passing the same road sign.

"That's our destination, too. Brownsville," he told Callie, though it would take them nearly two hours to get there.

She looked at him, eyes coming to life again, and

broke her silence. "Why all the way out there? You have a contact?"

"I don't know a soul there," he admitted, "but I do know it's big enough that we shouldn't have much trouble disappearing, and there's enough international business, I should be able to find a same-day courier service to transport these DNA samples to the lab without much trouble."

"Seems like a lot of miles to drive out of our way," Callie countered, "and it's pretty desolate country, too, isn't it, between here and there? All out in the open?"

"They'll be expecting us to run back toward Corpus Christi, definitely not toward the border," he said. "This is the safest option I can think of."

She nodded. "Let's do it, then."

As they sped along a lonely state highway, he nervously watched the rearview mirror for any sign of pursuit. His heart raced when they spotted flashing lights ahead.

"What's that?" Callie asked, her words clipped with fear. "Should we turn around and go back?"

"If we do that, we'll only make things worse," he said, his legs feeling like jelly until they drew nearer and he recognized the markings on the vehicles. "Just get out your driver's license. I think we'll be okay."

They pulled up to what appeared to be a routine border patrol checkpoint, where a uniformed agent motioned for Jude to lower his window. After asking if they were US citizens and their destination, he told them to have a nice day, while his partner, the one handling the dog, waved them through.

They both released huge sighs once they were on their way.

"I thought we were toast," Callie said.

"We're both going to end up locked up if we can't get our acts together and quit getting so nervous around anyone in uniform," he warned.

"Thanks for that brilliant insight, Rookie. I'll be sure to keep that in mind, you know, while we're dodging guys who want to kill us while driving a *stolen vehicle*." She slanted an annoyed look his way. "What are you grinning at? What's so funny?"

"Nothing, Red. I was just thinking that if we really get backed in a corner, you can always whip out your charm offensive and I'm sure they'll let us off the hook."

She snorted. "One thing's for sure. We'd have a better chance with that than relying on your sense of humor."

When he caught her half smile out of the corner of his eye, he decided it was safe to make a practical suggestion. "Why don't you take out your phone and see about finding us a place to stay? Preferably someplace off the main drags, where someone will be less likely to come looking."

A few minutes later, she said, "I'm checking out some of those by-owner vacation rentals to keep us away from hotels and motels where they might be looking."

"Great idea," Jude said. "The more private, the better. I don't suppose they'll let you pay in cash, though."

"Hmm," Callie murmured after messing with her phone for a few more minutes. "There's no way to book without a credit card, but I think we'll be safe enough."

"Safer than getting caught sleeping in this Jeep," Jude agreed, noting how exhausted she looked, though it was not yet noon. But there was no discounting the physical and mental toll an ordeal such as the one the two of them had survived would take, not to mention the emotional shock of seeing the car that had meant so much to her demolished. "So go ahead and pick out a spot that looks good—just for one night, though."

"One night?"

"We'll have to figure out something else tomorrow," he said, wary that the use of plastic could give anyone in law enforcement, including those beholden to Beau Kingston, the opportunity to trace them if they happened to look in the right direction. Jude could only hope that it would take whoever was looking long enough to give them the chance to move on tomorrow morning, because they were going to need a place to lay their heads. "For this afternoon, though, I'll leave you to rest while I run over to the courier."

"Who says I need a rest? Did I?" she demanded, bristling at the suggestion. "You're the one who's sounding wheezy."

"Come on, Callie," he told her. "It clearly scared the heck out of you when you figured out they'd found your name and address, especially with your mother home with—"

"Fine. I have a lot on my mind," she sounded aggravated to admit. "Today has not turned out at all the way I thought when I came up with that crazy plan."

"Daring isn't the same as crazy. We both knew it was high risk. We just decided to accept those risks and chance it anyway."

"Right. Which means that I'm perfectly capable of hanging in there as long as you do while you go and deal with—"

"You're *absolutely* capable," he assured her. "You've more than proven that already. But that doesn't mean that when there's an opportunity for one of us to catch a break—say, take a nice shower, and put her feet up for a couple of hours while the other handles a few mundane tasks—she shouldn't take advantage."

"What sort of 'mundane tasks' are we talking, Jude? Other than getting those samples sent off to the lab?"

"This Jeep has to go."

"You're going to get rid of it? How?" she asked him.

He shrugged. "I'm still not completely sure about that. Maybe I'll remove the plates and then park it somewhere—say, down the road from the bus station, where I'll just happen to leave the thing unlocked with the keys in the ignition and the windows down."

Callie sighed. "I sort of hate that. You know there's a car seat in the back and one of the little boy's toy plastic dinosaurs."

"After what those thugs did to your car, you're worried about Emma Kingston's stuff?" he asked, though it touched him to realize that behind her sometimes icy and abrasive front, she harbored enough tenderness to care about a small child's lost toys.

"I know, and I'm torn, too," she said. "On the one hand, she's in the enemy camp—and she did call security on us. The kind of security that was willing to shoot first and ask questions later. But I really can't blame her for being frightened. As far as she knew, we were a couple of home invaders, people out to steal things or maybe even harm her or kidnap the new baby after she'd been so kind. And I can't imagine she directed those guards to do what they did to the Mustang."

"I'm with you there," he said, remembering how genuinely concerned the woman had seemed when she'd stopped and gotten out of her vehicle in the rain, all because she'd spotted a sick and stranded stranger and her partner. "And if we ditch the Jeep, it does leave us with a transportation issue. But if we're caught driving this thing— You may've seen on the news that a lot of police departments now are using these license plate scanners. If some computer pops up that plate number as stolen—"

"What if it had *different* plates? Do you think…?"

"Why, Callie Fielding—" As they passed some scruffy-looking goats browsing on what passed for forage, a spotted brown-and-white one popped its head up to watch them pass. "—what you're suggesting is definitely illegal."

"Then based on what I've seen today," she quipped, a hint of playfulness in her voice, "you should be just the man to make it happen while I take my shower and— how was it you put it? Oh yes, put up my feet for a couple hours while you attend to those mundane tasks."

After leaving Callie to get settled in the private backyard guesthouse they had rented in a modest but quiet and well-kept residential neighborhood, Jude first risked driving to the address listed on the same-day delivery service Callie had also looked up for him online. Once there, he filled out the online paperwork and packaged up the items, along with a cheek-swab sample of his own DNA for comparison, and paid for a couriered delivery to the lab.

Afterward, he started up the Jeep but hesitated in the parking lot, his stomach churning at the thought of the enormity of what he had just done. Because of the amount of the charge, he, like Callie, had had no other choice except to use a card, even though he knew fully well it might at some point be traced by someone working for Beau Kingston. Would anyone doing so realize— as soon as they saw the charge was to a courier service on the heels of Jude's mysterious visit to the Kingston mansion—what it was that they were really up to? Or by that time, would they know already, because Jude would have already confronted his half brother, Beau, with the results, along with his demands?

He took a deep breath, trying to allow himself to imagine how he'd accomplish such a thing without ending up buried somewhere on the vast acreage grazed by countless generations of Kingston cattle. The smart move, he realized, would be to find an attorney willing to work out a deal with him on the legal fees. Maybe having confirmation that he had actually been born a Kingston would, if nothing else, improve his creditworthiness.

But that was a problem for another day, Jude decided. Relieved for the moment to have Beau Kingston's potential DNA out of his hands, he next set his mind to the issue of the license plate. Lingering in the lot for a few more minutes, he started looking up the addresses of salvage yards but was interrupted when his phone began to vibrate, the words *Private Caller* appearing on the screen.

Annoyed by what he assumed to be a junk call—a few always seemed to get through each day despite the spam-blocking service he used—he rejected the call, only to have the phone stubbornly vibrate again twice more.

The third time, he picked up, irritated enough to want to give whichever telemarketer was calling a piece of his mind, though he knew the odds were high it would turn out to be a recorded message from an illegal robocaller.

"Don't even think of hanging up, you thieving bastard," said a distinctly male voice, one that was definitely both live and human and so thick with scorn that it turned Jude's guts to ice water. For one heart-stopping second he suspected that his grandfather hadn't died at all, that everything, from the old man's supposed heart attack to Jude's discovery of his mother's private papers had been no more than a colossal laugh, one last chance to mock the grandson he had so resented being stuck with.

But however filled with hate it was, the speaker's voice was stronger, surer and definitely more educated than Jude's grandfather had sounded as he went on to say, "We know it was you who dared to set your filthy feet in the mansion this morning, you and your—is Callie Fielding a lady friend you talked into joining on your con job? Or was it her idea in the first place?"

"It's no con," Jude insisted, struggling to keep his voice calm and even, though it chilled him to the marrow to hear Callie's name spoken with such contempt, especially knowing that they had her address. "And if you didn't want me coming for you, you damned well shouldn't have come after me instead of simply answering my letter like a normal person would have."

Though he expected a swift denial, the man Jude suspected was his half brother hesitated, giving him the chance to press his case. "I've sent you proof, Beau, if you'll only listen to me," he said. "I've sent the proof my mother was your father's first wife—and they were married in the months before my birth."

"*Everybody* knows your mother was hot and heavy with Winthrop. Everyone but you, I guess." The throaty grunt that followed was heavy with disdain. "So let me educate you on that, why don't you, Castleman? She was running around behind Big Jake's back, denying him while spreading her legs for her own physician. It's

Get up to 4 FREE FABULOUS BOOKS You Love!

To thank you for being a loyal reader we'd like to send you up to 4 FREE BOOKS, absolutely free.

Just write "YES" on the Loyal Reader Voucher and we'll send you up to 4 Free Books and Free Mystery Gifts, altogether worth over $20, as a way of saying thank you for being a loyal reader.

Try **Harlequin® Romantic Suspense** books featuring heart-racing page-turners with unexpected plot twists and irresistible chemistry that will keep you guessing to the very end.

Try **Harlequin Intrigue® Larger-Print** books featuring action-packed stories that will keep you on the edge of your seat. Solve the crime and deliver justice at all costs.

Or **TRY BOTH!**

We are so glad you love the books as much as we do and can't wait to send you great new books.

So don't miss out, return your Loyal Reader Voucher Today!

Pam Powers

LOYAL READER
FREE BOOKS VOUCHER

YES! I Love Reading, please send me up to 4 FREE BOOKS and Free Mystery Gifts from the series I select.

Just write in "YES" on the dotted line below then return this card today and we'll send your free books & gifts asap!

➡ YES ⬅

Which do you prefer?

☐ **Harlequin®**
Romantic
Suspense
240/340 HDL GRHP

☐ **Harlequin**
Intrigue®
Larger-Print
199/399 HDL GRHP

☐ **BOTH**
240/340 & 199/399
HDL GRHZ

FIRST NAME

LAST NAME

ADDRESS

APT.#

CITY

STATE/PROV.

ZIP/POSTAL CODE

EMAIL ☐ Please check this box if you would like to receive newsletters and promotional emails from Harlequin Enterprises ULC and its affiliates. You can unsubscribe anytime.

HI/HRS-520-LR21

no wonder she hung her head from all the gossip and slunk out of town without even looking back to check in on her son."

"You weren't even born back then, so you didn't know her, not like I did—" Though in the back of his mind it hit him that this detail, the supposed lover's identity, was new information, Jude could focus on nothing but the slander. "—or you'd *never* believe those filthy lies about her. She was absolutely faithful until the day she died."

Jude's mind skipped back to the sound of knocking, his own eleven-year-old fist against her locked door. The echoes of his own voice, cracking with panic as he called for his mother, because he'd known somehow, he'd absolutely *known*, when he had found her car still parked in its spot after he had gotten off the school bus, when she had never in his memory dared to miss a workday, not with her father always harping on her about contributing her fair share to the household. And then there'd been that note she'd taped to the bedroom door, the handwriting recognizable but so messy, the paper marked with what he'd later come to realize had been some of the last tears his mother had ever shed.

Don't come in, Jude. Wait for Grandpa to get home.

How he would always wish he had, instead of finding a knife in the kitchen and frantically forcing the cheap lock open. Finding the horror that would ever after remain seared into his memory, the way his mother had fashioned the belt of her own bathrobe into a slipknot to end her pain...

"I know you don't want to believe it," said the caller, sounding older than Jude had at first believed. Old enough to make him doubt he was actually speaking to Beau Kingston in the first place, especially since that man had referred to Big Jake Kingston by his first name. "But it's all right there in the court records from the divorce proceedings. The doc even gave a deposition admitting his involvement—his wife left him over it, as well."

"I know it was a lie. A lie cooked up to gain custody of Jake Jr.," Jude said, his heart beating faster. Because there was something about that name the caller had mentioned, Winthrop, some connection his overheated brain was currently incapable of making. "My mother would never— She wasn't capable. If you had any idea how that accusation haunted her, a woman of her faith and morals."

"People slip up. That's how bastards like you happen. There's no shame in that on your part." The voice turned abruptly harsher. "But no damned payday, either. Only a damned *casket*, for you and your girlfriend both, if either of you comes anywhere near the ranch again, or dare to steal any more Kingston property."

"Don't you threaten me, and don't get so damned self-righteous. You. Sent men. To kill me," Jude rasped, his voice once more straining. "Your thugs trashed my apartment, destroyed a vehicle for no damned—"

"I have no idea what you're talking about."

Not buying a word of the predictable denial, Jude bet his life—both his and Callie's—on the best bluff his brain could scrape together. "You touch either of us, and I promise you, this whole story's spilling on the airwaves, every ugly word of it. The attorney I've hired has instructions—and copies of the original documents ready to send key members of the media—and post online in a website I've rigged a dead man's switch on."

The threat sounded so persuasive that he wished he'd

actually had the time and money to arrange it…if such a thing were even possible.

But the caller's laughter was harsh with scorn. "If you imagine that whatever low-rent hack you've dredged up can't be bought off, you'd better think again—or that anybody in their right mind's going to believe that some broken-down bastard without two nickels to rub together is deserving of the family name, much less a share of one of the richest estates in this part of Texas—"

"I've *never* asked you for the damned name. Or one dime of Kingston money, either."

"But you *will*. Of course you will. Trash like you— what choice do you have?"

As the connection abruptly cut off, Jude gritted his teeth, raw hatred seeping through every atom of him…

As it hit him that, for all his hateful arrogance, the caller had a point.

After spending a few days relaxing in an upscale Las Vegas resort where he was welcomed as a frequent guest, Armbruster took a car to the airport, where he waited for his flight to the Central American country he currently called home. Though he might normally have been disappointed at the sudden cancellation of the Castleman job—and the large payday that would have come with its completion—he'd been exceptionally fortunate at the tables this trip, a pleasant surprise, since he was normally more inclined toward poolside diversions or the latest headline shows.

So it was, he was feeling content and ready to retire to the tropical resort condo that he'd chosen for its stunning ocean views for the remainder of the winter… or perhaps to retire for good this time, when the phone vibrated in his pocket—not the client contact burner phone, which he had disposed of before leaving Texas, but the one his handler used for reaching him when a situation called for more haste than their usual dark-web messaging system allowed.

Drop this one in the trash, too. Finally leave this life before you end up assigned to shepherd another slow-witted burden like Trigger, with his onion sandwiches and monosyllabic conversation. Or dead or incarcerated, like so many others who have gone before you.

But Armbruster had tried retirement before, three times in the past decade. Like companionship, he had found unbroken leisure satisfied him no more than an endless banquet filled with nothing but desserts.

No, he decided, as he raised the phone to take the call. Even after all these years, sweet needed salt to balance out life's flavors, to allow him to savor it in all its richness.

And the finest salts were surely distilled from tears and human blood.

By the time Callie heard Jude entering the small but welcoming guesthouse they'd selected, she was stretched out on the queen-size bed, tangled in a coverlet, blinking her way free from a dream that had left her breathless and disoriented.

"Sorry to wake you," he said, his tall form silhouetted by the sun's last golden rays slanting through the open doorway behind him.

"Don't be." Blinking away sleep, she pushed herself upright against the headboard and shoved damp strands from her face while he locked up. "My hair's going to be a complete wreck if I don't get up and do something with it before it dries like this. And I was—the dream I was having…"

He frowned at her. "Nightmare?"

She switched on the light above her head and frowned, straightening the long-sleeved tee she'd thrown on with a pair of black leggings after her shower. "Not exactly," she said, kneading at a crick in her neck. "More like a visit…from my husband. He kept asking if I'd seen his keys. Asking me and asking me, and I—I didn't know how to tell him what happened and how sorry I am."

On second thought, she realized, remembering how helpless she'd felt, that was probably the very *definition* of a nightmare.

"Someday, Callie…" Jude said, sincerity etched into the lines across his forehead. "Someday, I'd like to buy you a new Mustang—"

"I don't *want* another—another Mustang," she said, her voice breaking.

"What *do* you want, then?" he asked. "Because, when all this is over, if it's in my power to make it happen—"

"Not unless you have a way to turn back time."

Their gazes caught and lingered a few moments before he coughed as if to clear his throat.

"You all right?" she asked, hearing a rattling she didn't like.

He nodded before saying, "Maybe this is too hard. Too tough and too dangerous. I should never have involved you in this."

But along with the regret packed into his rasping voice, she imagined she heard longing, too. A longing for something they had both agreed could never be, no matter how difficult she sometimes found it to go on alone.

"I *wanted* to be part of this, practically demanded,"

she said. "I won't pretend I didn't just because we've had a few bumps in the road."

"*Bumps* in the road?" His brows rose at her understatement.

"Mountains, maybe," she admitted, before straightening her spine. "But I'm not going anywhere. Not until we see this through."

"Brave woman," he said, taking a step nearer. When their gazes met, her heart skipped a beat before she forced herself to look away from a face that made the last remnants of the nightmare—and the memory of her husband—dissolve like a sea mist touched by sunlight.

Desperate for a distraction, she pointed to the top of a small cabinet, where she'd left the wide-toothed wooden comb she used to untangle her hair. "Would you mind handing that to me?"

Jude brought the comb, but instead of giving it to her, he said, "Why don't you let me? I'm an old hand with this, or at least I helped my—my wife with hers when she had a stiff neck the way you do."

"Um... I..." she said uncertainly, unable to recall Marc ever making such an offer.

"Afraid I'll bite?" he asked, a challenge in his smile.

She made a scoffing sound and rolled her eyes in an attempt to hide what she really did fear as he settled down behind her.

"Just relax," he said, "and let me explain where things stand now with our situation."

"Sure, all right. I guess so," she said. "You did get those items sent off, didn't you?"

"No problems there," he answered, motioning for her to turn her back to him.

Their gazes caught for a split second, long enough

for her to feel the skin along the backs of her arms pebbling with goose bumps.

After turning away, she felt his hand carefully lift a section of her hair off her neck and back. As the tines gently glided through it, he said, "Tell me if I'm pulling too hard."

"Okay," she said, trying to ignore the pleasant tingling where he'd barely touched her. Trying even harder not to think back to what it had felt like when she had pressed her lips to his so briefly before they'd both agreed the two of them would never cross that line again.

Still, a chill rippled through her as she imagined him bending forward to press his lips to her neck.

"You all right?" he asked. "You're awfully quiet."

"And what about the license plates?" she asked quickly, desperate to get her brain back online. "Did you—did you steal a set or something?"

"Not exactly," he explained, dropping his question to continue working through the tangles. "I went by an auto salvage yard and offered cash to a guy who worked on the grounds there to make a plate trade while his boss wasn't looking. He ended up making me an even better offer."

"What kind of offer?"

"He'd take the Jeep off my hands, make sure it never turned up anywhere anyone could trace it—"

"You mean south of the border?"

"Or parted out. Seemed unwise to ask which," Jude admitted. "In exchange, I'd get a vehicle with a clean salvage title. Not exactly a sweet ride, but—"

"I thought we'd agreed we weren't going to ditch the Jeep."

"We did. But the more I thought about it, the less

I wanted either of us exposed to the kind of risk that came along with keeping hold of it. We can't afford the luxury of being sentimental, not about people who've already shown they're willing to destroy anyone who gets in their way."

Callie thought about the evening she'd seen Jude wheeled into Emergency, pale and sodden and nearly lifeless, about the devastation that Kingston's men had left behind both in his apartment and with the car that had once meant so much to Marc. "I hate it, but I know you're right. We can't afford to be soft when it comes to Kingstons, not if we expect to come out of this alive."

"I was hoping you'd see it that way," Jude said, "because I'm now the proud owner of an old silver Ford with one blue quarter panel and a good-sized dent in the trunk. But the engine's practically brand-new, the tires have deep tread and the thing runs like it could do a few laps around the Equator."

"I'll trust your judgment on that. But this guy you made the trade with. Are you sure you can trust him?"

Jude shrugged. "I got the impression that this sort of deal making is a little sideline he'd rather his boss at the salvage yard knows nothing about, let alone the law. Since he stands to get in a world of trouble if he's caught handling what he has to know is stolen property, yes. In a strange way, I *do* trust him."

"That's good news then."

"It's not *all* the news, though."

When the comb flicked free of one damp lock, she turned to look him in the eye, worry pulsing through her at the tension she saw written there. "What's happened?"

"A blocked call happened, on my cell phone."

"What?" Straightening abruptly, she leaned forward. "From them, you mean? Those people?"

He nodded. "I'm not sure which one of them, but yes. He was definitely from the Kingston camp, maybe whoever's running his security."

"Like those thugs who wrecked the car?"

"And tried to shoot us on our way out," Jude reminded her, passing the comb back to her.

"What did—what did he say?"

"That we're dead—both of us—if we come anywhere near Kingston property again."

"Tell me something we don't know already," she said with a disgusted snort. "Do you think he had any idea why we really came—or what you managed to steal out of Beau's study?"

Jude's eyes narrowed, his mouth flattening. Shaking his head, he told her, "I don't think they've put it together quite yet, or maybe they haven't missed the comb and the bandanna."

"They might never, with small, everyday items like that in a household with kids in it, especially with Beau out of town for a few days."

"I'm betting he won't *stay* out of town once he hears that we've come calling," Jude said. "I know *I* wouldn't if strangers had entered the house while my wife and child were at home."

"Which means he could turn up the heat on finding us."

"And likely killing us, if he realizes we've got a sample of his DNA. Otherwise, he's got entirely too much to lose."

Chills rippled over her skin, causing her to rub at her arms. "So how do we get out of this alive?"

"There's only one way I can see," he said. "We beat them—all of them, by revealing the facts and the results of the DNA test so publicly and indisputably that they'll never be able to deny my claim. Or refute the lies my father used to destroy my mother."

"You seem—you seem awfully confident this thing's going to turn out the way you've—" Callie drew a deep breath, understanding she might upset him. "—the way you've already decided this test is going to come out a match. But what if, somehow, it doesn't, Jude?"

"It *will*," he insisted. "It has to."

"But you saw those photos of Beau Kingston, didn't you? Inside the house?" she asked. "I'm sorry, but did you notice any resemblance? Because if there was one, I didn't really see it."

"Have you ever seen photos of the old man, Big Jake Kingston, when he was younger?" Jude asked before shaking his head. "The first time that I looked them up, other than the big hats and boots—he was way into the cowboy regalia—it was almost like looking in a mirror."

"That must've been a shock."

"Kind of took me aback, I'll admit," Jude said before coughing into his hand. Afterward, he shrugged. "Maybe Beau just so happens to look more like his mother."

"Okay," she allowed, but privately, she was praying that Jude hadn't been deluding himself this whole time about his family history and his resemblance to the stranger he believed to be his sire. Because the more she thought about it, the more she realized that having lost his mother in such a tragic manner so many years before, he'd never gotten the chance that most children did, to come to terms with his parent as a flawed human being. Only this mistake could leave them nothing to bargain with at all.

"You don't believe me. I can see it. But the test will bear me out. I guarantee it," Jude said. "And then I'll prove that Big Jake Kingston lied about my mother all those years ago when I go public with the results."

"But if you *are* right and you do this, if you put it out for everyone to see, that'll make you…" Her heart fell as her world shifted, as for the first time it hit her that this man she had partnered with for revenge against the Kingstons, this man she'd allowed to comb the tangles from her hair, and to touch her heart with his story, was far more than a poor, unwanted bastard fighting for the honor of the mother he had so loved. He was now determined to be… "You'll be one of *them*," she forced herself to finish.

He shook his head. "Inside, I'll always still be the same Jude Castleman I've always been," he said, pressing his closed fist to his own chest, "but it's only Jude *Kingston* who will have the power to keep us both safe."

Callie pulled him into a tight hug, her arms shaking with a new fear. "Not if they find a way to kill you before you get your hands on the money Beau Kingston sees as his."

Chapter 11

Over a dinner of Mexican food at a nearby café, the two of them decided that, despite the threatening phone call, they would still spend the night in Brownsville resting and recovering.

"After all," Jude reasoned, trying to convince himself as much as Callie, "the warning was more of a 'don't come back or else' than any indication they might know where we are yet. Besides that, I have reason to hope that my threat might at least slow them down enough to confer on their next move."

"I think you're right," she said. "We'd most likely only attract more attention if we stay on the move."

By the time he'd finished his tamales, Jude had convinced himself that there was no point in continuing to second-guess their decision any longer. With the guesthouse hidden behind a tall backyard privacy fence and the Ford parked out of sight behind the homeowner's detached garage, they were unlikely to find anyplace safer.

"Tonight, you're taking the bed," Callie insisted once they made the short walk back to their rental, aided by starlight and the few security lights on the mostly residential street. "I'm not hearing another word of argument about it, either. Your wheezing's getting worse, and I can see from the way you're moving that your back's sore from that fall you took off the fence. Or was it the truck accident?"

"The fall," he reluctantly admitted, rubbing at the aching spot he'd been trying to hide from her for hours.

"I can't imagine what you were thinking, shoving that dresser up against the door on your own just now." Gesturing toward it, she shook her head and muttered, "You men all think you're indestructible."

"I was *thinking* of our safety, and you're very welcome," Jude said.

"We would've been exactly as safe if I'd given you a hand," she pointed out, "and you wouldn't be wishing we had something stronger than that generic ibuprofen from my bag."

"I'll be fine," he insisted before looking toward the sofa. "But that thing's so hard, I wouldn't even want to *sit* on it and can't imagine either of us getting any sleep. Maybe we could— If I promised you I wouldn't..."

Before he could make a suggestion that was likely to make things between them more awkward than they were already, she crossed the room and pushed aside the curtain on hooks that served as a makeshift closet.

"Here's our solution. I found this neat little rollaway bed back here earlier. This is where I'm sleeping."

"Only if we both agree that I'm taking it tomorrow," he insisted.

"If that makes your chivalrous heart beat a little easier, Rookie." She flashed a sassy grin. "But as for tonight, try to get some sleep. After that plate of cheese enchiladas I just put away, I'm pretty sure I'll be out cold as soon as my head hits the pillow."

After Jude helped her set up and make the narrow rollaway bed, they both got ready to turn in for the night. In spite of Callie's proclaimed fatigue, he found her propped against the pillows in her bed, scowling down at her phone when he emerged from the shower a short time later wearing the navy T-shirt and gym shorts he intended to sleep in—along with freshly washed hair much closer to its natural dark blond hue.

"Everything all right?" he asked.

Already dressed for the night in a pair of purple-trimmed gray pj's, she nodded before shaking her head and then sighing. "I hope so. I just checked in with my mother, and she *claims* she's done as I asked, but I can't reach my aunt Jane to confirm that's where she is."

"You don't think she'd lie to you about it, do you? Stay at your house, where she might be in danger?"

Callie shook her head. "My mother's *not* a liar."

"I didn't mean to offend you. I wasn't trying to imply—"

"Hear me out," she said, gesturing for him to hold on with a raised finger. "What I meant to say was, she's not a liar in her own mind. She just doesn't want to disappoint me, so she tends to tell me what she thinks I want to hear."

"A shame you can't get her to put PB on the phone."

Callie chuckled before saying, "I'd probably have a

better chance of getting the straight story out of Baby than my mom—or certainly Lonnie." Her expression soured at the mention of her mother's husband.

"You haven't spoken to him, have you?" Jude asked.

"He'd only hang up if I called," she said, waving off the thought. "I did try shooting him a text, though, something to the effect of, 'Hope you're doing okay. Have you talked to my mom lately?' in the hope that he might let on if Mom might've— I pray I'm wrong about this, but it wouldn't be the first time she's gone back to a situation she shouldn't have."

As he sat down on the larger bed, he nodded, having seen from his years as a paramedic how difficult even severely abused women—and sometimes men—often found it to break away from their partners. "So how'd that olive branch you offered go over?"

She snorted, slanting a look up toward him. "Pretty sure he'd love the chance to break that particular tree limb over my head since he responded, and I quote, 'Unless you're about to tell me where I can pick my wife up, how I am and who I talk to are none of your damn business.'"

"So I take it your dislike is mutual."

She made a face. "He's always accusing me of sabotaging their marriage, when all I've done is make certain she understands that she deserves to be treated with respect—and has other options if she isn't."

"That's nowhere close to sabotage. That's being a supportive daughter," Jude defended. "Do you think she'll be okay for now? If she really did go back home?"

"'Okay' is a relative term, isn't it? I doubt he'd risk doing anything physical after the police have warned him, at least for a while. And if he does forget himself,

I'm pretty sure PB would take a chunk out of anybody who tried to hurt his grandma. He loves her to pieces."

"Good dog," Jude said with feeling, though from her worried look, he could see she was as aware as he was that no animal was any guarantee against a man intent on violence.

About an hour later, while Jude was trying not to bother Callie with his restless shifting in the bed, he heard the quiet buzz of her phone vibrating on the nightstand beside her.

"Don't worry about waking me," he told her, speaking in the room's near-total darkness. "I'm certainly not sleeping."

She took the call, but kept it short before profusely thanking the person on the other end.

"Good news?" he asked.

"The best," she confirmed. "That was Aunt Jane, telling me she's received my earlier text and she has Mom and PB safe and sound at her place. Actually, 'under house arrest' was the way she put it."

"I'm beginning to like your aunt Jane."

"She's kind of on the intense side—my mom claims I inherited my bossy tendencies from her—" Callie snorted at that "—but her heart's in the right place. And I'm beyond relieved to have her standing between Mom and trouble. Now, at last, I feel like I can finally breathe again."

"That's great," Jude said, wanting more than anything to cross the dark room, to go to her and give her a hug. He thought better of it, though, all too aware of the late hour and how little they were wearing. Within these intimate confines, it was more important than ever—and tougher, too—to maintain their carefully constructed boundaries.

In the silence that followed, he wondered if she felt the same pull and whether she might be wondering what would happen if they decided to bridge their fear and loneliness for just a little while?

Apparently, she had more sense, or else the day's stress and exhaustion caught up with her. Either way, the smooth sounds of her breathing told him that she'd dropped off to sleep.

His brain, though, remained restless, the growing tightness in his lungs less bothersome than the doubts that returned to gnaw at him, this time regarding what she'd said earlier about the DNA sample he had taken to prove his relationship to Beau Kingston. *"You've already decided this test is going to come out a match,"* Callie's voice floated up out of the darkness to accuse him. *"But what if, somehow, it doesn't, Jude?"*

His gut turned cold and queasy as he thought back, too, to what the anonymous caller who'd phoned today while he'd been out running his errands, had insisted.

"She was running around behind her husband's back, denying him while spreading her legs for her own physician."

Though it turned Jude's stomach to remember, the name the man had mentioned came back as well, the name that had so briefly made him wonder where he'd heard it before. This time, however, he pulled out his cell, tapping out *Winthrop* in the memo program so he wouldn't forget to ask Callie about it in the morning.

That was when it hit him, why his sleep-starved brain had connected the name of the man who'd allegedly been involved with his mother with the woman lying in the bed such a short distance from his own.

It was because Dr. Winthrop—Walter Winthrop, it must surely be—had been the patient who had died in that helicopter crash four years back—

The same "old friend" that Big Jake Kingston had claimed he'd *accidentally* shot in the face while hunting.

Callie was awakened before dawn by the sound of Jude's coughing. Deep, harsh coughs that had him getting up and staggering to the bathroom, where she heard him struggling to get the rattling spasms back under control.

Fully awake now, she climbed out from underneath the covers and went to switch on a lamp. Tapping at the bathroom door, she asked, "Is there anything I can do? You have your inhaler?"

It turned out that he didn't, so she hurried to find it for him and, afterward, encouraged him to take another shower. "Make it a pretty warm one, too. The steam will help to loosen things up."

But privately, she was worried that the prior day's exertion, including the time spent in the rain, had set back his recovery, and by the time the sun was fully up, she was starting to think Jude's situation might be far more serious.

"We need to get you to an urgent care center," she told him around seven when she went to his bedside and felt his forehead, which seemed too warm to her. "I have a bad feeling you're heading for pneumonia—if you're not already there. I'm sure the doctor warned you you'd be especially vulnerable until your lungs recovered."

He shook his head. "No more doctors. We can't afford to leave those kind of footprints—have to keep moving."

"We're not going anywhere today, Jude. Don't you get it? This could kill you if it gets bad."

"It's not going to get bad." Turning his head away, he hacked into his elbow, his wheezing audible. When he could speak again, his eyes were watering. "I still have my meds from the hospital, the inhaler and the antibiotics both. Plus, I have the best emergency nurse in Corpus Christi by my side."

"A nurse who's telling you, you stubborn mule, that you need a fresh set of chest X-rays and possibly a different antibiotic, not another day on the run."

"What if we compromised and laid low here for another day or two?" he asked her. "I'll admit that I could stand a little rest."

She nodded. "I'll see if I can book this guest cottage for an extension, then, and run out and pick up a little food for the minifridge and whatever supplies we might need."

"That's fine, but there's no need to go overboard, Ms. Nightingale," he teased. "I've always had an iron constitution."

"Even iron rusts when you dunk it underwater long enough, Rookie," she said, thinking that listening to his bravado was almost as annoying as her late husband, who'd always acted as if the world was coming to an end whenever he came down with a minor man-cold. "And I can tell you now, if you get too much worse, I'm not stopping to argue with you. I'm dragging your sickly carcass straight to the nearest ER—"

"If it does come to that," Jude told her, dropping the cocky act as he was interrupted by more coughing, "I want you to promise that you'll just dump me there and take off, get somewhere safe. Because I won't let some stupid illness be what ends up getting both of us tracked down."

After dressing, Callie headed out into the cool, overcast morning with the keys to the old Taurus. Though her mind was mostly occupied by the running list of what they would need, she couldn't help scanning the light traffic, her heart leaping whenever she noticed anyone looking her way or appearing to follow as she changed lanes or made a turn. Soon, however, she admitted to herself that her jitters had far more to do with her paranoia than the reality of the situation.

"You're fine. See?" she asked aloud, talking herself through the moment as she might to calm PB when he was spooked by approaching thunder. "That truck's pulled into that drive-through. You just need to take a deep breath."

Following her own advice, she sat outside the drugstore and waited for her trembling to subside before going in. After picking up several over-the-counter medications, a thermometer and a handful of other items, she headed to the grocery store in the same shopping center before returning to the guesthouse.

Throughout the day, Jude's cough continued to concern her, with the medication she gave him putting him to sleep. But during those intervals when he was awake, he continued to insist that he only needed time to rest and heal.

Callie only prayed that she was doing the right thing by allowing it—and that they'd be safe here while they waited to see if he would turn a corner.

Jude hated the thought of taking a chance by remaining in place, but in the hours that followed, Callie demonstrated exactly what her mother must have meant about her so-called bossy tendencies, insisting that he give both his lungs and his sore back the chance they needed to recover before they moved on.

"First off, if Kingston's goons were going to come and kill us in our sleep, I'm pretty sure that they already would have," she'd said. "And if you insist on pushing forward, you really will end up in the hospital."

"I'm not some useless little kid who needs your mothering," he said, feeling too out of sorts to be pleasant.

"Do you want to be some useless *corpse* who needs my burying?" she'd fired back, her hands on her hips.

"I told you already. Iron constitution." He thumped on his chest before the damned coughing made a liar of him once again.

"Just eat your chicken soup and get some rest," she insisted. "And leave all the worrying to me for the time being."

Whatever she'd dosed him with—some sort of over-the-counter nighttime syrup—left him little choice about the rest part. He dropped off into a troubled sleep, one punctuated by nightmares where he struggled to find Callie among the muck and weeds along the shoreline back in Corpus Christi. In others, she watched from the other side as he struggled to climb a Jack's beanstalk version of the gate they'd scaled to escape the courtyard of the Kingston mansion—one that kept growing taller as the security guards behind him took aim.

During those brief periods when Jude was awake, his brain thick with fatigue, he blinked at the clock or the window and tried to remember…something…

Something he was forgetting to tell Callie. Something

about the phone call. Some detail that he was terrified would come back to bite them both if he could not remember soon.

Chapter 12

"Just like you figured, they did dump Mrs. Kingston's Jeep," said Trigger, who had taken their latest ride out looking while Armbruster grabbed a few hours of shut-eye at the Brownsville motel where they were staying and gone out scouting for any sign of the Jeep stolen from the Kingston mansion.

Personally, he had figured it for a fool's errand, sending them both back here to find Castleman, who had surely only been passing through the day he'd used his credit card to pay a delivery service, according to what some friendly law enforcement type had told the client. But since there had been no sign that he had returned to his Corpus Christi home as of yet, it made sense to start their search at the last place Castleman, now likely in the company of the same woman they'd spotted him leaving the hospital with last week, was known to have been.

"So you found the Jeep itself?" Armbruster said, running a comb through hair that was as thick as ever, though the once rich dark brown had given way to silver. Still, he kept it neatly trimmed, along with the neat chinstrap beard that gave his jaw definition. Combined with his slim-cut sports jackets and silk ties, it gave him a polished, respectable look that opened doors and put people at ease—even those who had every reason in the world to fear his presence.

Trigger chuckled. "Parts of it—after I leaned hard enough on this little tweaker who gave me a weird vibe when I started asking questions over at the junkyard."

"Junkyard?"

"Hell, why not? It's where I'd go if I was desperate to score a little cash or maybe transportation in a pinch, and this dude looked just sketchy enough to bend a few rules if there was something in it on his end."

"So what *was* in it for him, taking you to Mrs. Kingston's Jeep?"

"He got to keep on walkin' with a coupla unbroken kneecaps." Trigger laughed uproariously, his breath once more reeking of onion, until Armbruster felt obligated to at least smile back. Then, the thick-necked younger man waved off the moment of camaraderie and explained. "Not really, man. I slipped him a couple fifties and the dude was like my best friend. Tossed in a few more twenties and told him to score an extra hit on me, and he told me all about the car Castleman's drivin' now."

"Just Castleman?" asked Armbruster, who was beginning to understand that Trigger possessed more in the way of subtlety than his coarse appearance might suggest. "So the Fielding woman wasn't with him?"

"Not that the tweaker ever saw. Could be he's ditched her someplace."

Armbruster shrugged his shoulders. "If that turns out to be the case, that's just one less for us to kill."

During the darkest predawn hours of their third night at the guest cottage, Jude woke to an eerie and disorienting silence. But there had been something before, something that had woken him from a deep and dreamless sleep. Had it been the sound of the guest cottage's front door closing? Was that the smell of fresher, cooler air?

Then he heard a softer noise, the padding of a nearby footfall.

Fully awake now, he opened his eyes to see a head and shoulders looming just above him, silhouetted by a shaft of moonlight filtering through the window blinds. Adrenaline shot through with panic blazed white-hot in his veins.

When a hand reached toward his face, he yelped and grabbed the intruder by the arms, yanking him off balance—

The spell was broken by a shrill scream.

"Jude!" cried Callie as she fell hard onto the bed beside him.

"Callie! Did I—did I hurt you?" he asked, his heart flipping as regret flooded through him.

"I—I think I'm okay."

"You don't sound okay," he said, hearing her voice trembling. Pushing himself upright, he pulled her into his arms. "You're shaking like a leaf."

He drew her even closer, instinctively needing to make up for manhandling her the way that he had. "I'm so sorry. I hope you know I'd never intentionally hurt you, not for all the world."

"It's all right. I know. I'm fine. I was only startled. We're both all right." She stroked his arm, the contact igniting an awareness of the hour and their isolation.

"I heard—" He fought to focus on the situation, reminding himself he could have badly injured her in his confusion. "I was sure I'd heard the door close. I thought—I thought you were—someone out to kill us."

"I was missing my phone charger and remembered I'd left it out in the car earlier when I went out to get some food," she explained. "When I came in, I went to check on you again. I guess we scared each other."

"I'm still on edge," he admitted, chuckling in his relief. Or maybe it was his nervous awareness of the fact that he was still holding her in bed, just as he'd been dreaming off and on while his body had fought to overcome its illness.

Disentangling herself from his embrace, she reached up to feel his forehead. "You're so much cooler than you felt last night. Feels like your fever's finally broken."

Jude struggled to pull back from the adrenaline overload to assess how he was feeling, other than bereft, now that she had pulled away. "I guess your rousting me out of bed last night for soup and a shower and those fresh sheets you put on were a good idea after all," he said, even though every moment of it had felt like an ordeal. "I'm breathing a whole lot better, too."

"Watch your eyes," she cautioned before pulling away from him to switch on a bedside lamp.

He squinted at her, looking rumpled in her pajamas with her hair wildly tumbled. Maybe he had lost perspective, but she looked more beautiful than ever to him—perhaps because he was so touched to think of her watching over him so closely these past few days. He saw that once again, the rollaway bed's sheets remained smooth. Instead, she'd left a blanket tossed in the upholstered chair she'd pushed close to his bed.

"I told you I'd be fine. You should've slept in your own bed," he scolded. "You must be exhausted by now, not to mention stiff and sore."

She shrugged. "I've had too much on my mind to sleep much, anyway."

"Worrying about me." He was meant to be the caretaker, not somebody else's burden. It was a lesson his grandfather had drilled into him early and his ex-wife had only reinforced.

"About you, our situation, what we're going to do next," she admitted, "and then there's… It's a lot of things."

"Well, let's at least knock one off your list," he said, realizing that he no longer heard the wheezing that had plagued him. "I'm definitely much better, thanks to your excellent care." He only hoped she didn't resent him too much for it.

"If you want to give somebody credit, maybe you ought to say a prayer," she suggested, her lips curving in a small smile.

"I'll be sure to do that, but I'm thanking you right now. If it weren't for you forcing me to rest, I would've likely run myself into the ground before I'd slowed down." Noticing the smudges of exhaustion beneath her eyes, he ran his fingers over the top of her wrist to caress it. "I never meant to run *you* into the ground, though."

"I'm fine," she said, sounding as anxious as she did fatigued, "just a little… It's been a stressful few days, worrying over my mother, you and whether Kingston's people might manage to track us down somehow and kick the door in while you were sick and helpless."

Sitting up straighter, he raked a hand through his unruly hair, looking into the face he had come to care so much for. "That's why you've been afraid of sleeping, isn't it? Well, I'm damned well not any kind of helpless now, so trust me, Callie. Trust me to return the favor and keep us both safe from here on out."

Scooting over to make room, he patted the bed just beside him, his heartbeat picking up speed as he anticipated her sniff of outrage or the sharpness of her voice as she said, *Nice try, Rookie, but did you forget we had a deal about keeping things between us strictly business?*

But she didn't speak of that deal, perhaps because she understood, as he did, that something had shifted in the last few days between them. That their forced dependency, the confidences and the danger they had shared, had made far more of them than casual work acquaintances or even partners in a desperate scheme to exact revenge on Big Jake Kingston's heirs.

He held his breath as she lay down beside him, allowing him to drape an arm over her waist. His pulse drummed with awareness of her scent, her softness, and how long it had been since he had held a woman who meant so much to him. A woman who he sensed would either heal the broken places in him or crush his heart beyond repair.

Beside him, Callie tensed, a shiver rippling over her skin.

"I shouldn't," she said, sounding so nervous, he feared she might break the spell, bolting up from the bed and springing away from him.

Leaning close, he whispered into her ear, "Rest easy, Callie. Just rest." He gently kissed her temple, feeling her warmth against his lips and vowing that with him, she would be safe from any danger...

Including the urges he suspected would keep him awake throughout the remainder of the night.

Callie had almost forgotten what it felt like, letting her guard down and experiencing the warmth and comfort of a man lying by her side, his arm draped protectively around her. A man she realized she trusted with her life, if not all her secrets. A man who'd come to mean more to her in just a short time than she ever would have imagined possible.

It's only the fear talking, the fear and loneliness you've felt these past two nights.

Nights spent on edge, propped uncomfortably as she kept an ear cocked for the sound of a car door outside, or a cough or rattle from Jude that might indicate she'd made the wrong choice, trying to tend him here herself.

That was when she'd understood that as hard as she had fought against it, Jude's dreams had intertwined with hers. They mattered, just as he did. How could she have been so foolish as to let her emotions get entangled, when she'd told herself from the beginning she was only doing any of this for Marc?

But it isn't Marc that you're in bed with, is it? Nor was it her late husband she was thinking of as she felt warmth spread through her body—warmth and what she recognized as need, too, heaven forgive her, desire igniting in places that ached for another's touch.

Half hoping and half fearing that Jude would forget the promise he had made her, she lay there for a long time, waiting. Yearning. Feeling the promise of a balm that might finally ease the pain she'd carried for so very long inside her. Or at least help her find some way to live with it.

So it was that she shifted, nuzzling against the stubble beneath his firm jaw, where she pressed a kiss to his neck. Feeling his swiftly indrawn breath and the quickening of his pulse, she whispered, "I can't rest with you. Can't sleep."

Beneath her hand, she felt his heart bump harder beneath his T-shirt. Breathing in the scent of him, she found herself unable to resist the temptation to taste the salt on his skin, mouthing the hollow just above the neckline.

"Funny thing," he murmured. "I've been sleeping so much these past couple days, yet somehow I feel like I'm dreaming. Because I've been dreaming of this almost from the first time we spoke, dreaming I could taste you, too."

With that, he turned his face toward hers and claimed her mouth with a kiss so all-consuming, it left no doubt of the sort of dreams that he'd been having.

Afterward, there were no more words, no room for fear or doubt or worry, as sensation banished all else. Eagerly, Callie peeled off his T-shirt to explore the irresistibly sculpted contours of his broad chest, with its sparse coating of golden hair.

Soon, she was distracted, moaning appreciatively as he reached under her pajama top to cup the fullness of her breasts. Back arching, she wriggled free of the material, which got in the way of the hungry kisses trailing toward her aching nipples.

When his mouth found them, she nearly came apart

then, tears of pleasure leaking as her vision splintered into white dots. Instead, she focused her energy on the urgent need to kick off her bottoms—to remove every impediment between her and what she needed, and needed quickly, before she could overthink this and ruin everything.

Jude took her nakedness as an invitation to explore the source of her heat, dropping clever fingers to her center to stroke and thrust inside her. When his mouth joined in, she cried out, spasming around him until she was exhausted.

When her eyes would focus again, she slipped a hand inside his tented boxers. Stroking the rock-hard length of him, she heard his groan of pleasure as she looked up and smiled at him. "I think it's past time we did something about that. You have protection on you?"

Groaning with need, he leaned over to reach for his wallet and fished out a square packet. As he held it between his fingers, his gaze feasted on her, a slow and hungry smile spreading across his face. "I'm not *that* much of a rookie, Red."

"Then how about you prove it?" she challenged playfully.

To her great delight, he set about convincing her completely…and repeatedly.

She awakened the following morning, the scents of soap and aftershave hovering in the air. And, more faintly, sex. The kind of sex that left her no place to hide from all the feelings she'd been fighting for so long. Her senses spiraled with unfolding memories from the night before.

After vowing not to let her emotions get involved with him—with anyone—what was it she had done?

But when Jude stepped out of the bathroom, his smile handsome as sin, her stomach did another kind of cartwheel.

"Finally awake, sleepyhead?" he asked, now freshly shaven and dressed in a pair of jeans and a long-sleeved T-shirt from the laundry she'd done yesterday while he was out cold.

Awake and half wishing you'd come back to bed. But she clamped down ruthlessly on the invitation on her lips, telling herself there was still room for withdrawal from a late-night indiscretion. Room to get out of this with both their hearts intact.

Because the terror nibbling at her insisted that retreat was the right move. The only move if she were to preserve the buffer zone she needed to maintain the safe space around her heart.

"Guess I was really exhausted last night," she managed. "I definitely—definitely wasn't acting like myself."

She saw his smile falter, the hurt flickering through his eyes and making her want to take it back. To tell him that last night had been beyond amazing, the kind of night that reminded her how transporting sex could be with the right person.

Telling herself this would be kinder in the long run, she stretched and sat up instead. "You're certainly looking a lot better this morning. Healthier. How's the breathing?"

"The breathing's great, but—is this how it's going to be between us, Callie? Something that meant everything to me, you're just going to blow off as if it didn't matter? As if nothing's changed at all? Because I don't operate that way. I—"

"I told you from the start what I'm capable of…and what I'm not," she said, her heart racing. Because this was exactly what she hadn't wanted. The kind of entanglement she'd avoided for years, for good reason.

In the back of her mind, she heard the thumping rush of the helicopter's rotors, picked out her husband's last words from the other panicked cries. *"Brace for impa—!"*

How could she forget that pain—forget *Marc*—even for a moment?

"That's what you'd been trying to convince everyone, including yourself, for four years now," Jude said. "But I can tell you from last night—and from every minute I've spent getting to really know you—you're capable of a hell of a lot more than you give yourself credit for."

"Last night," she said, enunciating each word with utmost care, feeling herself balanced on a knife's edge, "I was tired, lonely. And I'd been scared that I'd guessed wrong about which way you were heading, health wise. But I can't do this again. Can't let someone else's life mean more to me than my own. So just back off now, please, will you?"

As she stared at him, his image trembled with the tears in her eyes. Still, she saw his disappointment as he nodded.

"If that's how you need things to be this morning, all right," he said gruffly. "But I won't pretend I'm happy about it. Or that I'm giving up."

"All right. I just don't want you…to be too disappointed," she said, "because you deserve—deserve a whole lot better, Jude. That's one thing I'm sure of."

He sighed before changing the subject, sounding

somewhat awkward. "I don't know about what I *deserve*, but right now, I'm absolutely starving. So what would you say if I walked over to that little Mexican café where we ate on our first night here and picked us up a couple of to-go breakfast orders?"

"I'm glad your appetite's better, but why don't you go over and have breakfast while I shower and wash my hair," she said, thinking it would be easier to swallow if she weren't sitting across from him, knowing how much this morning's about-face had hurt him. "If you'll just bring me back a pastry and maybe one of their hot chocolates when you're done, I'll start to get things organized around here, too."

"You're sure?" he asked.

After she nodded, he agreed, "You're probably right. I do want to be ready at a moment's notice, in case today's the day we hear about that DNA test."

She gave him an assessing look. "You getting nervous about those results?"

"Anxious is more like it," he said. "Eager to finally get the proof I need to convince some lawyer to take the case on contingency."

"So you won't have to pay up front?"

He nodded. "And even more importantly, so I don't end up dead while presenting my case to Beau Kingston."

Sometime later, Callie emerged from the bathroom feeling more human now that she'd cleaned up and changed into a soft pink sweater and a pair of yoga pants.

As she ate the pastry Jude had brought her, she noticed him staring out the window, in the direction of the parked car. The tension in his body sent a ripple of apprehension through her.

"Everything all right out there?" she asked him.

"Fine," he said, sounding anything but. "I was just remembering that phone call the afternoon before I got sick and realizing there was something—something important that I completely forgot to tell you."

"What is it?" Callie asked, slowly lowering the *pan dulce* she'd been about to finish.

Turning to face her, Jude shook his head. "I could kick myself now for not putting it together sooner, but there was a name the anonymous caller mentioned—a name and a possible connection that didn't click with me until later."

What was left of her appetite drained away. "What connection?"

"He claimed that a married man named Winthrop had given a deposition admitting he'd been involved with—with my mother."

"*Walter* Winthrop?" She shook her head, her heart thudding as the distant past collided with the more recent unraveling of her own life. "The same Dr. Walter Winthrop from the crash? Are you *serious*?"

"I'm not absolutely certain it's the same guy. Not yet," Jude said, his brow furrowing. "The caller didn't mention a first name, but he did say the guy had been my mother's physician. *If* the bastard wasn't lying about that, too."

"Too?" She raised her palms in a bid for elaboration.

He shrugged before reminding her, "It doesn't matter who Big Jake Kingston talked into coming forward so he could get rid of his wife without losing custody of his heir. I told you before, my mother was never having an affair."

"Of course it matters—when that man ends up shot

in the face by Big Jake Kingston decades later. And for your mother's *physician* to have come forward…" Indignant at the thought, she scowled. "That's a huge ethical violation. If there's any justice, he would've lost his medical license for getting involved with a patient."

"And you said this Walter Winthrop who died in the crash was reported to have *been* a friend of Big Jake Kingston's, right?"

When she confirmed it, Jude said, "Seems like an awfully strange way to characterize the man who broke up your first marriage, doesn't it? If this Winthrop is really the same person—"

"We need to get over to the public library right away." Callie wiped the stickiness from her hands on a napkin. "We can use the computers there to start digging up as much info as we can find. You can search for old news reports, anything to do with both the helicopter crash four years back and any other items related to Walter Winthrop, maybe see if we've got the same person, at least."

"What about you?" Jude asked.

"I'll start out focusing on Texas Medical Board records, which should have information on licensure and records of any disciplinary actions."

"That's available to the public?"

She nodded. "Absolutely, to allow patients to check out providers to make sure they're legit, although I'm not sure how far back their records go. The librarian may have some ideas to help send us in the right direction."

"You sure you can trust some stranger?" he asked.

"A librarian?" As a memory cut through her anxiety, a smile pulled at the corners of her mouth. "My mom was always parking me in public libraries in all the towns we lived in when I was a kid when she went off to rehearsals and interviews, and I'm telling you, the people working there will almost always bend over backward to help you find out anything you need. They don't give you the third degree about why you want to know whatever you need to know. They're just there to help you find it, and best of all, there's never a bill."

"Sounds right in my price range, too," he said. "But are you sure you don't want any more to eat?"

"I'm fine," she said.

"I'm glad *one* of us is."

"What is it?" she asked.

He shook his head. "It kills me, thinking about the lies this jackass was talked into telling to destroy my mother."

Lowering her voice, Callie dared to ask the question that had been weighing on her. "What makes you so sure…now, after all these years? I mean, isn't it possible, if the marriage was in difficulty, and this doctor offered sympathy— Taking advantage of a professional relationship, that's not a matter of immorality on her part. It's ethical and criminal abuse, plain and simple, but unfortunately, there have been cases—"

"I get what you're saying," Jude said, shaking his head, "but you're wrong about my mother. After she— she died, you see, I found this—this note she'd left inside the pocket of her bathrobe. It was— She'd addressed it to my grandfather."

He paced the room, old grief lining his handsome face. She sipped from her tea, waiting for him to get past the moment.

Once he had, he told her, "I still remember every word of it. She'd written, 'I know no one believes me, least of all you, but it was all a lie, a lie meant to make me disappear. And now he's got his wish. You both have.'"

"I'm so sorry, Jude."

"At the time, I didn't understand what it was about. I couldn't."

"Were you ever able to ask your grandfather about it?" she asked.

He shook his head. "I never even showed it to him. I knew he'd take it away from me forever, the last thing that she'd ever written. And there was no way he was going to accept any sort of blame or offer any real explanation for what my mother did. Not when it was so much easier to go on blaming me."

Her eyes burned as she imagined what the shattered young boy he must have been had suffered. "Afterward, living in that house with that man…"

Jude stopped his pacing to look at her. "It might've been hell, but there was one thing he couldn't ever take from me. I knew that my mother and I, we'd loved each other. She loved me with everything she had. Maybe it wasn't enough to save her, but it's saved me every day since."

She squeezed his arm, heart overflowing at the strength of a bond that had outlasted even death. "When we look for the evidence, any court records or anything linking this man to your mother, why don't you let me be the one to read it? That way—"

"I appreciate the offer," Jude said. "But if I'm going to finally put these lies to death, I have to be strong enough to face them."

If he could manage that, she swore to herself, then she could somehow find the courage to read whatever back articles they might find related to the helicopter crash in an effort to find any additional information she might have previously missed on the late Dr. Walter Winthrop.

"You okay?" Jude glanced over at Callie as they walked out of the public library after three that afternoon, once they had finally exhausted all avenues of research. In the brilliant winter sunlight, her light freckling stood out more than usual, since her face had gone dead pale.

"I'll be fine," she said, her voice as washed out as her color.

He wondered, though, if she was still back at the LifeWings helicopter crash site in her mind, transported by the articles she had insisted upon reading. Articles about an event that they both now knew for certain had ties to the relationship between the man he believed to be his father and his mother's family doctor.

An archived online death notice had turned out to be a valuable source of information regarding the late Walter Winthrop, who was described as a "beloved physician who practiced for many years in Kingston County and in Fort Worth, prior to his retirement."

"'Retirement' might be how his family put it in his obituary," Callie had whispered as she'd made use of a second computer beside the one that Jude had claimed in the uncrowded library. "But according to this other article, it looks like Walter Winthrop did indeed have his license suspended following allegations of improprieties with patients in Fort Worth about a dozen years ago. Groping during exams, according to the complaints."

"Wait a minute. He was assaulting *patients*?" Jude had emphasized the plural, loudly enough to draw annoyed looks from other library patrons before he once more dropped his voice. "You mean there were others besides my mother?"

Nodding grimly, she added, "It looks as if there were a series of similar reports, over a span of years, before anybody really listened to these women."

"Makes me wonder who a woman would most likely tell first, if her doctor pulled something like this. Not an affair at all, but—" Jude had mused, trying to imagine how deeply upset a modest, deeply private and religiously oriented woman like his mother in particular would have been by such behavior. "What if my mother actually went to her husband, looking for support, a champion after she was…touched, but instead of doing what any decent husband would have, Big Jake Kingston saw the whole thing as some kind of sick, pathetic *opportunity*?"

Callie made a sound of pure disgust. "So you're thinking he *betrayed* her, making some sleazy back-door deal with her attacker?"

"It's almost inhuman to imagine, but that's exactly what I'm thinking."

"I can definitely see this creep of a doctor going along with whatever Big Jake wanted," Callie said. "He'd probably do anything for a chance at a fresh start in a new town, with his medical license still in hand—at least until he started up again with his habit of preying on his female patients."

"Leopards and human predators never change their spots," Jude said darkly, wishing like hell that both Winthrop and Kingston were alive to answer for what they'd done. "But the real question is, what changed that made Winthrop head back to Kingston County for a visit?"

"I'm betting the doc ran out of money. After all, he'd

lost his license years before by that point. So what if he came back with the idea of shaking down his 'old friend' under the threat of confessing that he'd lied about your mother in that deposition?"

Callie nodded. "Blackmail does sound like a recipe for ending up shot in the face. Then Kingston must've panicked and used his influence to force LifeWings to sending out my crew in bad weather."

Seeing her eyes haze with painful memories, Jude quickly changed the subject. "So let's talk about our next move. Maybe over lunch?"

She frowned. "I don't think I could, Jude. The thought of eating right now, after reading all that, turns my stomach."

He shook his head. "You barely had anything this morning, and it's already long past lunchtime. And I'm betting you weren't taking great care of yourself while I was sick, either."

"I'll be fine."

"That's what I said, too, if you'll remember, before I came down sick for days."

"Fine," she said, in a tone that said she would rather give in than listen to his nagging. "I'll try a fast food sandwich, as long as the place has some kind of veggie option."

"Sounds like a plan," he said with forced cheer. "Then maybe we can drive over to that little park we spotted on the way to the library and eat there."

"A little fresh air sounds good to me," she agreed. "After being cooped up in the guest cottage for days, I'm in no hurry to head back there."

After picking up their late lunch, he pulled out of the

drive-through lane and then immediately tensed after glancing in the rearview mirror.

Callie straightened in her seat. "What's wrong?"

"Don't stare," he said as they continued through an area dominated by fast food restaurants, gas stations and convenience stores, "but there's a silver Cadillac, older model, three cars back with a couple of guys in it. I noticed them before, the driver with the wraparound sunglasses, as we were leaving the library."

She shifted the bag with their lunches to the floor of the rear seat, sneaking a peek over her shoulder. "You're sure it's the same pair?"

"I couldn't swear to it, but let's find out." Without using his turn indicator, he hit the brakes and made an abrupt right—causing the driver behind them to loudly blare his horn—and then sped along as fast as traffic would allow.

"I don't see him following," said Callie a couple of minutes later, as Jude was beginning to breathe a little easier. "Maybe recent events have made us both a little paranoid."

"And here he comes." Jude's pulse raced as he spotted the same sedan waiting at a stop sign just as they drove past it. Speaking to the driver, he said, "Thought you were being sneaky, didn't you?"

"Apparently, he's done with stealth mode," Callie reported as the car pulled out just behind them, wheels squealing.

"Wait a minute," Jude said, his gut tightening as his mind flashed to that day along Oso Bay. He fought to calm himself, reasoning that their pursuers wouldn't dare to make their move amid the bustle of midday Brownsville traffic.

Then he noticed something that threw his adrenaline into overdrive. "Where's the other guy?" he asked. "The one who was in the passenger seat before?"

"Are you sure there were two?" Callie said. "Because I didn't see—"

"There were *definitely* two," he said. Had the passenger moved to the rear seat, where he was even now readying a sniper's long gun to fire on them? Or had he transferred to another vehicle that would cut them off at any moment?

Traffic thinned as they left the commercial area and entered an older residential neighborhood. "We've got to get off this street, find our way back to more traffic," he muttered. "Or better yet, a police station."

Even as he spoke, Callie warned, "Watch out, ahead," staring at a tiny, silver-haired man who was obliviously backing his ancient station wagon out of his driveway— and right into their path.

Too afraid to stop, Jude hit his horn to warn the driver, which apparently startled the elderly man into stomping the accelerator rather than the brakes. As Callie screamed in alarm, the wagon sailed across the street, its rear end jumping up the curb and crunching as it toppled a neighbor's brick mailbox.

"Oh no!" cried Callie. Jude swerved around the car's front end and raced off—more afraid the poor man might be hurt in a potential shootout than he was about the possibility that he'd been seriously shaken up by the minor fender bender.

"That's it. I'm calling 9-1-1," Callie said, sounding breathless as she fumbled with her phone.

Jude didn't respond. He couldn't, not with the Cadillac picking up speed, looming in his mirror. He gave the

Ford more gas, but it wasn't enough to avoid a pair of light taps at their rear bumper, the second making them swerve slightly.

"What's he's *doing*?" Callie burst out.

"Trying to cause a wreck so they can take us out," Jude said as their pace surged toward highway speeds. Seeing a stop sign dead ahead, he hit three long blasts on the horn to warn any oncoming drivers, because his instincts assured him that slowing down now was sure to prove a fatal error.

As the Taurus entered the intersection, the Cadillac moved up as if to pass, and sure enough, the rear passenger window came down, a jutting barrel giving him an instant's warning.

"Get down! Gun!" Jude bellowed, before he jerked the wheel aggressively into the Caddy's direction of travel.

Almost instantly, a huge jolt shuddered through the vehicle. Metal screeched as fender panels tangled. An earsplitting cacophony of pops and groans and Callie's shrill cry rose, overlaid with the splintering of window glass behind him.

He wrenched the wheel again, and with another shriek of metal, the two cars separated, sending the Cadillac bouncing up a curb into a front lawn before the driver managed to get it back on course.

"You all right?" he yelled to Callie, who still had her head down and seemed to be fumbling around for something.

"I dropped the phone! It slid somewhere—I can't find it to call for help!"

Hearing a thump and clatter outside the car, Jude glanced at the rearview and saw that the Taurus's rear bumper had just fallen off in the street. Too close to avoid it, the driver of the Cadillac ran over it before instantly losing control, his car careening to slam into the rear end of a delivery van parked along the shoulder with its lights flashing.

"They've crashed!" Jude hit the brakes, looking to see the van's driver, who'd been halfway down the sidewalk, gaping in shock but unharmed, and the wrecked Cadillac emitting a thin plume of dark smoke from its badly crumpled hood.

Callie, who had popped up from her crouch to look, said, "They're not going anywhere in that thing, so hurry! Let's get out of here, in case one of them is in good enough shape to bail out and start shooting at us!"

Though Jude would've given a lot to get some answers from the killers, he knew good sense when he heard it. Driving away, he took a deep breath and forced himself to moderate his speed to avoid drawing further notice, especially since the police would soon be racing in this direction in response to reports of the wreck.

"Are you—are you all right?" Callie asked, about a block away. "I don't mind telling you, I thought we were both history."

"I know." His gut twisting with the thought of how close they had come, he smiled wryly. "Guess this means my grand plan for a picnic in the park is off, then."

"You think?" Her laughter sounded shaky, her voice strained and high. "And finally, *there's* my stupid phone—" Plucking it out from beneath the seat, she held it up for him to see.

"Better keep it close by, just in case," he advised. "Since we invaded Kingston home turf, there's a chance he might've sent more than these two hunting for us."

"Please, don't tell me things like that right now. I'm not sure my heart can take it."

"I'm sorry, but we can't afford to make any more mistakes—like sitting around in one place waiting to be tracked down."

"We had no other choice before, not as sick as you were."

"Maybe," he admitted. "But we can't risk going back to the guest cottage now, not even to pick up our things before we head out."

"So we'll just leave, then, with nothing but the clothes on our backs?"

"I'm sorry, but I don't see a better option," he said.

"What about a destination then?" she asked. "Because if Beau Kingston is this serious about trying to have us both killed, is there anywhere on earth we can be safe?"

Chapter 13

As they rolled up to a red light, Jude looked at her and flinched, a look of pure horror on his face as he answered, "There's absolutely nowhere you'll ever be safe as long as you're with me. That's why I'm taking you back so I can finish this alone."

"Wait. Back *home*, you mean?" She shook her head in disbelief. "When we both know those people have my address?"

"I'll drive you to your aunt's, then. You'll be safe there with your mother."

"You totally misunderstand me if you think I'm only looking for a better spot to hide out," she argued. "I'm not going anywhere until we can *both* head home and back to our real jobs."

"You're going," he insisted, his voice gruff, "if I have to drag you there myself."

"I don't know what's gotten into you," she fired back. "But don't you dare drop into Neanderthal mode with me, Jude Castleman."

A car behind them honked, alerting them that the signal had changed already. As they proceeded, he moved into the right lane before pulling into the lot of an office supply store and shifting into Park.

"I'm sorry if I raised my voice, but, Callie, *look*— look, right above you, at the car's headliner." Ducking his head, he cursed, venting his frustration. "Don't you understand how close we—how close *you* just came to dying?"

Scooping shallow breaths, she looked up…and took in the roughly round hole just above her head. A bullet hole, she realized, though she hadn't even heard the gunfire over the noise of the collision.

"It p-punched all the way through the roof," she stammered, "and look at this. Here's another in the door post by my elbow."

Turning to peer behind Jude, she gaped at what must be the entry holes in the passenger window about a foot behind where he was sitting. She hugged herself to keep her body from shaking to pieces.

"Now do you get it?" he asked, sounding equally rattled. "Why I have to take you back?"

She laid a trembling hand across his forearm, where she found his muscles taut as steel cables. "You're shaken up. We both are, but you need to remember, I came into this of my own free will, knowing there would be risks."

"Not anymore, not for you. I'm sorry, but I can't let you—"

She glowered at him. "Is this what you're like when you're with a woman?"

"When I *care* about someone and don't want to see her *murdered* before my eyes? *Yes*," he said. "I'll damned well own that."

"Then I guess it's a good thing that we're not really together, because I make my own decisions, Jude."

He opened his mouth as if to argue, but she didn't give him a chance to escalate an argument that was doing neither of them any good.

"Listen to yourself—to both of us. To what we're doing. We're *reacting* instead of *acting*, when we both know how that usually ends up working out in an emergency setting."

By choosing those particular terms, she hoped to snap his mind back to their training and the years of experience that each of them had dealing with patients who were often experiencing the most traumatic moments of their lives. She'd dealt with Jude during enough emergency calls to know he absolutely had it in him to handle this—if only he could set aside his protective instincts long enough to use that sharp, efficient first responder's mind of his.

"Just imagine we're on the LifeWings helicopter again," she added, "en route to some accident or even a mass casualty scene. What are our goals, our priorities? And how do we address the most critical needs without causing further harm?"

Nodding, he blew out a deep breath. "As much as it pains me to admit it, you're right. Now that we've collected the DNA sample, we have to come up with a new plan, one that's better and more focused than hiding out and running from our pursuers until they catch up to us."

She nodded her approval. "That sounds a whole lot better."

"Let's check the damage to the car first. Wherever we end up going, we don't want to end up breaking down—or getting stopped because we're missing something critical."

After several attempts and a hard shove failed to open the driver's side door, Callie said, "Why don't you let me check so you won't have to climb over the shifter twice?"

Exiting the vehicle, she walked around it before returning with a report. "Between the mashed-up driver's side and the bullet holes in the window there behind you, we look kind of like the loser in a demolition derby."

"What about the rear end?"

"Considering that the back bumper's missing, I was pleasantly surprised to find the rear license plate's still hanging in there."

"That's something," he said. "Taillights?"

"Left side ones are definitely smashed. You want me to step back out to see if the brake lights or the right-side turn indicator work?"

He shook his head. "There's really no point, since we're not in a position to repair or replace right now. We'll just stick to the back roads and try to reach our destination before dark."

"What destination did you have in mind?"

A wicked smile spread across his face, one that had her body tingling with a red-hot memory of last night's encounter. Distracting herself from temptation by pinching the tender flesh inside her forearm, she forced herself to focus on what he was saying.

"The one place they won't ever imagine that we're running—back to Kingston County to beard the lion in his den."

* * *

With his emotions now locked behind that same fire-wall he'd used in so many previous emergency situations, Jude felt an eerie calm take over, giving him the clarity he needed to finally see the issue he'd been missing all along, along with a tantalizingly simple solution to the problem—if they could pull it off.

As they wended their way toward a less-traveled road that would keep them off the main highway, he explained, "When I first reached out to Beau Kingston with my letter, it was a huge mistake. I should have gone to him in person instead of giving him time to decide I was a threat, no matter what I claimed, and figure out that having me eliminated was more expedient than an expensive, drawn-out legal battle."

She shook her head. "But he could've buried you in attorneys' costs, eventually forcing you to give up any claim on the estate you might have, and it would've been completely on the up and up. Instead, he risks everything to try to have you outright killed. *Why?*"

"Because, for some reason, my existence is a bigger threat to him than I imagine. And he's not going to believe I don't want money—"

"The only language any of the Kingstons apparently understand."

"Right," he said. "He won't buy my claims unless I present a binding deal to him in writing."

She made a skeptical face. "Hmm. So you're planning to use a *contract* to try to stop a bullet?"

"I know it sounds crazy, but hear me out. We'll need to come up with a list of concrete demands to offer in exchange to give the whole deal credence."

"So what *do* you want, exactly?" she asked. "I know

you came looking to clear your mother's good name, but what would that look like to you, exactly? And how could Beau Kingston help to make it happen—you know, if he decided to quit trying to have us murdered long enough to cooperate instead?"

As they passed through scrub-dotted fields of golden grasses, Jude turned the question over in his mind, trying to imagine what would bring his mother's spirit the peace that had eluded her in life. What would restore the pride she must have once felt in being the wife of a successful rancher and mother to a young son, before a physician's unwanted touch and a husband's ultimate betrayal had shattered her faith in herself?

"I'll want him to use whatever influence he has to make certain you stay on the job at LifeWings."

"Forget that trivial complaint for the moment," she insisted. "Just tell me what you're after."

"A story on the front page of the local paper," he said, "an admission of what his father did, right there for everyone she ever knew to see, so they'll understand that she was set up, that she didn't abandon her child willingly."

"So you're asking now for Beau to confess to his *father's* sins?" she asked gently. "Sins he couldn't have had knowledge of, since he wasn't even born at the time?"

"But people need to know."

"*What* people?"

"Her—her old friends, her neighbors, the people who knew her back at the time."

"You mean the community who believed the worst of her then and, I don't know for certain, but I'm guessing turned their backs on her? *Those* are the people whose good opinion of your mother matters to you now?"

"I—I never stopped to think of it like that," he said, his dreams of redemption for his mother falling to pieces like wet newspaper in his hands. They'd been no more than a child's fantasies, he realized, based on an orphan's pain, for his mother was at rest now, far beyond the reach of shame or heartache. Perhaps in death, she'd somehow been reunited with her lost son, the brother he had never had the chance to meet.

Beneath the lengthening shadow of an oversize live oak tree, a pair of grazing deer raised their heads to observe their vehicle's passage. Somehow the peaceful sight felt like a benediction, easing a little of the tension he'd been carrying between his shoulders for as long as he could remember.

"You're absolutely right," he said. "Beau can't testify to something he had no knowledge of, and even if he could, my mother's beyond their judgment now with the child she lost. What *does* matter is that back at the time, even though she had money, status and a husband, she found herself completely alone and powerless when it came to dealing with abuse."

"A lot of women are," Callie said, "or at least they feel that way, for so many different, complicated reasons. When I think of how hard it's been with my mother, getting her to see herself as someone whose rights and dignity are worth standing up for—and she has plenty of support."

"It was probably even harder back at the time."

"In a rural community like Kingston County, I doubt that even now there's much in the way of resources women can turn to. It's a huge problem in smaller towns."

"That's it," Jude said as inspiration struck him.

"*That's* what I can ask Beau Kingston for in exchange for my giving up, in writing, any future claim on the estate."

"What do you have in mind?" she asked him.

As the miles rolled past, he outlined the rough idea, as well as his reasoning for his request. "What do you think?" he asked her once he'd finished.

"I think it's a wonderful thought, Jude—it's concrete, achievable and utterly unselfish. There's only one small problem I can see with your plan."

"What's that?" he asked her.

"How are we going to force a man who lives on a security-patrolled compound, a man who's shown absolutely no inclination to *listen* to a thing you have to say to him, to pay any attention to our terms?"

"As soon as I have those DNA results, I'll have all the leverage I need to call for a meeting…if we can only stay alive until then."

"Then we'll just have to pray his hired goons don't catch up with us until you have the proof."

Once the two of them checked into a small motel in the same neighboring town where they'd stayed when they'd first come to the area, Callie took one look at the room's two queen-size beds and covered her mouth when a reflexive yawn slipped out.

"I know," Jude said with a look of sympathy. "It's been one heck of a long day already."

"You're the one who should be wiped out," she countered. "I wasn't even driving."

He shook his head. "I'm too keyed up to wind down yet, and there's too much to be done before it gets too late. Why don't you hang out here awhile? You can put your feet up, maybe check in with your mom while I head back to that discount store we passed to pick up enough supplies to hold us for a couple of days?"

"That'd be great. I'll definitely want a toothbrush and a few things."

"I'll see if I can find some heavy-duty plastic, too," he added, "to tape over the car window to make the bullet holes less obvious and keep out any weather."

"Sounds like a plan," she said. "While you're gone, I'll try to contact Dr. Norris, too, to see if he has any results for us on the testing."

"Great idea. Thanks." But his expression had clouded at the mention of the confirmation on which he had staked so much. The proof that he was descended from a man the world may have respected but Callie understood that he felt nothing but contempt for.

"Sure you're okay on your own?" she asked.

"Probably better off that way," he said, "in case Kingston has people watching for the two of us. I will need a list, though, of what you'll need and your sizes, you know, in socks and shirts and underthings."

"My *sizes*?" she asked, abruptly self-conscious.

"Are you actually *blushing*, Red?" He chuckled. "It's not as if we haven't—"

"I know it's ridiculous, especially considering how we nearly *died* together today, too." She turned up her palms, a sheepish smile pulling at one corner of her mouth. "But we're talking my *panties*, Rookie. This is uncharted territory."

He laughed but stopped abruptly, the pain of longing in his eyes. Longing for a connection she had been a fool to risk. A connection that had her suddenly aching to reach for him.

"Let me get you that list," she said instead, turning

away before her body gave in to an impulse her heart was not prepared to back up. "And how about in a couple of hours, I call out and order pizza for us?"

"That sounds like the best idea I've heard all day." After being chased and shot at, neither of them had had an appetite for the sandwiches they'd picked up at the drive-through window and later tossed, cold and untouched, into the trash at a roadside rest stop.

Once he'd left, Callie kicked off her shoes and propped up pillows against one of the bed's headboards, making herself comfortable before calling Dr. Norris. Though she fully expected to end up leaving a voice mail, she was surprised when he personally picked up on the second ring.

"I was wondering how long it was going to take before you called to start riding me the way you always did the hospital lab for your patients' test results," he said.

"Don't tell me after all these years, my nagging's the one thing you still remember about me?"

When the doctor chuckled, she could almost see his overly bleached teeth flashing against his deeply tanned skin, which had an almost leathery look from all the years he'd spent indulging in a serious sport-fishing hobby. "I didn't say it was a *bad thing*, or the only thing that I remembered. I distinctly recall you marrying that flyboy before you even gave me a fair chance to show you that I can be dazzling, too, when I really put my mind to it."

"I believe you were busy dazzling the third Mrs. Norris at the time," she said mildly, since for all his vanity and flirting, Graham Norris was nearly thirty years her senior.

"Well, I'm afraid she saw the error of her ways soon

after, but you, my dear—I understand you're currently sing—"

"Only calling to pester you about those DNA results," she interrupted, deciding to cut short his fun before he could embarrass himself any further.

"Yes, of course," he told her, clearing his throat before pulling on his professional demeanor like a lab coat.

"You did promise you would expedite it."

"I moved it to the head of the line, but the extraction process itself, I'm afraid, cannot be rushed."

"But you're still staying on this personally? Monitoring the progress and will let us know the minute you've completed the comparison?"

"*If* there's enough genetic material," he told her. "I'm afraid I won't be able to say for certain until we're finished. If there were any way of collecting an additional sample—"

"There's definitely not," she was quick to say.

"Understood." He didn't question it, no doubt used to dealing with clients in a variety of personally sensitive situations. "I promise you, I'll do everything I can."

"You have to," she said. "These results are absolutely crucial, a matter of life and—"

"If you're hoping for expert testimony, don't say another word about it," he warned.

"I'm sorry," she said. "Of course. Jude only wants the truth, that's all."

"And that's exactly what I'll give him, the moment I have results that I can back up. Until then, I have his contact information on the paperwork he sent us."

His phrasing served as a reminder that, though her personal connection with one of the lab's directors had allowed him to get the process expedited, Jude was the actual client of record. As such, he was the only person to whom Graham would deliver the results.

Once she'd thanked him and completed the call, she phoned her mother, who didn't answer until the fourth ring.

"Did I catch you at a bad time?" Callie asked her.

"To be honest," her mother said tartly, "I was trying to decide whether I had anything to say to you, since you've abandoned me in my hour of need while you're off on your little *sexcapade* with that hunky paramedic."

"Wait a minute," Callie said, resisting the urge to argue her mother's embarrassingly unsubtle way of summing up a far more complicated—and dangerous—situation. "I thought *you* were the one who's been hounding me for years to get out there."

"That was before I realized you meant to stick me here with Jane and all her Mrs. McJudgy looks over the rims of those English-teacher glasses of hers whenever I mention how much I miss Lonnie."

"Miss him?" Callie asked, struggling to keep herself from shrieking, *After everything he's put you through?*

"Not the browbeating or the demands, of course," her mom admitted, "but the sweet little surprises he brings me, the fun we still have when he's in a good mood."

"Mom, the man refuses to give you access to your own bank accounts." Callie kept her words cool and controlled, the way she always had felt forced to, since childhood, to compensate for all her mother's drama.

"He was raised differently, and he gives me an allowance. It's to help us both stick to our budget."

Callie let that slide, though the defense made her blood boil. "What about locking you out of the house because he was mad you'd gone to happy hour with the other ladies from your office after work?"

"Everything's so cut-and-dried with you," her mother accused. "You don't have the fire in your veins like we do. I yell and break things, too, sometimes, so who's to say what's normal and what's passion?"

Callie resisted the urge to gag at her mother's choice of words. "*Passion* should never involve the sort of screaming that has the neighbors calling the police, and it should *never, ever* leave the kind of bruising I saw on your neck."

"The shouting was a onetime thing, I told you."

"The police came at least two times, that I know of—"

"And you were wrong about that bruising. I've told you and I've told you, he would never touch me that way."

"Mom…" she pleaded, her vision hazed with tears of frustration.

"You don't understand. Lonnie would be lost without me. He's told me I'm the only reason he has for getting up each morning. If I don't come back, he might—I can't bear thinking of it."

Callie curled her hand until her nails bit into her palm. "We've talked before about emotional blackmail."

"Isn't that what you're doing to me now? Withholding your approval unless I live the way you think is right?"

"It's not about what Aunt Jane or I approve of. It's—how do *you* want to live, Mom?"

There was a long pause before her mother whispered, "Not alone…because you need to understand that I can't do that, baby. I'm not built the same way you and my sister are."

"After the crash, I didn't think that I could do it, either," Callie said, her mind returning to the pain and darkness. "Don't you remember? I wanted to be gone, too, my ashes spread with Marc's? But it was *your* hand, holding on to mine, *your* presence at my bedside."

"I wouldn't let you go... I couldn't," her mother whispered, "my poor, broken baby."

A single tear broke free, streaming down to Callie's jaw as she recalled the words her mother had said to her then. Loving words she'd clung to when there had seemed no other reason to keep breathing. "I'm not broken any longer," she swore, willing it, for both her mother's sake and her own, to be true, "and I swear to you that no matter what else is going on in my life, I won't let go of your hand—or your heart. I'll hold on to you forever if I have to."

When Jude finally returned to their room several hours later, carrying a number of shopping bags, he found Callie sitting cross-legged on the sofa, chewing on a slice of pizza.

Looking up sheepishly, she said, "Sorry I didn't wait, but I couldn't hold out any longer. It smelled like heaven, and my stomach was singing the song of its people."

Dropping the packages onto the foot of the unrumpled bed, he laughed and sniffed appreciatively at the warm, cheesy aroma. "I can't say as I blame you. I didn't mean to be so long, but I decided to make an extra stop."

"Well, grab a slice while it's still hot," she invited. "I had them make half of it with sausage and pepperoni."

"If you really don't want me falling in love with you, that was the wrong thing to say."

Blushing at his words, she said, "But the deal is, you

can't make fun of the pineapple and green peppers on my side."

"Fruit on pizza is barbaric." He flashed a teasing smile. "But I'll accept your terms."

As they ate, she said, "It's getting dark. I was starting to get worried."

"You didn't get my text saying I was stopping by the pawnshop?"

"I guess I must've missed it," she said. "My mom kept me on the phone for quite a while."

"Everything all right with her?"

Callie took a swig from her water bottle before shaking her head. "I'm afraid she's weakening about leaving Lonnie. Or just plain scared to be alone."

"Do you think she'll stick out the separation?"

"I wish I could say for certain. It breaks my heart, watching her go through this, knowing she's the only one who can say when she's had enough."

"If I were you, I'd probably be in jail by now for kicking Lonnie's tail into the next county."

"Trust me, it's crossed my mind, but she'd only feel so sorry for him that she'd end running back to tend to the big jerk's wounds out of pity." She sighed, putting down a half-eaten crust. "I tell myself she just needs time now, and maybe a little space to help her put things in perspective, but I'm terrified she'll make a choice that eventually gets her really hurt—or worse."

Seeing the anguish in her eyes, he said, "It sounds like you're doing everything you can. I'm just sorry you're having to deal with this, especially while you have to stay away from home."

"Believe me," she said bitterly, "there's never a good

time for any of this, but thanks for understanding. It means a lot to talk to someone who really gets it."

"Maybe you should try it more often, then," he suggested gently, "opening up instead of walling yourself off to the friends who care about you. You have them, you know, myself included."

She dropped her gaze. "I'm not all that great of a friend, Rookie. You could seriously do better."

"You're full of more than pizza and pineapple, you stubborn woman." Putting down his slice, he wiped his hand and laid it overtop hers.

When she stiffened, he realized that he had pushed too hard, so he withdrew before offering the mercy of a change of subject. "Did you happen to reach Dr. Norris about the DNA testing?"

"No news yet," she replied, visibly relaxing with the reprieve, "but he promised he would call you the moment he knows anything."

"I only hope it's before those goons Kingston has hunting us don't find us again first. Every time I think about what happened this afternoon, how close the bullets came to hitting you…"

"To hitting both of us," she said.

"It's why I made that second stop today, because I wanted some way, just in case I needed to protect you."

She shook her head. "What do you mean?"

He went to the bed, where he'd set down the plastic bags, and pulled out a zippered case.

"Is that a—?"

"A pistol, yes." He showed her. "A nine-millimeter Glock—"

"And you just—you just waltzed into the pawnshop and bought it, just like that?"

He shrugged. "I had to fill out the instant background check paperwork and give the guy my ID."

Her stomach flipped. "So there's a paper trail."

"It was unavoidable."

"Along with another credit card purchase that might potentially be traced?"

"That, too," he admitted. "But with both of us out of cash, it's either that or ATM withdrawals. We just have to hope they aren't tracking our movements that way."

"It's not just a hope," she said, a sudden edge to her voice. "It's gambling, Jude. Gambling with our lives for some macho mirage of safety."

As the evening wore on, Jude tried to convince himself that he'd been right to buy the pistol, that he should have taken their safety into his hands before they'd ever left for Kingston County. Instead, he'd relied on Callie's plan, along with what he'd naively thought of as their moral high ground, to keep both of them alive.

But as she disappeared into the bathroom, taking what seemed like an eternity in the shower, he began to wonder if her sudden chill was more that the strain over their situation or her apparent disapproval of his purchase. He sensed a struggle inside her, a war she was fighting to distance herself from him, to give her heart the space she'd need to finally walk away from him forever.

"It's damned well not as if she hasn't warned you she means to kick you to the curb," he muttered to himself as he stared at the bathroom door, listening with longing to the hum of the hair dryer just behind it.

He raised his fist to knock, thinking it might help if he apologized for not discussing the purchase with her and getting her take on its risks before his cell phone rang.

Since he'd given virtually no one the new number, his first instinct was to ignore the call until he remembered about his DNA test. Sure enough, the screen showed the name of the private testing lab.

A jolt of pure electricity surging through him, Jude felt his knees loosen. This was it, what he'd been waiting for, the confirmation that would give lie to his grandfather's cruel words throughout his childhood, words he'd carried all these years. *Worthless bastard.*

"This is Jude Castleman," he answered, his mouth as dry as ancient bones as he dropped down to perch on the bed's edge.

"This is Dr. Graham Norris calling from Surety Cybergenics," came a measured, male voice, speaking in the reassuring tone of someone who routinely delivered life-altering news to nervous clients.

To confirm Jude's identity, the caller asked him for his birth date and a four-digit security code that had previously been selected. With his palms sweating and gut churning, Jude stammered the first and drew a complete blank on the second until the numbers came out in a garbled rush.

"What was that again?" Norris asked.

Screwing shut his eyes, Jude forced himself to carefully repeat the digits.

"Very good," Dr. Norris said. "I'm pleased to inform you that both sample items you provided, the comb and the bandanna, yielded sufficient DNA for comparison to the swab taken from your own cheek."

Jude found himself sighing, relieved beyond measure that the risk he and Callie had taken hadn't proven pointless. "Go on," he urged.

"Because we were trying to determine the relationship between two males suspected to have been fathered by the same individual," Norris went on, "we did a very specific type of testing focused on the Y chromosome of each."

"The one passed down through the male line," Jude said, confirming he still remembered the basics from high school biology.

"Exactly," the doctor went on, "which is why I can say with one hundred percent confidence that the probability that you and the tested individual share a common male parent is zero."

"Zero?" Jude said, rocketing to his feet. "What're you saying? That we aren't—"

"Half brothers," Norris continued. "In fact, the two of you share no DNA segments that would indicate that you're related in the slightest, not even going generations back."

"Not related? But that can't— That's impossible!" Jude countered, everything he'd been so certain of, as well as all the plans he'd made, the risks he'd taken with his and Callie's life both, crashing down around him.

"I assure you, the results on the samples provided are accurate. If you'd prefer to try again, however, perhaps using a voluntarily submitted sample from the other party..."

The remainder of the doctor's words were lost to the booming of his pounding heart. Somehow, he managed to thank the man before cutting short the conversation.

As soon as he had disconnected, he turned to see Callie standing near the bathroom doorway in her bare feet and the oversize sleep tee he had bought her and staring at him with a stricken look that told him she had caught the gist of the conversation. "Oh, Jude," she said.

Slipping past her, he shut the door behind him and proceeded to bring up everything he had just eaten. It was some time before he stumbled out, empty and exhausted, shaking his head when he saw Callie rising from the sofa to stare at him.

"I'm so sorry," she said, her arms crossed over her own stomach, as if in sympathy. "I can't imagine what a shock it must've been to find out that—"

"This could be a mistake, right? Isn't it possible that the samples I collected might've come from someone else? One of Beau's boys, maybe?"

"But if that were true, wouldn't those boys be your nephews?" she asked, moving close. "If so, then Dr. Norris should've detected some degree of relationship."

"What about his wife's, then? Or maybe some household employee's?" Sure, it seemed unlikely that this mystery person would have both dropped a man's comb beneath Beau's desk and left the blood-spotted bandanna, but that didn't make it *impossible*.

Callie's gaze captured his, and she reached out to lightly touch his forearm. "I hate to poke holes in your theory, Jude, I really do, but Beau Kingston—he looks nothing like you. The two of you are *not* half brothers, which means…"

"Which means that my father is most likely—" He thought back to the anonymous phone call. "—my mother's doctor, Walter Winthrop. And that it's altogether possible that I could be the product of her rape."

Her eyes gleamed as she covered her mouth. "Surely, you don't think…"

But he wasn't listening any longer. Couldn't hear a word over the roaring in his ears as it came to him that the photographs that had run with the articles on Winthrop's death, and one earlier report related to the sexual misconduct allegations, had shown a man with light-colored eyes and silver-streaked hair that looked to have once been some shade of blond.

Not unlike his own, he thought ruefully, though his mother's coloring had been even fairer.

And the accusations that had cost Winthrop his license—inappropriately touching women in his care—was it really such a leap to think that he'd gone even farther? Given her own father's harshly judgmental brand of faith, particularly when it came to women, whom he'd so frequently referred to as "fleshpots," "temptresses" and worse, his mother's silence made sense. It crushed Jude, imagining she had blamed herself and that she'd had no one she could trust to turn to.

"Jude, please talk to me," Callie said. "Tell me what you're thinking."

"I'm thinking my grandfather had it right about me. I really am a bastard—"

"I hate that word," she told him. "You know, my parents weren't legally married to each other, either, but it never had a thing to do with any choices I made. Or any child ever born."

"I didn't mean it that way," he said, raking his fingers through his thick hair. "I meant for putting you at risk for nothing."

"Don't ever say it was for nothing," she said, attempting to pull him to her and then giving him a pleading look when he remained rigid and unyielding. "If we've accomplished nothing else but to make a Kingston lose sleep at night, to realize that people like us can and do sometimes push back and push hard when they're walked on, that alone was worth the effort."

"But what've we really accomplished?"

"You've clearly scared him to death, firing that shot across his bow with your initial letter. And after we conned our way inside his house, I wouldn't be at all surprised if he figured out what it was you'd taken, and that's what's scared him enough to double down on his efforts to have us killed."

"But it was all for nothing. He has nothing to fear from me."

"He *never* has, though, has he?" she asked. "The reality has never mattered. It's all in his perception."

Jude frowned, thinking it through…and realizing she was right. And that tomorrow, Friday morning, might be his one and only shot at using that fact to his advantage…

Because he knew exactly where the *best of men and the most generous* was going to pick up his employees' breakfast.

Chapter 14

Though Jude appeared to have physically recovered from his shock, Callie could see he hadn't yet begun to process what he'd learned, let alone decided what to do about it. When she tried talking about it further, he abruptly told her that it was getting late and he needed to get cleaned up for the night. After hitting the shower, he immediately headed for the second bed, turning his back to her as he pulled up the blankets.

"Jude?" she called quietly, sitting up in her own bed, where she'd been texting with her aunt over the situation with her mother. "If you need to talk some more, I'm here…"

"I'm good, thanks," he mumbled, turning to glance at her with his tousled hair flopping down onto his forehead. Raking it back with a hand, he added, "Just wiped out, what with everything. Mind if I switch off this light?"

"Sure, go ahead," she said, but after he did, his back still to her, she continued sitting there, imagining she could feel the misery radiating from him, the confusion over who he really was, as the potential son of a man who'd forced his attention on his female patients.

She felt, too, Jude's searing shame over what he clearly considered his own flawed judgment. The injustice of it had her rising, her feet carrying her seemingly of their own volition to his bedside, where she stood, poised to tell him that she couldn't care less how tired he was. He could darned well lie there and *listen* to her explain in no uncertain terms how his willingness to champion the mother he had lost in such a tragic manner, his insistence on fighting to restore her dignity and honor, was one of the things that she loved best about him.

Loved best...

The truth of it unfurled inside her...the undeniable realization that all this time, while she'd been fighting, she'd been falling somehow, too. Slowly yielding to another attachment that could crush her, when she'd sworn that she would never risk putting herself through that kind of loss again.

Then quiet your breathing, so he won't hear you standing so close. Back off and creep back to your bed now instead of peeling off your nightshirt and sliding, naked and willing, into his.

Coward that she was, she slunk away, her eyes burning and her ears ringing with the distant thrumming of helicopter blades and the screams that would never fade from her mind. As she lay in bed, she rubbed incessantly at her wrist, not caring that the tattooed flesh would be raw and red by morning.

She felt as if she'd barely slept when she awakened sometime later to what sounded like the patter of soft rain on the roof and window of their room, which was located off the upper-level balcony of an older two-story motel. The slight squeak of a door hinge had her cracking her eyes open and noticing that Jude had turned on the bathroom light. Hearing him moving around in the room, she checked the time and saw it wasn't quite 4:30 a.m.

"You're not feeling any more nausea, are you?" she asked, her voice still thick with sleep.

Standing beside the bathroom door, Jude turned, his elbow bumping it open wider. In the expanding beam of light, she saw that he was fully dressed in his jeans with a fresh T-shirt and his jacket. But what sucked the breath from her lungs was the sight of the pistol in his hand and the grim set of his jaw.

"What are you *doing*?" she cried, a surge of pure adrenaline shooting her upright in an instant.

He shook his head and tucked the gun out of sight into what she thought might be some sort of waistband holster. "I'm getting ready, that's all. Getting ready to make this right."

"With a *gun*? At this hour?" she demanded, her pulse racing. "What are you talking about?" She spotted the car keys on his nightstand next to the gooseneck lamp. "And were you about to go somewhere, without a word to me?"

"No, of course I would've told you before I left."

"Left for where?"

"You remember," he said, "that little taco stand, the

one where Beau Kingston's biggest fan works? Flavio's, I think it was called."

"What are you talking about?" she started before her sleep-starved brain filled in the blanks. "Wait a minute. I remember the place. You—you're planning to *ambush* Beau Kingston when he goes to pick up his employees' breakfasts?"

"I'm planning to go talk to him," Jude told her, "preferably without getting myself killed during the conversation—because you cannot tell me that the owner of one of the largest ranches in the state, the man who hires gunmen to knock off anyone he considers a threat, is running around without some kind of sidearm on him. Or for all I know, a damned bodyguard at his side."

She shook her head. "This is crazy. You pull a gun on that man, you're going to get yourself killed. Or end up killing someone, no two ways about it."

"I didn't say I necessarily planned to pull a gun on anybody, but I did tell you I meant to beard the lion in his den, didn't I?"

Rising from her bed, she stalked toward him. "I thought you meant through an attorney, once you had those test results."

Jude laughed bitterly. "Yeah, well, that possibility's flown straight out the window, hasn't it?"

"What if we found someone—or wait a minute— maybe I could *pose* as your attorney, make the call pretending like you *were* his half bro—"

Shaking his head, Jude interrupted. "I need to make it crystal clear to him, face-to-face, why it's time to let this go."

"So he's just supposed to, what? Forget the fact that

we scared his wife—a new mom—half to death, stole her Jeep and made off with a sample of his DNA?"

"Considering the fact that his men nearly killed both of us, destroyed both our vehicles and trashed my apartment, I'd say that the almighty Kingstons are getting off damned lucky—and if he doesn't want everything we've learned leaked to the press immediately, he needs to call his dogs off now."

"I still don't like it," she said, "but I'm coming with you. Someone needs to watch your back."

He shook his head. "That's not happening. You're staying."

"But we're partners in all this," she argued, closing in to grasp his bicep, "*partners*, start to finish."

Pulling away from her, he crossed the room to grab the car keys. "Then let me make it easy for you, Callie. As of this very moment, our partnership is over."

Though Jude knew it was the right move, it was all that he could do not to take Callie into his arms and beg forgiveness when he saw her face crumple. But as painful as it was to hurt her like this, the memory of the bullet holes near her head gave him the strength to stand firm in his rejection.

As the rain outside intensified, he turned away from her, unable to look into her eyes as he said, "I'll call you once it's over. Then I'll drive you back to your aunt's so you can be with your mom and PB."

"Damn it, Jude, don't you dare walk out of this room," she said.

"If anything happens—if you don't hear from me within a few hours—there's a car rental office I looked up in town, over by the discount center—"

"I know you're trying to keep me safe. I get that. But after everything we've been through, you can't just—"

"It'll be all right. I swear it," he said.

"Don't give me that garbage. Because if you walk out on me, Jude Castleman, you're as good as dead to me right now."

He swallowed hard and strode out, feeling something curl and wither in him, some threadbare hope he hadn't even known had taken root inside him. Hope, that maybe after this was over, there might be some way forward. That he might have earned enough trust to eventually convince her to let him into her life and perhaps, eventually, her heart.

The rain was coming down now, both colder and harder than he had expected as distant lightning flickered. Yet he was too miserable to care much as it sluiced down through his hair and over his face.

Standing in the parking lot, he heard her call his name. At the balcony's edge, she stood shivering hard in her wet nightshirt, her eyes, her face, every aspect of her body language pleading for him to come back.

He looked up at her, his mouth full of the taste of ashes, knowing that if he succumbed, he would never again find the strength to leave her. And knowing that if he didn't take this chance now, he would have missed his very best shot at keeping both of them alive.

Giving her one last, regretful look, he mouthed the words *I'm sorry.* Then he turned and trudged into the chill darkness, his gut telling him he'd just killed something precious beyond measure.

How very interesting, Armbruster thought, as he watched from the parking lot. The young woman at the railing had wiped at her eyes before turning and running back inside.

Though he'd hoped to have the opportunity to eliminate the pair together, this evidently traumatic separation left him with some interesting decisions.

If he'd still had his partner with him, the choice would be quite simple. Leave Trigger behind to force in her room's door and throttle her before she knew what hit her. This would free Armbruster himself to trail the primary target from a safe distance, waiting for an opportunity to gun him down the moment he arrived at his destination and left his vehicle.

But thanks to the yesterday's accident in Brownsville, Armbruster's partner was no longer part of the equation. Though the injuries he'd sustained when the Cadillac slammed into the delivery van hadn't been life threatening, Trigger had been left bellowing in agony, his right ankle and arm both bloody and contorted.

One look had told Armbruster the oversize enforcer wasn't going anywhere, except to the hospital, where the police would undoubtedly show up with their questions. So without a moment's hesitation, Armbruster had pulled out his gun and silenced his young partner's cries with two quick bullets to the temple.

Afterward, he'd leaped from the car, taking a wild shot at the startled van driver, who'd bolted for cover while Armbruster himself had raced in the opposite direction. In under twenty minutes, he managed to find and steal an older model Honda. It had taken him considerably longer—and a significant cryptocurrency transfer to the hacker he had hired—to monitor both targets' use of credit cards. But the outlay, though significant, would be well worth it, he decided.

He was more than ready to be finished with this cursed job, and then to embark on what he vowed was going to be a permanent retirement in his tropical paradise. As he watched Castleman run through the rain to climb into the Taurus—which he entered from the undamaged passenger's side—Armbruster marveled at the thought that after thirty years of killing, his ticket to nirvana was only two stopped hearts away.

The only question left to answer was, which one of the squabbling lovebirds did he kill first?

In spite of the cold rain, and the fact that she was standing half-naked in her nightshirt at the railing, Callie turned back for a moment, unable to keep herself from watching Jude drive away. Unable to suppress the fear—which felt more like a bone-deep premonition—that she would never again see him. At least not alive.

When she spotted the silver car gliding out of the lot after him, she tried to tell herself that the icy core of terror low in her gut was nothing, that the vehicle's sudden appearance was coincidental. But the fact that the headlights were turned off in these conditions suggested otherwise, and when the male driver passed the motel's security light, for a single moment, she glimpsed a face that had her body erupting instantly in gooseflesh.

She recognized that thin beard, the neatly trimmed gray hair and narrow face. It was the murderous driver of the crashed Cadillac from Brownsville! Before she could do so much as scream, the silver car was gone.

Racing back inside the room, she grabbed her cell and called Jude's number, desperate to warn him that he was being followed. But try as she might, she couldn't make her phone connect. Seeing she had a full charge, she checked the cellular signal and saw no bars—perhaps the bad weather had caused some sort of area outage.

In a last-ditch effort, she picked up the motel's landline and was relieved to find it working. After getting an outside line, she tried Jude's cell, in case only her mobile was affected, but groaned in frustration when his phone didn't ring.

"No, no, *no!*" she cried, rushing to pull on her jeans and a long-sleeved charcoal-gray top with her jacket before whipping back her hair into a messy tail. Her panic escalated when she sat down to jam her feet in socks and could only find a single shoe. After forcing herself to take a few deep breaths, however, she managed to clear her head enough to locate it tangled in the edge of her bedding.

Now fully dressed, she forced herself to take a moment. *Stop. Think. Come up with a plan of action, or you'll have to live with the memory of shouting at Jude, you're as good as dead to me!*

First, she tried Jude's number again, but the phone still wouldn't connect.

Digging in the nightstand drawer, she pulled out a small directory, marveling for a moment at the fact that such things still existed, and looked up the number of the car rental company location Jude had mentioned and prayed that she could get them to deliver a vehicle to her.

To her immense relief, her call to the number went through, but instead of connecting with a live human being, she reached an answering machine, where a cheerful recorded voice informed her that representatives would be available to assist beginning at 8:00 a.m.

But if her instincts were on target, in three hours, Jude could be dead already. She had to find some way to get a warning to him—or get to him herself—before then. But how? How could she hope to do it, with no vehicle at her disposal, nor any hope of convincing the authorities, should she try calling them, that she was not some raving lunatic?

After pulling on her jacket, she grabbed her purse, deciding on the spot to run down to the lobby and try to beg or bribe—despite her lack of cash—someone to help her, or to call the police to plead her case. Heading out, she started down the metal staircase. But in her hurry, she slipped on one of the wet steps, falling onto her rear end, then tumbling to the bottom, where she landed in a tangled heap.

To her surprise, a dark-colored Lexus passing by in the lot stopped short, and a petite, dark-skinned woman wearing a rain jacket flung open her door and ran over to the bottom of the stairwell, where Callie sat trying to gather her wits and rubbing a bruised elbow.

"My goodness, that was a nasty fall! Did you break anything, do you think? I was just heading in to check out, but I'll have them call an ambulance if you—"

As a flash of inspiration struck her, Callie cradled her head with her hand and moaned before slumping to one side and doing her best imitation of a seizure.

"You poor thing!" cried the woman. "Don't try to move! I'm heading in to get help, and then I'll be right back!"

In her hurry, the Good Samaritan rushed toward the nearby door of the motel office, leaving her car running and the door open.

The instant she disappeared, Callie rolled to her feet and jumped into the sedan. Praying for forgiveness for an act of desperation she'd never imagined she'd resort to, she put the car in gear and roared off into the darkness, trailing guilt—and the first glimmers of hope she might save Jude—in her wake.

Chapter 15

As Jude cruised a lonely, two-lane road, he kept his speed down in deference to the increasing rain and the clouds that hugged the ground so thickly it was impossible to make out any of the numerous wind turbines he knew dotted these grassy plains. Still, he sensed the presence of the hulking structures, along with the vast herds of grazing cattle, all on land controlled by the powerful ranching heir he had come to finally face.

Though he knew the coming meeting should fill him with anxiety, the need to focus on the road—where thick mud had washed over one low spot—kept a lid on his emotions. Or maybe it no longer mattered to him how this morning turned out, since he understood he had already destroyed whatever slim chance he might have had with Callie.

Still, he was grateful when he finally pulled to the

roadside about thirty yards short of the still-dark wooden taco stand and spotted a pair of headlights approaching from the opposite direction.

When the aging SUV slowed, he smiled, pleased to recognize it as the same vehicle parked outside the building when he and Callie had visited before. Sure enough, the same dark-haired young owner who'd professed such a debt to Beau Kingston emerged and started toward the stand's brightly painted door.

Driving up, Jude climbed awkwardly from the Taurus's passenger side and skirted the edge of a large mud hole.

"Glad to see you back," the owner said, a grin splitting his round face. "Come inside, out of this weather."

Hurrying to unlock, he ushered Jude in ahead of him and flipped on the light.

As he pulled off his rain-beaded jacket and traded it for a white apron hanging near the door, Flavio said, "And here I thought you and your *esposa* were only passing through the area."

Jude winced inwardly to hear Callie, who had been feigning pregnancy at the time they'd come here, referred to as his wife, a mistake that had him recalling the joy he'd once felt, all too briefly, in looking forward to being a father. And the happiness he'd known, until this morning, over being so close to Callie.

"It was your egg-and-*barbacoa* that reeled me back in," Jude said, forcing himself to go through the motions. "You'll have to tell your friend Señor Kingston that I commend his good taste—and your cooking."

"Stick around long enough to have a taco and some café out of the rain, and you can tell him yourself. Jefe should be by to pick up his standing order for the Kingston office staff soon, maybe twenty, thirty minutes."

"I'm sure a busy, important man like him won't want to be bothered with such a simple conversation," Jude said.

The owner chuckled and nodded, a look of fierce pride warming his dark gaze, "Señor Kingston is a man of many responsibilities, but you will see he is a man to meet the eye and shake the hand when it is offered, a man whose word is worth far more than the cow manure on his boots."

"So…he's not the old man, then. That's what you're saying?" Jude asked, recalling the cook's prior speed in coming to the defense of *this* Kingston.

Posture stiffening, the younger man studied him with a look somewhere between curiosity and suspicion before murmuring, "Not his *father*. No, he is not," putting an odd emphasis on the relationship.

"Then how about that taco, then, with a large coffee?" Jude asked, though he was so nervous he wasn't even certain he could choke down so much as a bite.

Turning away, Flavio plugged in the drip coffee maker, which immediately began brewing, and nodded toward a small collection of mismatched mugs hanging on hooks along the wall. "Please make yourself at home while the grill heats," he said, turning to head behind the counter.

His progress was interrupted, however, as he stopped to answer a ringing phone, mounted on the wall. After a brief conversation, spoken mostly in rapid-fire Spanish, he jotted down the details of what Jude took to be a takeout order before ending the call and bustling away.

As Jude waited at one of the three stools near the

counter, he pulled his cell phone from his jacket, where he tapped out a quick text, thinking that as upset as Callie had been with him, she'd probably appreciate the update that he'd made it here and Beau should be arriving shortly.

Jude hit Send, only to see an icon appear letting him know the message couldn't be delivered. Seeing that his cell had no signal, he grimaced and pushed himself to his feet, thinking he might get enough reception outdoors, where the rain seemed to be petering out, to help to case her worry.

As he stepped outside, a dark blue pickup pulled in beside the owner's, the high-end model with its chrome trim causing Jude to shove his phone back inside his jacket, his heart beating double-time when he spotted the rear license plate, which read KINGSTN.

The man who emerged easily matched Jude's own height—and was possibly even a little broader through the shoulders. But with his dark eyes, coal-black hair, straight nose and chiseled jaw, the rancher's face bore witness to both Callie's assessment and the results of the DNA test. There was no way, Jude's gut told him, that this man was a close relation.

Even so, Jude found himself stepping forward and calling out, "Beau Kingston? I need to have a word."

Dragging a broad-brimmed Stetson hat from his truck, Beau pushed it down on his head and turned to face Jude, curiosity rather than hostility in his expression.

Eyes flaring at what he saw, Kingston abruptly stiffened, his curious gaze morphing into a fierce scowl. *"You."* His fists curled, his voice edged with a growl.

"I damned well recognize you from the security cameras in my *own* house!"

Leaving the truck door open, he advanced on Jude, waves of raw fury rolling off him.

"If you'll just give me a minute, I can explain that," Jude told him, some instinct—or perhaps it was Callie's warning that if he pulled the gun, someone would end up shot—prompting him to raise his palms instead.

But Beau Kingston just bore down like a freight train, his fist rising—and then rocketing toward Jude's chin—so quickly there was no time to get another word out.

As a fighter, Jude was strong and nimble, with a talent for sidestepping haymakers and using his opponent's momentum against them. But Beau Kingston's strike was so swift and true that Jude's head snapped back and he found himself splashing down onto his back into a puddle in an instant.

"Considerin' the stunt you used your pregnant lady friend to pull on my wife, I oughta stomp you flat into that mud hole, you damned car thief," Kingston sneered at him. "But you can count yourself lucky I'm only gonna call the law."

Seeing and hearing such contempt—the same contempt his mother had faced from Beau Kingston's father—had Jude thrusting forward from his knees, tackling the rancher's legs with a shout of pure rage. As the rancher tumbled down next to him, Jude hammered blows, shouting, "You started this whole thing, you greedy, arrogant jackass, sending your paid thugs to kill me!"

"K-kill you?" Beau panted, rolling him over and landing another punch to his shoulder before aiming for his face.

Jude narrowly avoided his fist, one of his own knees crushing the rancher's fallen hat into the mud.

"What the hell're you talking about?" Beau asked.

Too busy grappling to respond to his ridiculous denial, Jude heard a splash at his side. Before he could process the sound, Beau was twisting to reach past him, to snatch the dripping gun—which Jude realized, in a panicked rush, that he must have dropped.

Adrenaline spiking, he lunged for the weapon, but Beau clambered back and rose, taking aim at Jude's mud-soaked chest. Though the muzzle appeared clogged with thick muck, he didn't dare to gamble that the weapon wouldn't fire.

"Hands up, you son of a bitch," Beau demanded, "and if you're betting on my good nature to keep me from blowing a hole clean through you, you should've taken your chance before I ended up coated head to toe in mud."

A little blood, too, Jude noted as he rose to comply, absurdly pleased to see the redness dripping from the rancher's nose in spite of his own far more serious situation. *At least I managed to drag him down into the mud, too, where the Kingstons rightly belong.*

"Now tell me," Beau ordered, the sky still slowly dripping on his bare head, "what did you mean before, about me trying to kill you?"

"Don't pretend you don't know that after I mailed you that letter, you sent your men to Corpus Christi, where they pointed a gun out the car window and forced me off the road, damn near killing me."

"I don't even know who the hell you *are*," Beau protested, "much less have the first idea about some traffic issue you had hours away from here."

"It's not a simple traffic issue when you send thugs to trash my place while I'm in the hospital. What'd you send them after? The originals? Because no way I'm dumb enough to leave those documents lying around my apartment."

"I have no idea what you're talking about. *None*," Beau insisted, "And as far as some letter—the ranch gets hundreds of pieces of correspondence a week. You can't possibly imagine I handle it myself."

"I sent it to you, not the ranch, and marked the envelope *Personal and Confidential*."

"Which means it would've been routed through my attorney, Ed Franklin."

"Inside a large envelope with copies of documents," Jude continued, though in the back of his mind, the name of the longtime Kingston lawyer registered, "including the certificate from our father's marriage to my mother."

Kingston flinched at that, his gun hand wavering, but only for a fraction of a second. "What the— What's your name anyway? And I don't mean the fake one you gave my wife, either."

As the rain petered out, Jude hesitated a few moments before he decided he had little left to lose at this point. "Jude Castleman. My mother was Millie Castleman Kingston. I only learned quite recently that she'd had another son, Jake Jr."

"So you're saying JJ was your *brother*?" Kingston snorted, giving him a look that dripped with skepticism. "Ed's been warning me since I inherited that guys like you would come crawling out of the woodwork."

"Guys like me?" Jude echoed, a dangerous edge to his voice, despite the weapon pointed at him.

"Scheming opportunists, yeah." Beau sighed and

shook his head, a look of disgust coming over him. "Always looking for a handout. You can't imagine you're the first who's shown up with some kind of tall tale."

"Except I *told* you straight out in the letter, I didn't want your money. Still don't. And I offered proof of who I am, my birth certificate with my mother's name, for one thing, and I said I'd take any DNA test you want, if that's what it takes to establish that I'm exactly who I say I am."

"DNA," Beau said. "That's it. *That's* what you were after when you wormed your way into my house. To prove that *you're* the Kingston, so you could try to push me out."

"Push *you* out?" Jude scoffed. "Why would I—*how*? I'll sign whatever papers you want to prove it, Kingston. I'm *not* here for your land and cattle, and the very last thing on this earth I'd ever want is your old man's name."

Beau narrowed his eyes, peering into his face with a renewed intensity. "*My* old man's…?"

"*Jefe!* Señor Kingston, you need help?" shouted the cook, still in his apron as he came running outside, a baseball bat in hand. The withering look he sent Jude promised that his status had shifted from welcome guest to mortal enemy for daring to lay a finger on the young man's benefactor. An enemy he would happily flatten with that wooden bat should Beau simply nod in his direction.

"I've got this under control, Flavio," Beau assured him, "but if you wouldn't mind lending me that apron, I'd appreciate it."

The cook untied and stripped off the white cotton then extended it toward Beau.

Instead of accepting it, Beau ordered Jude, "*You* take it."

"What?" Jude asked, forcing a chuckle. "If you're going to put me to work cooking now, you'll need to know I'm nowhere near the wizard with the breakfast tacos that your friend is."

"Take it," Beau repeated, gesturing with the gun until Jude complied. "Now wipe that mud off your face."

"What do you—"

"Just do it," Beau ordered, his jaw clenched and his dark eyes blazing.

As Armbruster struggled to push the Honda out of the slippery mud hole it had slid into as he'd driven across a low spot, he cursed this wretched job once more—and himself for shooting the muscular partner whose strength could have easily freed them from this situation.

But what had happened to Trigger had been as unavoidable as the rain that had caused his stolen ride to hydroplane and slide off the road in the first place. And his efforts to move the car had so far gotten him nothing except angry, wet and tired...

And as relieved as he could be when he spotted the approaching older pickup, which slowed—as rural residents tended to do when they spotted a fellow driver alone and stranded. The gap-toothed cowboy behind the wheel—or at least the facial hair and hat looked cowboy to Armbruster—cranked down his window and offered, "Looks like you're good and stuck there. You need a lift somewhere, mister?"

"I've got a rope in my trunk. You help pull me out of this," Armbruster told him, gesturing vaguely toward the car, "and there's a hundred-dollar bill in my pocket with your name on it."

The cowboy frowned, seeming to consider. For a moment, Armbruster thought he might have to kill the rube inside the pickup, leaving himself a bloody mess to sit in, but the younger man flashed a grin and opened up the truck door, saying, "I reckon I've got time to help you, but it wouldn't be very charitable of me to accept your money for doin' somethin' that any decent person ought to."

The moment that he turned and started toward the Honda's trunk, the benevolent cowboy ended up taking two quick bullets to the back of his skull instead.

As Callie raced toward Pinto Creek, she hunched over the wheel of the stolen Lexus with her jaw clenched and her grip tight on the wheel. With the windshield wipers beating out a breakneck rhythm, she alternately peered at the road ahead and glanced at the rearview mirror. So far, she'd spotted no sign of the silver Honda ahead, nor any police pursuit behind her, but she was nearly sick with fear at the thought of having to deal with either situation.

When the phone beside her rang, it startled her so badly that she swerved slightly on the rain-slick road. Heart leaping like a jackrabbit, she fumbled to answer, grateful beyond measure that the cell service had been restored.

"Jude," she warned, her mind making the desperate leap that he was calling, "that man from Brownsville— he's on your—"

"Callie, this is Aunt Jane. I'm sorry to disturb you so early, but I'm —I'm afraid we have something of a situation here."

Callie's pulse surged even faster, prompted by the

quaver in her normally calm and controlled aunt's voice. "What sort of situation?"

"This morning, when I got up early to put on the coffee, I thought I'd let out PB so he wouldn't disturb your mother and—"

"Yes?"

"They weren't in the guest room, either of them. PB's leash was gone, and—"

In this weather? As Callie peered into the rainy darkness, she allowed that it might be clearer and brighter hours north of here. "What about Mom's car?"

"It's still here, and her purse, too. But that's not the—"

"Maybe she couldn't sleep and took Baby for an early walk," Callie suggested, her stomach twisting itself into a tight knot. "I know it's strange for her, but she was really wound up yesterday when I spoke with her. I'm sure she'll be—"

"Callie, I heard noises out front. It was PB, scratching and whining at the front door," her aunt said. "He was frantic, smudged with mud from last night's storm, and trailing his leash."

"What?" Callie's heart fell. "You mean *alone*?"

"I do, and he's acting…you know I'm not much of a dog person, but he has his head down, his tail between his legs, and he's been whining and hiding behind the furniture ever since I let him inside. I can't even make him come out."

Her stomach tightening, Callie was certain her aunt was reading PB's behavior right. "I can't imagine Mom purposely turning him loose somewhere where he might get lost or hurt. Do you think she might've twisted an ankle—or I don't know—had some sort of medical emergency?"

As terrifying as she found the idea of her mother falling on a dark trail, Callie couldn't picture the always protective PB leaving her. He'd stand guard if she knew him—unless her mother had been pulled inside a vehicle and taken away.

"I drove around the block, where she normally walks," Aunt Jane said, "but I didn't see her anywhere. And I can't imagine her straying farther. She'd certainly stick close to the streetlights."

"What about her phone? Does she have it on her?"

"I didn't see it on the charger, but when I tried to call her, it went straight to voice mail. I need you, Callie." The older woman's voice was shaking. "I need you to get back here and bring my sister home right now."

Choking back tears, Callie promised she would be home the first moment possible. "But in the meantime, call the police. And tell them to look for Lonnie—they need to find out where he is right now."

But as she ended the call, an even deeper fear rose up to chill her to the marrow. What if her mother's disappearance had nothing to do with Lonnie but was somehow related to the hired killers that had been chasing her and Jude instead?

Was it possible somehow, the men who'd chased them from the Kingstons', the same men who'd trashed Marc's car, had been given Callie's name and address? Could they have somehow tracked down and snatched her mother, thinking that her disappearance would be the swiftest, surest way to lure Callie and Jude back?

But even if it were true, if Callie knew beyond the slightest doubt that she'd be walking into some sort of setup, she would have no choice except to return. First, though, she'd have to warn Jude about the danger heading his way.

Praying it hadn't caught up to him already, she forced herself to pull to the side of the road to try his number and nearly cheered when, this time, the call started ringing. "Answer, please, please answer," she whispered, a lump thickening her throat when she reached a generic recorded message.

Disconnecting, she hit the gas again, fresh panic rising hot as bile. *He can't answer because he's fighting for his life—or maybe dead already.*

She realized she wasn't far now, maybe less than five minutes from the little taco stand where they'd once eaten. She knew, too, that if she pushed on, she could end up coming up on a situation that might not only break her heart, but cost her her life.

For a chance of saving Jude, of making right in some small way her ugly words when they had parted, Callie would willingly add that risk to the others she had taken...

But did she have the right, in taking that chance, to risk her mother's life, as well?

As Jude stood holding the apron in his hand, Beau glanced at Flavio. "Now that the rain's quit, you think you could maybe bring out a towel or two?"

The young man nodded. "Towels, yes, and fresh water to wash off with—or you can come inside to clean up. Don't worry over the mud."

"Just the towels for right now. Thanks," Beau said before returning his expectant look to Jude. "Go on. Wipe that muck off."

More mystified than ever, Jude used the white cotton to wipe the mud off his forehead, cheeks and mouth as the cook trotted away. "There," he said, lowering the apron to stare back defiantly at Kingston. "You satisfied now?"

As Beau studied him, his expression wavered, the look of hostile skepticism giving way to something that resembled sadness. As the gun's muzzle slowly lowered, he swore softly, his voice nearly breaking as he said, "You—you look so much like him."

"What? Like who?" Jude asked, shaking his head in confusion.

"You—you're damned near the-—the spitting image of my brother." Beau looked as rattled as Jude felt by the declaration. "Right down to those cheekbones and that little dent you've got in your chin."

"Jake Jr., you mean?" Of course, Jude realized, Beau would have grown up with him. Would have known the older JJ, as he'd called him, as his own half brother.

"He had the look of the old man, too, the blue eyes, the light hair and definitely that same chin. But he never had his nature, thank God. No, JJ was as kind and gentle as our father was a tyrant. He was a damned good brother to me, at least as long as he could stick it out here, with the old man riding him like he did."

From the haunted look on Beau's face, Jude could see there must be some painful story behind their separation. But it didn't change the fact the he had some basic facts wrong.

Facts that Jude now felt honor-bound to lay out on the table. Because his gut was telling him two things: that Beau hadn't lied when he'd claimed that he had never seen the letter and that Jude himself had only one chance at getting this right—and that chance lay in the truth.

"You and I—I had the DNA done, and it tells me we're not brothers," he admitted. "So it must be true, what my grandfather always told me. That I'm my mother's bastard."

To his astonishment, Beau blew out a breath and shook his head. "Not a chance—and it'd be as plain as day to anyone around here who really knew my family." Heaving a sigh, he shrugged, and, to Jude's relief and astonishment, slowly lowered the pistol in his hand. "Nope, more than likely, it's those rumors finally comin' home to roost."

"What rumors are those?"

"The rumors that *my* mother, Big Jake's second wife, had a lover among the hands. Heaven knows the old man more than half believed it, the way he treated me all my life."

"I—I'm sorry," Jude said, knowing how it felt to feel unwanted.

Beau shrugged. "It was never easy, but eventually, we worked out a sort of truce. I figure the old man didn't have much choice after JJ ran off and got himself killed in that wreck. Since Big Jake never would admit he'd raised a bastard, I was and always will be his legal heir, so Dad talked me into coming back."

"Sounds like he ran off a lot of people—and what he did to my poor mother…" Jude said. "The man absolutely broke her. Set her up to look like an adulteress—with the same doctor who abused her, of all people—so he could get sole custody of her child and drive her out of town."

Beau stared at him. "You—you're sure of this?"

Flavio returned before he could answer, offering Beau a pair of plain, white kitchen towels and asking, "Should I call the sheriff to come lock him up?"

"Thanks again, but I'll handle this," Beau said, "in private."

"You need anything at all, I will be inside."

As they watched his receding figure, Jude continued, "I'm as sure as any man can be about—about what happened with my mother."

Haltingly at first, and then with increasing confidence as it became apparent that Beau was neither going to shut him down nor shoot him, he told him about the note he'd found after his mother's suicide—and what he and Callie had later learned of Walter Winthrop, the physician who had confessed to the so-called affair.

"Wait a minute," Beau said. "I know that name. Surely you aren't telling me this is the same Dr. Winthrop killed in that chopper crash a few years back."

"*After* he just happened to end up shot in the face in the middle of the stormiest winter night in—"

Intense as their conversation was, the sound of an approaching engine—no, *engines*—disrupted Jude's concentration. Looking up, he saw a pair of vehicles: the older-model pickup roaring toward them and the big sedan swinging out as it came up from behind—

"We'd better move, fast!" Beau said, racing for the cover of his own truck.

Less certain of which direction the swerving vehicles were heading, Jude held his ground long enough to see the dark blue Lexus swerve and smash into the pickup's rear driver's side wheel, hard enough that the truck was spun around, the struck tire collapsing with what appeared to be a broken axle.

As it came to a stop, the pickup's driver jumped out, raising a gun to fire through the windshield of the car as it sped toward him. The Lexus veered off, curving away before slowing to a stop, its unseen driver slumped to one side. But Jude's attention was on the armed pickup driver, who had turned in his direction, taking aim as he surged forward.

Panic rocketing through him, Jude realized, *I'm a dead man...*

A thunderclap of gunfire exploded, two shots, but impossibly, it was the gunman who dropped instead of Jude.

Whipping his head around, Jude saw why—in the person of Beau Kingston, tension radiating from his mud-stained body as he held Jude's smoking pistol.

"Holy hell..." Beau murmured, slowly lowering the weapon. "I guess that you weren't lyin' about someone gunning for you."

Heart jackhammering, Jude rushed to the fallen gunman, whose breathing rattled into silence as Jude pulled the weapon from his grip. Despite the spreading puddle of blood beneath the man's chest, Jude's training had him checking the carotid for a pulse. Finding no life signs, he shouted to Beau, "This one's gone," and then raced for the Lexus.

Chapter 16

When she heard the car door open, Callie cried out, certain it was the gunman coming to finish her off. Already, the pain was unimaginable—not only the burning agony that exploded with every attempt to draw breath, but the torment of knowing it had all been for nothing.

In the instant before the bullet struck her, she had spotted Jude, standing in the open. A sitting duck for the professional assassin that she had failed to stop. As she'd briefly blacked out, she'd even heard it—the shots that told her that she'd risked arrest, her mother's safety and even her own life in vain…

He's gone, she knew, the tears so thick they left her blinded—or maybe it was the black wave of unconsciousness rising to spare her the sight of her own approaching death. *Maybe at least then, I'll have a chance to tell him how very sorry I am, how much I care about—*

"Callie? Callie! How on earth did you get…" A panicked voice broke through the darkness. *Jude's* voice. Could it be a hallucination? "Let me— I'm here to help you now. We're going to get through this, together."

But it was his hands that convinced her he was real, for they were swift and sure as they moved over her body, the hands of an experienced medic checking vitals and then applying direct pressure to her left shoulder, which somehow started her choking, painfully coughing up what tasted like blood.

As her eyes rolled back, she heard Jude shouting, apparently to someone else, "We need medevac for her, stat! Get me LifeWings! Tell 'em I'm authorizing. I'm one of their medics—or pull whatever strings you have to, but get that helo here *now*, because I'm damned well not going to lose this woman!"

The thrum of the helicopter's blades beat a dark path to her awareness, telling Callie she was back again, on the helicopter *that* night, a place she had revisited so often. Except somehow this felt different, wrong, as if the dreamscape had reordered things, so everyone was sitting in the wrong seat. Marc was where she usually sat, and for some reason she was lying down, in the very spot where their patient Walter Winthrop should be.

"Where'd Larry go?" she asked Marc, realizing the late medic was nowhere to be seen.

She waited anxiously for some response, half expecting her husband to drift away like smoke or flake apart like a crumbling mosaic, as he'd been doing in her nightmares lately.

"There's a new medic now, remember?" he said softly, the voice she'd loved so long and missed so deeply bringing tears to her eyes. His lips turning upward in a sad smile, he added, "A damned fine one. You don't need Larry. You don't need any of us any longer."

"Please, don't go yet," she begged, lifting a hand to reach for him as he began to fade. But that moment sent pain spearing through her shoulder, a white-hot shaft whose tendrils spread out through her chest and snaked down her right arm.

And Marc, the helicopter, the night she had been stuck in for four long years all gave way to the sight of Jude's handsome face above hers, his blue eyes damp as he bent near her. Yet she still heard the helicopter—and glimpsed the familiar LifeWings paint scheme and logo nearby. Somehow, she was on a gurney, being pushed toward the waiting chopper.

"They—they can't let me fly with you," Jude choked out, as he trotted alongside her. "But you have to hang tough, Callie. And you have to swear you'll be there waiting when I get there, please… No matter what it takes, you have to be there…because I love you. I need you, and this can't be— This won't be the end of it, I promise."

More than anything, she wanted to reach up, to wipe the dampness from his face and tell him she would be all right. *They* would somehow be all right, even if she couldn't see how.

But she had another responsibility, one she couldn't let slide. Because if she didn't survive this flight, she had to know that he would be doing what he could.

"C-call Aunt Jane. M-Mom's miss—" Agony bubbled from her mouth, leaving her choking and coughing.

"Don't try to speak now," he warned.

Fighting to raise her head, Callie pleaded, "Call… her!" before her eyes rolled back as she lost consciousness once more.

Chapter 17

Though Callie had dim memories of briefly rousing in recovery, where a surgeon gave her a run-down of how incredibly fortunate she'd been to have received skilled trauma care so quickly, she didn't fully awaken until much later.

Or maybe she was still unconscious, because it was her mother's long, blond hair and out-of-focus face she spotted in the chair beside her hospital room bed.

Heart jumping at the sight, Callie blinked to clear her vision. Her mother's grip tightened on her left hand. It felt like she was holding on for dear life... Or was it something else? Had the two of them somehow met beyond the—

When her body jerked in her surprise, her hazy thoughts gave way to pain at her shoulder, a pain whose sharp edges had been dulled by what she thought might be morphine.

"Try not to move too much, my poor baby," her mother said, her brown eyes welling.

"H-how—did you—" Callie began, her voice so hoarse and dry that she started coughing.

Releasing her hand, her mother raised the head of the bed slightly and poured some water in a cup before bringing the straw to Callie's lips.

As she drank, her mother explained, "You gave us such a scare."

"Me?" Callie sputtered. "Wh-what about—? Where *were* you?"

"Oh, that." A deep flush crept upward from the neckline of her light-turquoise-colored blouse. "I am so, so very sorry. I don't know what it's going to take to get you and Jane to forgive me, but whatever I have to do, I'll—"

"You went with him, didn't you?" Callie felt her own temperature rising, and with it a burst of anger that short-circuited her pain. "Do you know how much you freaked out your poor sister? I had her call the police, for heaven's sake."

"It's not what you think! It isn't," she pleaded. "I only promised I would meet him that morning so I could tell him face-to-face I'd spoken with an attorney and I'm filing for divorce."

"You *are?*"

"I certainly am," her mother said, sounding furiously determined, "especially since he grabbed me and dragged me into his truck after kicking poor PB for growling at him."

"He kicked my dog and hurt you?"

"It all happened so fast, and I don't think his boot actually made contact," her mother said, shaking her head. "But the moment PB shied from his foot and pulled the leash from my hand, Lonnie had me in the truck—and he'd done something to the lock, so I couldn't get out, either."

"Couldn't you call for help?"

"I was afraid if he saw me trying to use the phone, he'd—he'd— I don't know what he'd do. He was awfully wound up."

"Are you all right?"

"Now that I know you'll recover, I am," her mother assured her.

"I mean, what did he do to you? How did you finally get away?"

"He left some bruises where he grabbed my arm, but other than that, he just drove and begged and pleaded. When that didn't work, he started with the yelling and name-calling—" Sniffling, she grabbing a tissue from the box on the rolling bedside table and wiped at her eyes. "—the same as always when he doesn't get his way."

"I'm sorry," Callie told her. "It's not—this isn't your fault."

"It *is* my fault, for choosing, over and over again, the kind of damaged men who can only make themselves feel strong by pushing down on anyone they see as weaker. That's what the book Jane has me reading says, and that counselor I've been seeing for a while."

"It doesn't mean that you're weak. And even if you were, no one who's mistreated is to blame for—"

"That's what the police said, too, after they tracked us down using my cell signal. Lonnie got upset and tried to run—and then he resisted when they caught us." She shook her head. "So now the fool's facing those charges as well as abduction and assault."

"You're going through with the complaint this time? You'll actually testify against him?"

With a final sniffle, her mother straightened her spine and flipped her blond hair back behind a shoulder. "If I can raise a daughter who's brave enough to steal a car and smash it into a stone-cold killer to save her man, I can be brave enough to do this. And to get the kind of help I need to avoid making the same mistake again."

"I'm so proud of you, Mom."

"And I'm crazy proud of you, too, even though I swear to you that if you ever try a stunt like this again, I will personally put you on permanent TV restriction and lock you in your room for a month," her mother threatened, reprising a familiar but never followed-through-on variation from the repertoire of threats from Callie's youth.

Remembering the kind woman whose Lexus she'd not only made off with, but damaged, Callie wondered just how much trouble she was going to be in once she had recovered. "So where'd you hear all about me?"

"From that handsome boyfriend of yours, of course. He's called me on your cell phone probably ten times in the past two days. He's—"

"Wait—Jude isn't here?" She shook her head. "And what do you mean, two days?"

"You've been—you've been sleeping mostly, because of the medication. They had to stitch up a hole in your lung and remove the—the bullet lodged inside you. But they gave you some blood, and now you're so much stronger."

"What about Jude? Where is he?"

"More than anything, he wanted to come straight

here," her mother said, "but at first they wouldn't allow him to leave Kingston County. There were things he had to see to there—"

"They? Who are they?" Had the authorities arrested him, or had Beau Kingston and his people done worse? Panicking at the thought, she tried—foolishly, it turned out—to bolt upright in her bed. *"Ungh!"*

Gritting her teeth, she sank back and closed her eyes against a wave of pain and dizziness.

"Easy there," came a new voice, that old bourbon and polished burl wood voice that she'd so longed to hear. Footsteps approached her bedside. "I'm here now, and so damned glad to see you—begging your pardon, Mrs. Stringer."

"I told you on the phone, hon. Call me Rhonda," said her mother. "And I'm so glad to see you were able to make it back."

"Yes, ma'am."

"Yes, *Rhonda*, you mean," Callie's mother pressed, "but we can work on that another time. Right now, I expect you and my daughter would like a few words in private, and to be honest, I'm about dying for a little dinner. Can I bring you anything from the cafeteria?"

"No, thank you," he said, "and it's nice to finally meet you in person."

When she left, Callie opened her eyes to see Jude slanting a look down at her, overflowing with such honest relief, such tenderness, that it broke her heart wide open.

As he bent to gently kiss her forehead, he said, "But being alone with you—seeing you alive and conscious—is one hell of a lot better."

Jude sat down beside her, enfolded her paler, smaller

hand in his. Giving it a squeeze, he asked, "How are you feeling?"

"I'm—I don't even know yet. Sore? A little weak?"

"I'm told you should be out of here fairly soon, maybe four or five days if there are no complications." The smile he offered her looked just shy of exhaustion, and she noticed he could use a shave, as well. "The doctors are saying you got very lucky."

"I know it wasn't only luck." She shook her head as it came back to her, his hand pressing against her wound, keeping her life's blood from pouring out of her. "Right after it happened, you were there to save my life."

He shook his head. "I was the placeholder, that's all. Kept you going long enough for Beau Kingston to bypass the usual protocols and get a helo sent from LifeWings."

"Beau Kingston? He did that for me?"

"That and so much more," Jude told her.

But she was fixated on the fact that, like his father before him, Kingston had used his influence to pull strings. "But it was storming, wasn't it? I remember rain and lightning."

"The line had passed through, and it was safe to fly. No safety protocols were broken. Though I can promise you, if your coworkers had had any inkling that you'd been the patient that day, they would have been clamoring to volunteer to take the risk—present company included."

"Thank you," she said, for the first time noticing the many balloons, stuffed animals and cards festooning the room. "But… Beau *Kingston* helped? Wasn't he the one trying to have both of us murdered?"

Jude sighed and shook his head. "Actually, we were

dead wrong about that. The initial letter I sent him was intercepted by a name you'll remember—Ed Franklin."

"His father's attorney?"

He nodded. "The very man who threatened you when you starting asking questions about the shooting of Dr. Walter Winthrop following the crash."

"So you're saying, what?" she asked. "That this family attorney was the one—that *he* sent the assassins?"

"That's exactly what Beau and I forced him to admit—we even got a recording—when we confronted the old man together."

"But why? Why would he do that?"

"To protect the family secrets he's been up to his neck in for decades. He was the man who called me anonymously, and not someone from Beau's security team the way I suspected."

Staring into Jude's face, she guessed, "So Franklin knew, then? *Knew* that Big Jake shot Winthrop because of a deal gone sour between the two of them to set up your mother the way they did?"

"There—there's even more," Jude said, grief carving deep lines in his forehead as he rubbed at his stubbled jaw. "Franklin told us why the bastard did it—why Big Jake was so desperate to pry his wife away from their son…"

Jude was shaking as he thought about it, partly with exhaustion since he'd been skating dangerously close to the edge to make the drive here, but mostly with rage at what had been done to his family. Not only to his mother but to the brother he had never known.

"You don't understand," the nearly white-haired Ed Franklin had pleaded, tears streaming down his wrin-

kled face after Beau had angrily demanded he tell all of it, *"either of you. Things were different in those days, and Big Jake had a billion-dollar legacy, not only that but the brand that was his name, to think of."*

"What is it?" Callie asked him. "Because whatever lies Franklin told about your mother—"

"She was gentle, kind and loving," he said, an unspeakable sadness twisting his heart, "so sweet natured that our father—and according to both Beau and Ed, Beau's most likely the one who was illegitimate, not me—that what he thought of as her *coddling* was bound to—to ruin his namesake."

"Ruin him?" Callie sounded as confused, as outraged as he'd been when he'd first heard it. "How can you possibly *ruin* a little child with love and nurturing? Isn't that what parents are supposed to give their babies?"

"Not a parent like Big Jake Sr.," Jude said bitterly, "who'd seen the signs and recognized— He was terrified, Franklin claimed, that Jake Jr. would turn out to be like Jake Sr.'s own younger brother. A younger brother who took his own life because he couldn't handle being gay."

"But it's not—" Eyes gleaming with tears, she shook her head. "Surely, people don't think like that anymore, and anyway, a mother's love or coddling or whatever some misguided fool might want to call it isn't what determines anybody's orientation."

"Of course you're right. We know that now. But too many people *did* think that way, not so very long ago," Jude said. "And as horrible, as unforgivable as what the old man did to my mother was, and what it ended up causing him to do when Winthrop tried to come after him for money, maybe, just maybe, there was a little love mixed up in there, too, at the beginning. Love and fear for a boy he didn't want to end up meeting the same fate as his brother."

"I'm sorry, but your father was a rich, entitled creep. A man doesn't betray his wife like that out of *love* for anybody. He probably just couldn't handle the '*shame*'—" She released his hand to furiously sketch out air quotes to underscore her sarcasm, though her right arm, where an IV was connected, wasn't up to the task. "—of having his heir turn out to be gay."

"I'm sure you're right about that part," Jude said, recalling Franklin's comments. "Beau said he was harsh with JJ, harsh enough that the kid took off and never looked back as soon as he was of age."

"And was he—was your brother *happy*?" she asked.

Jude shook his head. "Beau couldn't say. He knew that he worked overseas in the energy sector until he died in that motorcycle wreck a few years back. As far as anybody knows, he never married or had a family."

"I'm so sorry that you never had the chance to know each other," Callie told him, "and that both of you had your mother taken from you by one man's small-minded selfishness."

Given that that same man had cost Callie everything, Beau couldn't blame her for the contempt he saw in her eyes. Hatred he feared would spill over onto him as well, the moment it sank in that he was biologically the man's son.

"What happens to Franklin now, and those men, the ones he sent to kill you?" she asked.

"Both of the shooters who came after us are dead, Callie, the second man partly thanks to your distraction—"

"Glad to know my ripping off that car and almost getting myself killed accomplished *something*," she said wryly, "and that it turns out you're such a good shot."

"Oh, it wasn't me who killed the guy." Jude admitted. "Beau got my gun during our fight."

"You fought?"

"I consider it some consolation," Jude said dryly, "that his black eye looks way worse than my swollen jaw."

"Yet he still shot the hired killer?"

"He did indeed, or I wouldn't be standing here beside you. He also made certain that his *former* attorney is in custody, where Franklin will be charged with conspiracy to commit murder…and probably a number of other crimes, once they've all come out."

"So the killers are all dead or in jail," she said, "and you and Beau, I take it, have managed to come to some sort of arrangement where you're not at each other's throats?"

"Both of us have a lot to sort through, but yeah. We've been talking—and I've apologized profusely to his wife, Emma, for our actions—and about the Jeep we took."

"Speaking of cars…" Callie sighed. "I can't help noticing I'm not handcuffed to this bed."

"And you won't be."

Her brows flew upward. "How's that?"

"After Beau found out what his own security guys did to your Mustang—they were more than a little hot after we escaped them—he took it upon himself to take care of your issue with the Lexus by offering to buy the woman you, um, *borrowed* it from a brand-new model with all the bells and whistles to replace it."

"He did that? For me?" she asked, dropping her gaze and raising her hand to wipe her eyes.

"Yes, he did, an offer that she graciously accepted, but I still can't believe you faked a—what was it—a *seizure*? And jacked some stranger's car?" Jude shook his head, half horrified and half admiring of her ingenuity and sheer gutsiness.

"I know it was terrible, but with the phones out, I couldn't think what else to do. I had no other way to warn you that I'd spotted the shooter on your tail." Her reddened gaze rose to meet his, tears streaming down her face. "What I'd said to you, when you left—that you were dead to me." She made a strangled sound. "I couldn't bear it."

"Callie, you could've been killed."

"But *you* certainly would have been. Don't you get it? That's all I could think of, that you would die never knowing how much I —how much I've come to—to love you."

"*Love* me?" Jude's chest hammered out a breakneck rhythm. Surely, he had heard her wrong. Or maybe that was what she *had* thought, in the heat and terror of the moment when she'd been so certain he'd be murdered. Fear could do strange things to people, could make them forget who they really were and what they wanted.

"*Love you,*" she insisted, her beautiful eyes shining. "That's right, Rookie. I never meant for it to happen— thought there was no way that it ever could, not the way I'd barricaded myself behind a brick wall of bitterness over my loss. But somehow *you*, or the fear of losing you, finally broke down my defenses—and made me realize I can't bury myself alive in my grief another day."

He wanted this so badly, to believe in her, in the possibility she offered, but whatever hope had lived inside him had been crushed so often and so ruthlessly that he simply stood there, frozen, waiting for the other shoe to drop.

"But now that you're okay, I've realized..." was the way she would begin it.

Or maybe, instead, she'd lead with, *"Of course, I didn't know at the time that you were definitely a Kingston."*

Instead, a worried look crossed her face, one that had her elevating the head of her bed higher. "Jude, are you all right? Maybe you should sit down, because you're looking like you're about to fall—"

"I'm scared stiff, that's all," he admitted. "My heart's damned near beating its way out of my chest while I stand here, waiting for you to tell me you've come to your senses and realized you could never love the son of the man who cost you—"

"Oh, Jude," she said, squeezing his ice-cold hand in hers. "Don't you get it? I finally *have* come to my senses, and out of the shell where I'd been living far too long."

"And I'm so happy to be a part of that, but—"

"I told you before, Jude, it's never mattered in the least who sired you. You're clearly not that miserable excuse for a human being, or the grandfather who ran you down for so long, his words lodged in your heart." Shaking her head, she added, "You're your mother's son instead, a first-rate man she'd be so proud of, one of the finest, bravest men I've ever known…and it's long past time you had a woman in your life who let you know it, each and every day."

He cupped the face of the woman he would always love in his shaking hands and answered, "Only if you'll let me spend every one of them letting me show you what it means to be cherished."

"You drive one hard bargain, Rookie," she murmured as their lips came together, laying a foundation for the future they would build together. A future they would nurture with their dreams, their passion and a love that had the power to mend their grieving hearts.

Chapter 18

Pinto Creek, Texas
Eight months later

"**I** swear I have ten thumbs tonight," Jude complained, fumbling with his tie as if it were an anaconda he meant to wrestle into submission. Standing in front of the mirror in the two-bedroom adobe home they'd decided to rent until they were more settled in the community, he looked as nervous as Callie had seen him since that day in her hospital room.

"Let me help you with that, Rookie," teased Callie, who had just finished putting on a pair of sparkling earrings. "It's obvious you haven't had much practice in the tie department lately. Out of the way, PB—and watch the tail. I don't need your white hairs all over my black dress."

In response, the big dog half yodeled a protest and wandered away to find the latest of many chew toys his new best buddy Jude had bought him.

"Not much call for ties just lately, when I've been busy swinging hammers," he said, alluding to all the labor he'd put in on the old building that the two of them had poured so many months of hard work into rehabbing and remodeling.

"I'll remind you you're not the only one who's flattened a thumbnail or raised a blister," she said as she looped the silk around his neck and tried to remember exactly how to do this.

A flash of memory came to her, an image of her first husband smiling down at her, nodding his encouragement as her hands went through the motions. Giving his blessing as she went on with her life now, with the man she'd married just six months earlier, the two of them wrangling her excited aunt and mother as witnesses before running off to the justice of the peace simply because they couldn't bear to wait a moment longer to make things official.

"You're looking particularly stunning tonight," Jude said, ducking his head to steal a kiss as she finished snugging up the knot. "And you're right, too. You've put in every bit as much sweat equity as I have to make this thing happen. I don't know how to thank you, Callie, for helping me bring this dream to life."

"It was your idea, and your money that gave it its start," she said, though the dream had caught fire as well, in her imagination, inspiring her in a way that had made the decision to leave flight medicine a no-brainer.

"Not my money. I never earned it."

He'd held firm on his refusal to accept any part of his

father's legacy or his name, even after DNA comparisons to other known relations had confirmed Jude's heritage. Callie had been there when Beau had told them—and had offered to go with him to his new attorneys, *"honest* lawyers, this time," to figure out how to make things right between them.

"Right," Jude had insisted, "will be for you, and later on your children, to continue running the ranch and taking care of the employees you've grown up with. All I want from this life is to build a women's health and domestic violence center, right here in Kingston County, in honor of my mother, so no other woman in the community will ever again find herself in crisis and alone."

Hearing him say that and knowing he was turning his back on an offer that might mean a fortune to live by his core values, had made Callie fall in love with Jude all over again.

And her respect for Beau Kingston had spiraled even higher when he'd answered, "If that's the way you feel, I won't bring up your share of the legacy again on two conditions, my brother…"

Though the two didn't share a bond of blood, Jude nodded, acknowledging a connection that somehow, inexplicably, had come to transcend their genetics. "Let's hear them."

"First," Beau said, "you're going to accept the proceeds of your brother's estate. Compared to my father's, it was modest, but there's enough there—and not a penny of it's ever been touched since it was invested—for you to buy and equip a facility, secure yourself some decent housing, and put away a little something for the future to help out with expenses."

Jude considered for a few moments before agreeing, "And what else?"

"Since you'll be benefiting the community, the Kingston Foundation will want to be a big part of what you're doing. And that means——"

"Throwing your weight around by reminding us constantly that every dollar in funding comes with strings attached?" Callie had challenged, recalling his foundation's —and his obnoxious cousin's—history with LifeWings.

"Micromanagement's not my style," Beau had assured her. "Trust me, between running the ranch and that family of mine running me—" the fond smile he flashed showed he wouldn't have it any other way "—I've got no time to get in your hair."

"I'm betting Tammy Kingston-Hoyle has time," Callie said, though she'd learned the woman's mortified daughter had talked her mother into withdrawing her complaint against her and Jude.

"I'm sure she does, but you don't have to worry. She's been forced off the board by a cabal of other cousins who'd had enough of her high-handed ways."

"A cousins' coup. I like the sound of that," Callie said.

Beau grinned. "You make it sound way more entertaining and less annoying than it was, believe me. But I can promise you both that for your center, I'll make time to arrange for fund-raising advisers, organizational support, anything I can to help you make this work."

"That's very generous," Jude said.

"Honestly, the foundation's discussed creating something similar on and off for years. We've just never found the right people with the passion to spearhead it. So what do you say?"

That afternoon, they'd shaken on the agreement. And this evening, they would at long last be attending a reception celebrating the opening of the center the two of them would run together.

After scratching Baby's ears and tossing him a biscuit, Callie and Jude headed for the new ride he had insisted on buying for her—a four-wheel-drive SUV she found more practical for toting her dog and clinic supplies than the convertible that she'd once driven. In under ten minutes, they reached the vintage one-story brick structure, its lot overflowing with more cars than Callie had ever seen gathered in one place in this small community before.

Laughing nervously, she asked, "What is this? Did somebody tell them we were hosting the football play-offs here or what? And why are they all here so early?"

"I'm thinking Beau must've turned up the wattage on his influence," Jude said.

"It can't only be that," she said. "You've seen how many people have been showing up to help us out with getting this old building in shape. And I've had so many signing up for volunteer shifts, or calling about donations—if Emma Kingston hadn't pitched in to help, I don't know what I'd do."

"You'd handle it like a boss, the way you always do," he told her, as they made their way through the cool, clear night together, walking along the side street where they'd been forced to park. Slipping off his jacket, Jude laid it over her bare shoulders, feathering his fingers along the curve of her neck enticingly before he moved his hand. "Even if you had to launch another minor crime wave to get the job done, you desperado.

Or is the proper term *desperada* when speaking of a wild woman?"

Laughing at his teasing, she playfully elbowed his ribs before sobering abruptly. "Wait a minute. What's everybody doing out front? Shouldn't they be inside, grubbing up the wine and nibbles?"

Hurrying his steps, Jude said, "I sure hope we haven't had another water leak, or this is going to be a really short celebration—"

"And a damp one," she said, wrinkling her nose at the thought of dealing with the mess—which was sure to be as unpleasant as it was embarrassing—while dressed in their finest. Trotting to keep up with him in her heels, she caught his arm when she spotted Emma walking toward them, with Beau at her side, smiling with what looked like anticipation as they waved Callie and Jude forward.

"Come, come," Beau said. "We've all been waiting for you."

"But we thought—" Jude said, sounding as confused as Callie felt as he looked around, taking in the faces of volunteers, donors and a host of expectant-looking but less familiar faces, a good portion of them belonging to men and women in their sixties, seventies and older. "We agreed this wasn't to get started until seven thirty. *Didn't* we?"

"We might have told the two of you that," confessed Emma with a small shrug. After sliding a conspiratorial look in the direction of her husband, she added, "But that was just so we wouldn't spoil the surprise."

"*What* surprise?" asked Callie, though she already had her first clue, in the twin beams of a pair of spotlights pointed at what looked to be some sort of sign, currently covered by a white cloth, in front of the building.

"This center means a lot to many of us in the area," Beau said, his deep voice carrying as he spoke into what Callie realized was a small clip-on microphone so everyone could hear him. "Not only because of how it's going to help make this community a better, safer place in the future, but because it's given us a chance to come to terms with our failures of the past. Failures to protect those who need protecting. Failures to listen, when our gut instincts tell us something's wrong…or when someone powerful and respected is flat-out lying to us."

In the hush that followed, she heard murmurs, soft whispers in creaking voices. *"He means his father—he does."*

"I always knew she'd never…"

"I only wish I'd had the nerve to speak up then."

"I heard that doctor—he took liberties, and not just with the one patient, either…"

Callie took her husband's arm, and in his utter stillness, she knew he'd heard them, too. And understood they were in reference to the woman whose struggles had brought him full circle, back to the place where her suffering began.

"This center can't right those wrongs," Beau continued, "but it can serve as a powerful reminder to be better. To do better and be braver, and to honor those whose goodness will always remain with us as an inspiration."

With that, the tall rancher, looking handsome in his black Western-styled suit and matching Stetson hat, stepped forward and, in one swift move, whipped off the cloth that had been covering the new sign, a sign which read:

The Millie Castleman Memorial Women's Center
Offering Healing, Hope and Help

At the sight of his mother's name——not her married name, but one untethered to the man who had betrayed her—Callie saw Jude stiffen and then heard him exhale sharply, as if a blade of grief had sliced straight through him.

Oh no, she thought, pulling him into her arms as if she might somehow protect him. Beau and his wife, all of them, might have meant well by this, but their heartfelt gesture had surely instead brought it all back for Jude—the trauma that had shattered his young life and made her weep to think of even now...

But when he pulled back, a moment later, she realized she had been wrong as he used his thumb to wipe away the tears from her eyes. "No need to cry for her—because I know my mother's finally happy." Kissing her temple, he added, "I *feel* her, right here with us, smiling with pride."

"I'm proud, too," Callie told him, "so very proud of what we're building..."

As Beau and Emma, along with an entire community that had claimed them as their own, gathered to share their well wishes and congratulations, she felt her heart expand to take it all in...along with the family she and Jude hoped would someday take root on this same fertile soil.

* * * * *

WE HOPE YOU ENJOYED
THIS BOOK FROM

Danger. Passion. Drama.

These heart-racing page-turners will keep you guessing to the very end. Experience the thrill of unexpected plot twists and irresistible chemistry.

4 NEW BOOKS AVAILABLE EVERY MONTH!

#2151 COLTON 911: FORGED IN FIRE
Colton 911: Chicago
by Linda Warren

While Carter Finch is trying to investigate a potential forgery, Lila Colton's art gallery is set on fire. As a result, Lila becomes the main suspect. Carter stays by her side and they're drawn into multiple mysteries that threaten a possible future they could have together...

#2152 A COLTON INTERNAL AFFAIR
The Coltons of Grave Gulch
by Jennifer D. Bokal

Police officer Grace Colton is being investigated for unlawful use of force. Internal Affairs investigator Camden Kingsley is charged with finding out what happened—but there's more to this case than meets the eye...and romance is the last thing either of them expected.

#2153 STALKED IN SILVER VALLEY
Silver Valley P.D.
by Geri Krotow

Former FBI and current undercover agent Luther Darby needs linguist Kit Danilenko's talents to bring down Russian Organized Crime in Silver Valley, and Kit needs Luther's law enforcement expertise. Neither wants any part of their sizzling attraction, especially when it becomes a liability against the two most powerful ROC operatives.

#2154 COLD CASE WITNESS
by Melinda Di Lorenzo

When Warren Wright is caught witnessing several armed men unearthing a body, he has no choice but to run or be killed. His flight leads him to seek cover, and he inadvertently draws Jeannette Renfrew into his escape plan. The two of them must work together to solve a mystery with connections to Warren's past.

HRSCNM0921

"Kit, you misunderstood me. Let me try again."

He saw her shake her head vigorously in his peripheral
vision. If he could grab her hand, look her in the eyes, he
would. So that she'd see his sincerity. But they'd started
to climb and the highway had gone down to two lanes,
winding around the first cluster of mountain foothills.

"No need. Just take me back home." This version of
Kit was not the woman who'd greeted him this morning.
Great, just great. It'd taken him, what, fifteen minutes to
make mincemeat of her self-confidence? He felt like the
lowest bird on the food chain, unable to escape the raptor
that was his big mouth.

"I'm not taking you home, Kit. We're going on this mission, together. I'm sorry if I pushed too hard on your history—it's none of my business. None of it." He needed to hear the words as much as say them. The reminder that she was a mob operative's spouse, albeit an ex, would keep him from seeing her as anything but his work colleague.

She was nothing like Evalina.

The memory of how the ROC mob honcho's wife had used him, how stupidly he'd fallen for her charms, made his self-disgust all the greater. It was one thing that he'd allowed himself to be duped and his heart dragged through the ROC crap. It was another to cause Kit, a true victim of her circumstances, any pain.

"Are you sure you can trust me, Luther?"

Don't miss
Stalked in Silver Valley *by Geri Krotow,*
available October 2021 wherever
Harlequin Romantic Suspense
books and ebooks are sold.

Harlequin.com

Love Harlequin romance?

DISCOVER.

Be the first to find out about promotions, news and exclusive content!

 Facebook.com/HarlequinBooks

 Twitter.com/HarlequinBooks

 Instagram.com/HarlequinBooks

 Pinterest.com/HarlequinBooks

You Tube YouTube.com/HarlequinBooks

ReaderService.com

EXPLORE.

Sign up for the Harlequin e-newsletter and download a free book from any series at
TryHarlequin.com

CONNECT.

Join our Harlequin community to share your thoughts and connect with other romance readers!
Facebook.com/groups/HarlequinConnection